THE
Sleeping Beauty
PROPOSAL

**Center Point
Large Print**

**This Large Print Book carries the
Seal of Approval of N.A.V.H.**

THE
Sleeping Beauty
PROPOSAL

Sarah Strohmeyer

CENTER POINT PUBLISHING

THORNDIKE, MAINE

This Center Point Large Print edition
is published in the year 2007 by arrangement with
Dutton, a member of Penguin Group (USA) Inc.

Copyright © 2007 by Sarah Strohmeyer.

The text of this Large Print edition is unabridged. In other
aspects, this book may vary from the original edition.
Printed in the United States of America.
Set in 16-point Times New Roman type.

ISBN-10: 1-60285-027-5
ISBN-13: 978-1-60285-027-9

Library of Congress Cataloging-in-Publication Data

Strohmeyer, Sarah.
    The Sleeping beauty proposal / Sarah Strohmeyer.--Center Point large print ed.
    p. cm.
    ISBN-13: 978-1-60285-027-9 (lib. bdg. : alk. paper)
    1. Marriage proposals--Fiction. 2. Self confidence--Fiction. 3. Large type books. I. Title.

PS3569.T6972S55 2007
813'.6--dc22

2007008475

For the indomitable Kathy Sweeney

You're engaged to be married. You're radiant, feeling a bit like a celebrity. . . . Do not panic.

—Martha Stewart's Keepsake Wedding Planner

THE
Sleeping Beauty
PROPOSAL

Chapter One

If you ask me, the best part about the Sleeping Beauty fairy tale is that she didn't have to do anything to get a man. She just lay around for a hundred years. And one day a cute guy with lots of ambition and extra time on his hands rode up on an expensive horse, hacked through a bunch of brambles, ran upstairs, and kissed her.

Voilà! Instant husband.

This has been my problem. I'd like a husband in theory, but I don't want to have to work for one in practice. You know, keep my legs shaved and my figure trim. Dress well for all occasions. Learn how to grill a steak, twice-bake a potato, check my teeth for spinach, say no to desserts, look stunning in a bikini, bat my eyes, suck in my stomach, never burp, fetch beer, giggle at his every joke, wear thongs that ride up my butt, make nice to his sister, and play those games.

I am lousy at those games.

My mother loves them. She loves the whole challenge of baiting and trapping the elusive white-collar, upwardly mobile North American male. I think she wishes she were still single like she was back when she lassoed my father, the prudent bank president in a gray suit, the guy who never fails to lead strangers to the brink of suicide with mind-numbing lectures on the importance of building credit and pursuing equity.

For example, one day my mother sent me a present

with a note on pink stationery that said: "Be the first to hang up and he'll be the first to call back!" It was a white plastic egg timer. I sat on my front step and stared at it, baffled.

Then I called my best friend, Patty Pugliese, who said, or rather yelled, as she tends to do, "It's so you'll know when to get off the phone with a guy, you moron!"

Patty's a successful lawyer at a boutique firm in Boston, unmarried and determined to stay that way. As the oldest sister of seven kids growing up poor in South Boston, she likes to say that she's already raised her family. To her marriage means diapers and a husband who stops by long enough to get you pregnant again. She'd much rather sleep around and drive a Porsche.

I found a spot for the egg timer on my stove and there it sat for years, reminding me every morning, as I flipped my Egg Beaters omelet with salsa and low-fat cheese, of what I was doing wrong. Like putting it by the stove instead of the phone, for starters.

One by one my closest friends from college got married. Mary Ann went to Germany, married a doctor, and had two children named Louise and Hanz. Sara married Gary, who lived in the apartment above us junior year. (We'd all seen that one coming.) Julia married a guy she met in law school. Lorraine married her dentist. Only Ellie and I were left and Ellie was looking, hard. She had egg timers next to every phone in her apartment, and one by the cell in her car. (I am not kidding.)

It haunted me, my egg timer. I'd think about it as I went to work, riding the number 73 Waverly bus to Harvard Square and taking the Red Line up to Thoreau College, where I'm an admissions counselor. I'd ask myself, is it me? Do men not find me attractive?

Clearly, that wasn't true. Guys asked me out all the time and they'd tell me that they loved my hair, which is nothing spectacular, your run-of-the-mill brown, or that they thought my legs were really strong. (Just what does that mean?) They said I was funny and had a great personality. But something about me was not marriage material. We'd last four, maybe five dates discussing, as always, their ex-girlfriends and how to win them back, and that was it. They never called again.

Why? I mean, I had the timer!

Maybe it was my job. Maybe it wasn't exciting enough to attract quality men. In a college town like Boston, everyone knows there are two types of admissions counselors: the recent graduates biding their time until something more exciting comes along, or the hacks, like me, who have decided to make a career out of breaking kids' hearts.

Not that I'm one of those. I'm not. I'm the person on the admissions committee who votes for Suzie Plain Cheese of Dayton, Ohio, because she's a hard worker and a sincere student who didn't pad her resume. I

13

know Suzie will grow up to be a generous member of society, joining her community's school board and maybe leading a Girl Scout troop or two.

But Thoreau College is in a losing war against Harvard. (As if we could compete!) Inevitably, my Suzie is overruled in favor of the rich kid from New Jersey whose parents have paid for him to distribute clean needles in Ghana and for him to take classes that coach him to a perfect 2400 on the SATs.

So, I went to work and did what I could for the Suzie Plain Cheeses of the universe. I spent my lunch hours eating turkey sandwiches with diet mayo, lettuce, and tomato on whole wheat along with a Diet Black Cherry Vanilla Coke while reading their essays about the life-changing aspects of *To Kill a Mockingbird*. On the train home I read their explanations for why they bombed biology and, after a dinner of Lean Cuisine and a Skinny Cow sandwich, I read about their plans to take over the world while my overweight, diabetic cat, Jorge, barfed on the carpet by my feet.

I kept up this routine hoping that life might change of its own accord.

And then, just when I had given up and signed myself over to a limited existence in my Watertown apartment with my nearly blind cat, a miracle occurred.

I met Hugh.

Not any Hugh. Hugh Spencer. I'm sure you've heard of him or read one of his books. Though when we hooked up, he wasn't famous. He was just an

14

assistant English English professor. I didn't repeat myself. He taught English and he *was* English. How cool is that?

All the freshman girls had crushes on him. His office hours were booked faster than a Rolling Stones reunion tour. And they weren't there to discuss his brilliant analysis of Shakespeare's use of feminine foil in *All's Well That Ends Well*, either. The guy is the spitting image of Hugh Grant, heavy-lidded blue eyes, that naughty grin, even the stutter. (Though Patty thinks it's totally affected and she may be right.)

Better yet, I didn't have to put out bait or trap him. He came to me. Literally. He opened the door of my office one night when I was "working" late and there I was, naturally, with my skirt over my head inspecting my ass with a hand mirror.

Granted, it wasn't the best of circumstances to meet a future husband. That's not exactly putting one's "best face forward," you might say. But it was funny. Hugh had come looking for a flashlight to help Alice, our secretary, change her tire and what he got instead was an uncontrollable fit of hysterics.

I, of course, didn't find it funny at all. I was mortified! But no matter how hard I tried to explain that I was checking for cancer—having just taken a break to read a *Cosmo* article entitled "Killer Moles You Don't See"—the more he doubled over. I mean, it was a matter of life and death. And he was laughing!

To make up for his callous attitude toward my health, he took me out to dinner. (All clear on the ass-

15

mole front, by the way.) The next thing I knew we had one, two, three, four, five, and six dates. Then I stopped counting.

It was glorious. Saturdays we'd go to the North End and pick up fresh pasta for dinner. Sundays we'd sleep late and read *The New York Times*. We biked. We jogged. We had mind-blowing sex on fresh white 1,000-thread-count cotton sheets. It was like living in a catalogue.

Suddenly, I had Adirondack chairs on my front porch. I was wearing gray yoga pants and facing the morning sun with an earthenware cup of fair-trade espresso in my hand, Hugh kissing my neck, his abs chiseled above his Ralph Lauren striped boxers. My kitchen was bright with fresh vegetables, green peppers, red peppers, and organic garlic sautéing in heart-healthy safflower oil. I completely forgot the whole line of Lean Cuisine or my excitement when I learned that Swiss Miss Hot Cocoa now came in Cherry Cordial!

Then came the Big Hurdles. You know the ones I'm talking about—the meeting of each other's parents; the vacation at a beach house; the Christmas together, alone; the first anniversary.

Surely, I thought, he will pop the question soon.

Not that I was one of those desperate women who, having passed her thirtieth birthday, was anxious to get on with the next half of womanhood: being a wife and mother. I wasn't.

Really. It was merely that I enjoyed being with

Hugh and he seemed to enjoy being with me and, unlike Patty, I was of the opinion that two people in love in their thirties who had been together for over a year should probably start discussing things like whether it was better to raise children in the security of the suburbs or amidst the stimulation of a city, and if Labradoodles really were safe with babies.

But the first anniversary came and went and the only diamond Hugh gave me was the one patterned on a blue silk scarf (to match my "cerulean" eyes). Nor was the famous Spencer family diamond ring hanging from the tree on our second Christmas, no sapphire at the bottom of my champagne flute on New Year's.

Summer arrived, bringing with it warm and romantic nights. We took what had become our "annual" vacation on Martha's Vineyard, strolling hand-in-hand down the beach as the fog rolled in. No diamond in the sand, either. And I looked. Looked hard.

Three years later, I was still looking, my big toe turning over clam shells and crab claws, certain a diamond-and-platinum solitaire had been dropped somewhere. What was he waiting for? He'd told me he loved me. That was now a given. He often brought up our old age, how he could see us hobbling down the same Vineyard beach in our twilight years. I assumed that by then we'd be married, if only for the Social Security.

Did I push? No. Even after the FedEx guy started accepting Hugh's signature in lieu of mine and my answering machine said, "Hugh and I can't come to the phone," not once did I bring up the *M* word. I was so incredibly not that way.

Though plenty of women in my situation might have been that way. Might have feigned a pregnancy like Connie, a woman (shrew) I work with, who drew a tiny + sign in pink magic marker on her pregnancy test and left it by the toilet. (Not such a hot idea. Her loser boyfriend found the test, stepped outside to get the paper, and was never seen again.)

Nor did I leave the *New York Times* Weddings section about or conduct long, loud phone calls with Patty about my aging ovaries and whatnot.

Instead, I continued to play it cool. I shrugged when Hugh coyly asked if I ever thought about getting married. (A classic commitment-phobic boyfriend test to see if you're out to trap him, in my opinion. Don't fall for it!) I even managed to convince myself that marriage was not all that it was cut out to be. Women of our generation had no need for the financial support of men. Why be burdened when I could be free?

One day while we were lying by the Charles after a run, we finally had the Big Discussion and I learned Hugh had a "position" on marriage. It was this: Being unmarried keeps us fresh.

Turned out Todd, my older brother, had a corollary: Being unmarried keeps Hugh's options open.

"Mine, too," I said, defensively.

To which Todd snorted, "Right. You want to get married, Genie, and you know it. The only reason why a man in his late thirties doesn't want to commit is because he thinks, hopes, that there's something better around the corner. I know. I am that thirty-seven-year-old man."

It hurt. And for a while I was mad at Todd for being such a knuckle-dragging Neanderthal. Marriage was passé. Anyone with any intelligence knew that. Just because Hugh and I didn't have a slip of paper didn't mean we weren't committed to one another.

Like Hugh said, marriage was an anachronism left over from the days of tribal politics. (I have absolutely no idea what that means.) Our bond, he said, didn't need approval from the state. (Or commonwealth. We were in Massachusetts, after all.)

Besides, Hugh was working his heart out, teaching by day and drafting a new novel at night, a novel he needed to be a smashing bestseller so he could quit academics and write full-time. He was exhausted. Testy. It would have been unfair of me to pester him at this crucial point in his career with my neurotic whining about children and hobbling on the beach and just how long he planned on keeping his options open, anyway.

So I was patient. And my patience was rewarded with more abundance than I ever could have hoped for.

Hugh hit it big with his novel *Hopeful, Kansas*, a delightfully sappy romance about a handsome drama student named Dick Credo who's bent on becoming famous and who never noticed Dora Schlubb, the girl who tutored him in math who secretly had a huge crush on him.

Dick Credo leaves his Kansas hometown of Hopeful, goes to Hollywood and becomes a megastar, and then is felled by drugs and alcohol and his reputation is ruined. So he ends up back in Hopeful and wouldn't you know that Dora, the girl who tutored him in math, is still carrying the proverbial torch.

She helps him heal and he sobers up and realizes he missed his true calling to become mayor of Hopeful and clean up all the Hopeful crime and marry the nerdy girl. Only, right before their wedding, Dora's diagnosed with some mysterious and quick-killing disease—but she keeps it from Dick—and she collapses into his arms at the altar, "her face as pale as the virginal white wedding dress she had saved for herself and for him."

She didn't even get to . . . you know . . . with Dick, the Brad Pitt of Hopeful, Kansas. (If you ask me, there was more going on with Dick than just drugs and alcohol. But that's another book for another day.)

Anyway, Hugh's book landed smack at number 1 on the *New York Times* bestseller list and suddenly *People* magazine was interviewing him and he turned into an overnight celebrity, a kind of literary hottie. There were even groupies.

His publisher sent him on a book tour for three weeks, during which there were lots of questions from nosy journalists about which he preferred, boxers or briefs. (I would think to myself, "I know.") And then

20

there were the questions about me, which he handled artfully.

He'd say, "I have found the love of my life. We have a relationship that no novel, no matter how great, could do justice. It's the kind of love that makes my passion burn with unquenchable desire."

I would swoon whenever I read that. I couldn't wait for him to come home so I could rip off his clothes and personally quench his flames.

Hugh's last stop on the book tour was an appearance on whatever the show is with Barbara Walters. Barbara ended the interview with what would become the question that changed my life: "Are you ever going to marry your own Dora?"

I was on the edge of my seat. I could not believe what was happening before my very eyes, especially when Hugh said he would ask "Dora" to be his wife if he could be assured the answer would be yes.

Eeeeeek!

Well, of course the answer would be yes, silly. I wanted to reach out and grab him through the screen and shake him by the neck. That's when Barbara held up her finger, as if she'd just had a brilliant idea, and said, "Hugh. Why don't you ask her right now, here on live television? Ask your Dora to marry you."

My heart stopped. My vision became tunnel as I stared, riveted, at the screen. This would be a moment we'd describe to our children (Meg, Beth, and Amy), and that Meg, Beth, and Amy would pass down for generations.

Hugh hemmed and blushed some more. Then, at Barbara's cajoling, he faced the camera and said, "You know how much I love you, my Dora. I haven't been able to stop thinking about you since the moment we met. While I've been away, I've been consumed, obsessed, desperate to hold you, touch you, kiss your soft, warm lips."

Really? That's funny, because he only called once a day to ask if he had any voice mail and to make sure Jorge got his insulin shots.

"You know how much I admire perfection and you, sweet, are perfection personified. I feel like I will die unless you tell me yes, that you will be my wife so I can be your husband until death do us part. Make me happy, my love, like no one has until you. Marry me."

Barbara was weeping like a hog over a trough of hot slop. Tears were streaming down her cheeks and mine, too. It was The Most Beautiful Thing Ever. *Ever!!* I'd never heard Hugh so poetic. The imagery. The passion.

"Yes!" I screamed into the universe. "Yes! Yes! Yes!"

The phone blared and I leaped off the couch. This was it! This was it! This was Hugh asking me to marry him mano a mano. Finally, after four long years, my prince had come.

I snatched up the receiver, my hand shaking with anticipation. I could barely breathe.

"Honeee. You should turn on the TV. . . ."

My mother! I couldn't believe it. Her incredibly bad timing is legendary. "Mom. I can't talk now."

"You should turn on Barbara Walters. Hugh's on and he just proposed marriage. I think to you, dear. Wait. He's back."

I hung up the phone and spun around to the TV. Sure enough, there was Hugh. He was on the phone. He was grinning and smiling and there was Barbara Walters saying something I couldn't quite comprehend, something about "his Dora" saying yes and all the people at *20/20* wishing the couple the very best on their journey through life.

Holy crow. My prince had come.

And . . . gone!

Chapter Two

My phone rang. Again, I flinched and thought with stupid hope, "Hugh?"

But it wasn't Hugh because the phone was my cell and it was playing "Show Me the Way." Patty had bought the ringtone off a Peter Frampton fan site online.

I pressed send. "You're answering," she said cautiously.

"Yes."

"You're not talking to Hugh."

"No."

"You're finished talking to Hugh?"

"Hugh never called."

"No Hugh?"

"No Hugh."

Pause.

"I'll be right over. Don't do anything until I get there."

I snapped the phone shut and inched to the couch, every part of me feeling cold and numb as I digested Patty's two simple words. *No Hugh.* Still, I couldn't grasp their meaning, as if they were Chinese or Hebrew, which was odd because I was a smart woman. Not brilliant. But not paper-or-plastic either. I could calculate a tip and do my taxes. Why wasn't this making sense?

We were practically a married couple already, Hugh and I. This was a known and accepted fact around Thoreau College. If you invited Hugh to a cocktail party, you automatically invited me. My picture was on his desk. He was number 2 on my speed dial and I was number 2 on his. People asked what "we" were doing the following weekend. My mechanic knew Hugh better than he knew me because it was Hugh who brought in my car for oil changes.

Hugh took out my trash and cleaned Jorge's litter box. I'd thrown up once on his shoes and he didn't care. I got him ginger ale and Gatorade and changed his bloody cotton balls when he had his wisdom teeth pulled. I kept him from making long-distance phone calls to Malaysia while hopped up on Percocet. I even washed his boxers and, being an amateur skin care expert thanks to that *Cosmo* article, checked for moles in places where he never looked. We shared that kind of intimacy.

But tonight I'd learned that he was even more intimate with some other woman, someone more beautiful and thrilling, someone who sparked his passion, drove him mad with desire. Someone he fervently wanted to be his wife.

I haven't been able to stop thinking about you since the moment we met. . . . I've been consumed, obsessed, desperate to hold you, touch you, kiss your soft, warm lips.

Memories of his proposal were starting to rise to the surface of my consciousness, swirling and buzzing around my mind like a swarm of locusts.

Make me happy, my love, like no one has until you.

What was he implying, that I hadn't made him happy? I who had rubbed his back until my fingers were numb and done all the cooking while he wrote the book? I who had copyedited his stupid manuscript, organized his checkbook, *and* made sure he had clean shirts and lint-free jackets for teaching? I who had *scrubbed his toilet?*

If it hadn't been for me, why, I bet that damned book wouldn't have been half as successful. I can tell you this much, his first draft sucked and would have continued to suck if I hadn't showed him how to turn Dora into a real woman instead of a stereotypical shy Kansas farm girl with "down-turned eyes" and a "sweetheart's smile."

Yuk and double yuk.

Finally, I couldn't take it any longer. Despite Patty's orders to stay put and not do a thing, I called Hugh on my cell. I had to. I was going out of my mind.

He answered on the fifth ring sounding slightly rushed. "Hugh Spencer."

A big red bubble of anger popped inside me. "What just happened?"

There was a pause that telepathically I inferred as *Oh, shit.*

"Genie," he said. "Let me call you back. Now's not—"

"Don't even think about hanging up. For once be a man and be honest. Did you or did you not just propose to someone else?"

When he spoke next, he sounded different, as if he'd gone into a bathroom or maybe a closet. "The truth is . . . I did."

My other hand clenched into a fist. This was impossible. The logistics alone were unfathomable. Four years of constant togetherness and somehow he'd found another woman whom he loved enough to marry? It didn't make sense.

"Who?"

"Really, Genie. We can talk about this—"

"Who?" I needed a name, a face, an enemy on which to focus my rage and pain.

"I didn't mean for this to happen right now. I was put on the spot and I was going to say no, but then the moment kind of hit me and—"

"WHO?"

My front door opened and Patty walked in. Patty is short. Not midget short, but short. She has shoulder-length reddish hair that curls at her shoulders thanks to lots of expensive treatments that keep it from looking and feeling like Brillo. And she has big eyes and an upturned nose. She often reminds me of a Hummel figurine gone bad.

"Hugh?" she mouthed.

I nodded and pressed the speaker button on my phone so she could hear him.

She flipped him the bird. Then she proceeded to pull out two shot glasses from her humongous Tod's Tribu Shopper along with a very pricey bottle of tequila. It was going to be a nasty night.

"Who she is is not important, Genie."

"I'll be the judge of whether or not it's important for me to know who you've been sleeping with while we were, supposedly, in a committed relationship."

Patty's eyes widened.

"The operative word," he said, becoming testy, "being *supposedly.*"

"What does that mean?"

"You pushed me to be committed. You wanted to be committed. You told your parents we were committed, the entire school we were committed. But . . . *I never said I was committed to you.*"

The words hung in the air, frozen and crystallized. *I never said I was committed to you.* It was as if a flaying knife had sliced through my sternum and cut me in two.

Patty slapped her forearm in an Italian gesture of revenge. I shook myself, came to my senses, and realized he was still talking, perversely pressing his point, releasing pent-up anger that must have been boiling inside him for months.

"The difference between being with you and being with her is that I couldn't wait to be committed to her. This is what love is supposed to feel like, Genie. Empowering. Unquenchable. It's not supposed to feel like you're a wild animal, tagged and trapped, dying to be free."

"And that is how you felt with me?"

"Yes. I did."

Silence. Patty had poured the shots and was waiting on the couch. "Scum," she mouthed.

I wanted to get off the phone and collapse and cry, but didn't dare hang up. Likely, he wouldn't be answering any more calls from my number and, besides, he was flying to England the next day to finish his book tour. This was my last chance to uncover the truth in all its sordid nastiness.

I wanted to ask what made her so great that he wanted to commit, but it sounded too clingy, too *The Way We Were*. So, I said, "Tell me she's not one of your freshmen, because I'd hate to think I was the cover for some dirty old man."

"Who she is, how we met, how long we've been seeing each other, these are all irrelevant questions. You're missing the larger issue, the one that involves us."

Patty shook her head and said, "Bullshit."

"She is the symptom, not the cause, of our break-down."

I've always despised that line. It's so phony. "Oh, and what would you say is the *cause* of our break-down?"

"Please, Genie. Let's not go into this now. Give each of us some time to cool off and get ourselves together so we don't inadvertently say something we'll regret later."

My eyes felt hot and swollen and before I could help it, a few tears escaped and ran down my cheeks. Patty's cool hand grasped my hot one and gave it a squeeze. He must not find out he'd made me cry. "I know the cause of our so-called breakdown," I blub-bered. "It's that you're a jerk."

To this, Hugh exhaled a long, pained sigh. "Look, Genie. You know you're my best friend. There's no other person in the world who understands me so well, whom I can go to with any problem. You're my rock, right?"

"But?" I knew there had to be a *but* in there some-where.

"But . . ." He cleared his throat. "No matter how much I love you as a friend, the bottom line is that, at the end of the day, I'm simply not as sexually attracted to you as I should be."

Oh, God. That was worse than I expected. The floodgates had opened and, collapsing onto the couch, I let the tears come. Patty put her arm around me and made me rest my head on her tiny shoulder.

"Not now?" I managed to say. "Or not ever."

"Actually, to be totally honest, never."

That was it. I was gone. Big heaping sobs erupted from within me and there was no use choking them back.

"It's not anything you or I can help. It's pure chemistry. I've tried and tried to get past it, but I'm a man, you know, and the funny thing is that even though I consider myself more of a cerebral person"—he laughed nervously—"I still have these physical needs."

Like kindling tossed into a fire, whatever was left of my feminine confidence at that moment curled, shriveled, and burst into flames, leaving only a small pile of gray ashes. I didn't have the power or presence of mind to counter an attack, to wittily retort that maybe he wasn't man enough to bring out the woman in me or to wiggle my little finger, like Patty was always doing, to signal "inadequate" men with outsize egos.

I was flattened.

Because, aside from the way it worked in some out-of-the-way places in Kenmore Square, as far as I knew, sex was supposed to be between two people who loved and trusted one another. And I had trusted him. So trusted him that while I had been kissing and wriggling and licking and slithering all over Hugh, assuming I was hotter than Tabasco, I never imagined he had been merely lying back and thinking of England.

"Oh," I whispered, recovering a bit, though my shoulders were still heaving.

"I'm sorry. I never wanted to tell you that. Ever. It's just that you put me on the spot."

Yes. It was all my fault. Right.

Patty lifted a shot and raised a suggestive eyebrow. I shook her off. Later, maybe. For now I needed to be alert.

"Look," he said softly. "There will probably be questions about what happened and since I'm going home for several weeks, I won't be here to answer them. I'm sorry that you'll have to bear the brunt of this."

I hadn't even thought of this possibility—of my family and friends and all the people we knew at Thoreau, not to mention the press even, contacting me, asking if I was thrilled and if there was an engagement ring and whether we had set a date.

I'd have to tell them they should ask someone else. Hugh's real fiancée—whoever she was.

"I hope it won't be too hard for you," he added. "I never planned for this to happen. The last thing I wanted was for you to get hurt, Genie."

Too late. "Maybe they won't ask," I said. "Maybe they'll be polite."

"Maybe."

More silence.

Patty, having now given up on me, was downing the shot herself. This was it. This was going to be my last conversation with Hugh. I was definitely not going to call later tonight and beg for him to come back. Those days were over.

"Is *she* going to England with you?" I couldn't help it. "Because if she is, she should be prepared to know your mother does not like women who wear shorts. Also, about her rottweiler Scruffy . . ."

"Genie," he murmured. "Let it go."

"I can't let it go. It's four years. Four years ended in one night." The sobs were coming on again, involuntarily, like hiccups.

"I'm so sorry. Sometimes things are beyond our control. I wanted to love you in every way possible, but I couldn't. You have to believe me when I tell you I tried."

"I believe you," I said. But I didn't, really.

It was all a lie. We were a lie. And lies cannot last. Only truth.

Click.

I stared at the phone, the medium of my pain, lying so innocently on my coffee table. It was over. *We* were over. We would never again be Hugh and Genie.

Already I felt exhausted, as if my entire body had been run through Hugh's Italian Atlas pasta machine, leaving me flattened and folded. I had no idea how I'd make it through the night, let alone the rest of my life.

A shot glass filled with nasty-smelling liquid came into view and I remembered Patty was sitting next to me.

"Vengeance is mine, sayeth the Lord. Leviticus." She pushed the shot into my hand. "Until then, have a drink."

I downed the shot. It burned and tasted awful. It was perfect.

The phone rang, a number I didn't recognize.

"Let me handle this," she said. "You're in no shape."

"No. It's my responsibility."

Patty grabbed the phone. "Don't you trust me?"

"Why?"

The phone kept ringing and ringing. "I just want to know. Do you trust me?"

I thought of all the occasions Patty, my former college roommate, had come to my rescue—when I was flunking Soviet Economics and she tutored me to an A, when my car broke down on Storrow Drive in rush hour, when I got that nail in my foot down at the Y, when I missed my period and I needed an ultraexpensive early pregnancy test.

"Of course, I trust you."

"Then let me handle this." When she answered the phone, her voice immediately melted from tough litigator to Patty of the Belmont Junior League. "Why, hellooo, Connie."

Oh, crap. It was Connie Robeson, the only other single admissions counselor over the age of thirty-five in our office. Connie had been studying Hugh and me like we were a rare breed of mating African apes, curious and intrigued as to how I, with my outdated Etienne Aigner loafers, had attracted a prime specimen like Hugh when she had followed every dating book to the footnote with no matched success.

"Tell her I'll talk to her later," I said.

Patty flapped me away. "It is exciting, isn't it? Yes, she and Hugh couldn't be happier."

What? What was she doing?

"Very romantic," Patty gushed. "They do make a lovely couple. Dr. and Mrs. Hugh Spencer. He is a doctor, you know. A Ph.D."

I waved my hands in protest, trying to catch Patty's attention before she went on, but she just turned her back to me and kept on chatting.

"I don't think they've set a date yet, no, but I'm sure you'll be invited. Can Genie get back to you tomorrow? There's another call coming in and she's already on her cell to Hugh's parents."

That didn't even make sense. Hugh's parents were in London. Who calls London on their cell?

Patty hung up, reached into her purse, and pulled out her Palm Pilot. I watched dumbly as she scrolled through to her address book.

"What are you doing?"

"I'm calling your sister, Lucy, to make sure she knows you and Hugh are getting hitched."

I snatched the phone out of her hand. "You can't call Lucy. She'll turn right around and blab to my parents."

"Exactly. Then your parents will call all their friends, Connie will tell everyone at Thoreau, and then—bingo—no more questions. When he gets back

coworkers and bums off the street. Then I'd send the freaking huge bill to Hugh with a note explaining he could either pay for my so-called wedding or he could confess to his loyal female fans that he'd cheated on his girlfriend of four years."

Where did Patty come up with this stuff?

"But since you're so nice," she said, "don't think of faking your engagement as revenge. Think of it as therapy. Wedding therapy. In pretending to be engaged to Hugh, you'll hold him accountable and, meanwhile, you'll find out what it's like to be a bride, for once, instead of the bridesmaid you've been fifteen times before."

"Seventeen," I corrected.

"That's pathetic. Your closet must be jam-packed with ugly pastel satin dresses."

Couldn't argue with that.

I sat back and considered Patty's words. A fake engagement could be exactly like those twelve-step programs where you're supposed to fake it until you make it. I had to think: What if Hugh had really asked me to marry him? Would *I* be a different person? Would I stop putting my life on hold?

It was worth finding out.

I handed her the phone. "I'll do it. Call Lucy."

"Really?" Patty squeezed my arm. "You really will?"

"What the hell. I have nothing to lose."

After all, if my prince wasn't going to come, then maybe the next best thing was simply pretending he had.

Chapter Three

Panic!

I cannot believe I have let Patty talk me into her so-called Sleeping Beauty Proposal.

This is the first thought to trip across my brain as I lie in bed, sweating, while the morning sun slants through my window, exposing my web of deceit. How could something that seemed so justifiable last night seem so wrong this morning?

One of my few remaining brain cells raises its hand: *Tequila make Genie go crazy.*

Correct. Anyone else? Yes, you in the back by the cerebellum: *Patty Pugliese can talk a jury into believing O. J. Simpson really is innocent.*

Very good. All right. One more: *Hugh Spencer is a cruel cad and he deserves to be thoroughly humiliated.*

Possibly. Though I might be going too far because now the whole world thinks we're engaged. Like my silly sister Lucy—whose bazillion calls I've so far been able to avoid—and my mother, who, I'm sure, has phoned five hundred of her closest family and friends to spread the word.

It might be wise for me to tell Mom the truth now, before it gets too late. Yes, it will be humiliating, horribly humiliating, to have to admit that I concocted an engagement out of spite and, okay, on a sappier note, a broken heart.

I didn't want to admit this to Patty last night, but a teeny tiny part of me hoped that if I threw a wedding, Hugh would come. Kind of like *Field of Dreams* for brides. Only, in the cold, sober (I hope I'm sober) light of day, I realize that's just ridiculous. Hugh would never marry me simply because I sent out invitations. What was I thinking?

Of course, telling the truth will also mean enduring the gossip fest of all gossip fests that Mom and Lucy will throw as soon as I'm out of earshot. Hours will be spent rehashing how weird it is for an "otherwise normal woman" to fake an engagement, how I might need medication or maybe a stay up the street at McLean.

Lucy will act shocked that I fantasized Hugh proposed to me and then Mom will rely on her extensive medical background (soap operas, television dramas, movies, and Tuesday's *Science Times*) to diagnose me as suffering from a classic case of "Fatal Attraction Psychosis."

Not that I've really said "Hugh proposed." I didn't have to. All I had to say was, "Hello?" and the next I knew Mom was screaming and Dad was on the family room extension congratulating me with his gruff voice (to hide his emotion), spouting platitudes like "I'm glad you two have decided to quit shacking up and are making it legal" and "Guess my little girl's grown up." (Okay, Dad, I'm thirty-six. I think I'm grown-up.)

Meanwhile, Hugh—oblivious to the fact that half of

the East Coast and certain areas of the Midwest are under the impression we are tying the knot—is somewhere over the Atlantic, reading the morning paper and drinking his coffee on a flight to England, possibly with *her*, his real fiancée, Miss Hot Tamale. Likely she has a father just as proud as mine and a mother who also screamed nonstop for five minutes.

Or maybe not. Maybe she is from New York City, the Upper East Side, where engagements and marriages are all very passé. You know, they're what the masses do between buying megapacks of toilet paper at Wal-Mart and watching reality television.

Then again, I don't know anyone like that at Thoreau (we all steal toilet paper from the ladies' room). Wait. What if she's from Thoreau? When Hugh wasn't on campus, teaching or writing, he was hanging out with me, so where else could she be from?

It doesn't make sense. None of this makes sense. I mean, who can this other woman be?

Here, so far, is my list of potential candidates. Women I know who have harbored suspected crushes on my boyfriend. Or, rather, ex-boyfriend.

Alice, Admissions Department Secretary
Age: 25-55, no one's quite sure.
Weight: Permanent diet.
Marital Status: Living with on/off boyfriend, Trey Ray.
Favorites: White shoes. Extensive coffee breaks.

Tight pants. Kool Menthol Ultra Lights. The electric bull at the Somerville Tavern. Brandon, the guy who fixes the copy machine and other sundry appliances.

How she knows Hugh: Met when the rear left tire on her Grand Marquis blew out on Ballou Drive. Flat caused by Trey, who was ticked she threw out all his beer the night before. To this day, Alice considers Hugh her knight in shining armor and, until last night, she wasn't the only one.

Connie, Admissions Counselor
Age: 36, though claims 30.
Weight: Struggling to keep it under 129.
Marital status: Single and not loving it.
Favorites: Online dating. Speed dating. Coffee club dating. Books on How to Date and How to Meet Men and Why They're Not Into You When You Do Meet Them.
How she knows Hugh: Through me and she's none too happy about that—despite her claim that she finds British men "effeminate."

Isabel, Spanish Literature Professor
Age: Young.
Weight: A lithe 115, and one of those who can eat anything she wants and never put on a pound, curse her.
Marital status: Divorced.

Favorites: Swaying hips while walking. Talking with a thick, sexy Spanish accent. Looking like Penélope Cruz.

How she knows Hugh: Because she knows all the men on campus and they know her.

Simone, Women's Lit Professor
Age: Forty. Do you want to make something of it?
Weight: That's not important. Why are you concentrating on a male-defined paradigm?
Marital status: Do you always judge a woman according to her relationship with a man?
Favorites: Black coffee. Shawls. Using words like *deconstruct* and phrases like "employing the feminine speculum."
How she knows Hugh: Corners him at every chance to badger him about why he failed to include Anzia Yezierska in the freshman canon.

Nope. None fits Hugh's type. Except for Isabel. I'll have to keep an eye on her, the hot-blooded Spaniard.

Speaking of hot-blooded Spaniards, here comes Jorge the cat staggering through the doorway in his blind pursuit of a sun patch and leftovers. He collapses on my carpet of roses and green vines, exhausted from having hiked all of five feet, and looks up at me with the equivalent of feline disgust.

My alarm clock claims it's seven thirty, though as it is a largely untrustworthy piece of junk, that could

42

mean anywhere from seven twenty to seven forty. Still, enough time to make it to work and be reasonably efficient. I just need a cup of coffee, a shower, and a jiffy blood transfusion.

Oh, wait! It's not Monday. It's Sunday. Relief. I have one full day to recover and regroup. I could go back to sleep, but Jorge is having none of it. He is meowing relentlessly and won't let me rest until I've fed him and shot him up with insulin. (It's true. Jorge gets enough Humulin to treat a three-hundred-pound Snickers freak.)

Slowly, I ease myself out of bed, my head throbbing as I squeeze by the bureau. Gee. That brings back memories. Whenever Hugh bumped his knee on that damned bureau, he'd vow to get me out of this tiny apartment.

"You're a grown woman, Genie," he'd say. "The era of living like a college student is over. You need to get yourself a decent space."

No. Stop! I cannot spend my life like this, delving into nostalgia at the least little memory. I must move forward. Therefore, I march to the kitchen, grab a cupful of diabetic maintenance cat food, and dump it in Jorge's bowl.

"You're up!"

Patty, her hair sticking out in scary angles and with dark black smudges of mascara under her eyes, is holding a gigantic plant tied up in a white bow and yawning.

"Don't hate me because I'm beautiful," she says,

43

handing me the plant. "Who knew that FTD delivered at seven on a Sunday morning?"

My pathetic reaction is to hope that Hugh has sent the plant with a card ("It was all a joke. Of course I love you, you sexy vixen, you!") and a British Airways ticket to London. Jumping up, I grab the flowers and rip open the envelope while Patty collapses at the kitchen table.

"May today be the saddest day of your life!" Love, Aunt Jean.

Holy crap! I grip the counter for support as my entire body turns to petrified wood. I am both disappointed (that it is not a ticket to London) and terrified (that Aunt Jean has found out I am lying).

But how? I mean, I knew she did the Sunday crossword puzzles in pen and could guess all the answers on *Jeopardy!*, but I never figured she was this smart. Smart enough to smell a scam all the way in Jersey? I feel dizzy, as if I'm about to pass out.

Patty lifts her head from the table. She is wearing nothing but my old Supertramp T-shirt. "What's wrong?"

"Aunt Jean knows Hugh didn't propose to me."

"She does not."

"Read for yourself." I toss it to her so she can read for herself.

While she decodes Aunt Jean's threat, I try to determine how quickly I can pack up and head west. Of course, I'll need cash and an alias. How about Penelope Truehart? And then there will be Jorge. It'll be a drag to carry around his fat ass in a cat caravan, begging for Humulin and clean needles along the way. Motels won't look kindly on lending out rooms to a drug-dependent cat.

Patty is smiling. "Aww, that's sweet."

"Sweet?"

"Sure. It's an old expression. You know, now that Hugh's proposed to you, you're supposed to be over the moon with joy and the days only get happier. You are over the moon with joy, aren't you?"

"Not exactly."

"Well, you better start pretending, because brides-to-be are supposed to be over the moon with joy."

This raises a serious question. How can I pull off this charade if I cannot even fake being over the moon with joy in my own kitchen?

The coffeemaker orgasms and I pour us two cups, load both with milk and sugar, and head to the living-room side of my apartment. Patty follows me, along with Jorge, in case there might be food.

My apartment is in a brick walk-up designed for two units, divided into four. This means my kitchen is half its normal size and so is the bathroom. (My "back neighbor," as I call her, got the bathtub. I got a kitchen sink with a window.) Half of the original living room was turned into my bedroom, as was a walk-in closet where Patty slept last night. The dining room does double duty as a TV room and a place to eat. It's like living in the Soviet Union circa 1972.

Patty and I sit on the couch and look at Aunt Jean's plant.

"I went too far last night," I say. "With my mother."

"No, you didn't. Except for that part about claiming Hugh was related to Princess Diana. That might have been a bit much."

"I never claimed he was related. Mom asked and I said it was a possibility."

"You shouldn't encourage her. It's dishonest."

I give her a look.

"All I'm saying is you better disabuse your mother of that erroneous family trivia as I do not think the royal family is going to appreciate a call from Nancy Michaels of Belmont, Massachusetts, suggesting that they lend you Diana's sapphire-and-diamond engagement ring 'for the nonce.' "

That reminds me. "What am I going to do about a ring? People won't believe I'm engaged unless I'm wearing one."

I inspect my left hand with its inelegant short nails. I bet Hugh's fiancée has long fingers and a French manicure that perfectly sets off her fabulous diamond.

Gack! I hadn't thought about that before, them choosing the ring. Please, God, don't let it be Tiffany. Immediately a vision of an Audrey Hepburn look-alike springs to mind. She is holding a robin's egg blue box and smiling up at Hugh. There is a gap between her teeth, a sign that she's a sexual dynamo like Lauren Hutton. Or the Wife of Bath.

Patty takes my hand in hers. Unlike me, she has

46

always kept her nails long and painted in a tasteful pale pink. "You could splurge for once and buy yourself a diamond. I've often thought of doing that. Right-hand rings they call them, to celebrate being single. You know, your left hand's for love. Your right hand's for . . . I forget."

"Delivering an uppercut?"

"That's it."

I try to picture a diamond ring on either hand. "I dunno. Buying yourself an engagement ring is so Britney Spears."

"Hey. K-Fed wasn't going to step up to the plate. Then again, K-Fed did strike out looking."

There is pounding on the steps outside my door and a rapid knocking.

"I'm gonna clobber that FTD man," Patty says as I shuffle to answer.

Sure enough, more foliage. Only this time the flowers are being delivered by Todd, my older brother, a six-foot-three giant in running shorts and a sweat-soaked T-shirt. He could have changed after his run (he lives right around the corner), but he probably saw Patty's Porsche and decided to stop by my apartment to flex something. That's the way it is with him.

Todd's real name is Thaddeus. My real name is Eugenia and our baby sister's name is Lucinda. Todd, Genie, and Lucy. Thaddeus, Eugenia, and Lucinda. My parents, apparently, had no clue the nineteenth century had ended.

"I understand congratulations are in order," Todd

says dryly, producing the bouquet of flowers. "Don't think this means you won the bet, Sister Eugenia."

In addition to the flowers, he is carrying something even better—a white box with its trademark owl. Gesine's pastry. I *love* Gesine's.

"Ah, ah, ah," he taunts, holding the box out of my reach. "No sticky bun for you, not if you want to fit into your slinky wedding dress this September."

"September?"

"Yeah," says Patty from the couch. "Remember? Your mother picked your date. September fifteenth. It's Grammy Michaels's anniversary or something."

"But that's three months away!"

Patty shrugs and says, "What do you care?"

Oh, right. I keep forgetting that I'm not really getting married.

"Long night?" Todd walks in and nods to Patty's legs, bare and tan and smooth.

"Kind of."

"Most women I know get dressed after their one-night stands."

"Most women you know are *paid* for their one-night stands."

"I give that a C minus, but it'll do." He holds open the box for her, displaying two gooey cinnamon rolls. "Care to ingest two thousand calories?"

"Don't mind if I do." Patty, who has never counted a calorie, helps herself.

"You know, eat that and you're more than halfway to gaining yet another pound."

48

Patty gives him a dirty look. "Tell you what. I'll worry about my weight and you worry about when knuckle dragging's going to be back in fashion."

If I have any wish in the world (aside from being invited to spend a weekend with George Clooney on Lake Como), it's that my best friend and my brother would reach common ground. When they're together, all they do is snipe, snipe, snipe.

Personally, I blame Todd's insecurity. He's intimidated by Patty being a lawyer while he works in construction. Not that there's anything wrong with working in construction. There's not. It's just the way Todd was raised.

In my father's opinion, you're not *really* a manly income provider unless you're spending most of your life on the fifteenth floor of the Hancock building pushing paper around under fluorescent lights. I guess ripping out walls and building new ones is emasculating in the playbook of Donald Howard Michaels III.

The other theory has to do with Mom. She forever refers to Patty as "that horrid" Patty Pugliese. There is nothing about Patty my mother likes. She doesn't like that Patty's a lawyer who has made a career out of suing white-collar criminals, especially bankers like my father. She doesn't like that Patty knows what to do with an item you can buy online called the Fuzzy Teaser. She doesn't like that Patty's Irish and Sicilian and that half her relatives are under some sort of federal protection.

But mostly my mother doesn't like that Patty's so loud.

"You bring coffee for us?" Patty shouts. "Because your sister's stuff is shit."

Todd takes a sip from his own white paper cup and closes his eyes in exaggerated ecstasy. "Mmm. Mocha caffe latte. *Delicioso*. Too bad you can't have any."

"Be a hunk and get me one, would you?"

He shakes his head. "I know you're used to men waiting on you, darlin', but I'm not your errand boy."

"All in good time, my pretty. All in good time."

I take in the two of them munching on their cinnamon rolls and licking their fingers, both oblivious to the anxiety tearing at my soul, to my newfound failing as a sexual washout. Both oblivious to the fact that all they've left me are crumbs and cinnamon goo.

Snatching up the empty box, I shove it into the garbage loudly so they'll feel guilty, though they don't. "How'd you hear about Hugh's proposal so soon, anyway?"

"How could I not? Mom called on my cell when I was out last night to give me the lowdown and then Lucy called to talk about what Mom talked about." Todd wipes off his hands and swigs more coffee. "Trust me. There's nothing I don't know."

Patty says, "Wanna bet?"

Ever so slightly, I shake my head at her. Under no circumstances must Todd know I am lying. To do so would be to hand him an easy victory, one that could cost me beaucoup bucks.

50

The "Will Hugh Marry Genie" wager began years ago, the day after I'd carefully arranged a casual meeting with Todd at the Inman Square club Coco Joe's. He was there to hear my friend, Steve Taylor, play in his very loud, very bad "funkabilly" band called the Wily Coyotes, and Hugh and I were next door to sample some cuisine de Portugal. Hugh's not exactly a club type, but I managed to twist his arm with the bribe that Coco Joe's had lots of local color when really all it had of interest was my brother. (No offense to Steve.)

Here was my private hope: that Todd might find Hugh inspiring and that Hugh would find Todd interesting and that, together, we'd be the bestest of friends. I mean, even though my brother lives in the town where he grew up, he has led a fascinating life. He went to Harvard and then dropped out to see the world, traveling for two years in Asia, hiking mountains in Nepal, and even volunteering at Mother Teresa's orphanage in Calcutta (where he picked white maggots out of a villager's wound for days. Seriously).

And then there's the interesting side note that for a while there Todd was a practicing Sikh, which meant he believed we all have within us a spark that is covered by layers of greed and want and ego that need to be peeled away so that we can, finally, merge with the divine. Kind of like dermabrasion for the soul. Surely, Hugh would find that intriguing, no?

No.

Forget any talk of Sikhism or Mother Teresa; the men couldn't get past their differences in fashion taste. Todd wore a flannel shirt and jeans. Hugh wore khakis and a white, pressed, pinpoint oxford-cloth shirt. Todd pronounced Steve's band "kick-ass." Hugh opined that the Wily Coyotes needed its "ass kicked." Hugh worried out loud about hearing damage, to which Todd, an inveterate concertgoer, kept asking, "What?"

At the bar, I tried to explain to Todd that he needed to like Hugh because I was pretty sure he was "the one."

Todd was incredulous. "That wimp? Get out. There's not a genuine bone in that guy's body. Listen to his accent. Totally bogus. It's John Cleese clapping coconuts together and you know it."

I was rightly offended and told Todd what to do with his coconuts—insert them into a nether region of his anatomy. He said he was only trying to protect me from getting hurt. I told him promptly to fuck off.

The next day, after a fitful night of sleep, I showed up at Todd's apartment with two hundred dollars—the most I could get out of the ATM—and a bet that Hugh would someday ask me to marry him. Todd found two hundred dollars of his own and doubled it. So began the Will Hugh Marry Genie wager.

It has been four years of riveting tension ever since.

The closest Todd ever got to conceding that perhaps Hugh wasn't so bad happened last Thanksgiving when, in front of cousins, aunts, and even my

Grammy Michaels, my father asked him why he couldn't be more like Hugh. The implied question being: *Why can't you be more like Hugh, who had the stamina to graduate from Oxford, instead of being a Harvard dropout like you, loser?*

To Hugh's credit, he quickly interjected, "Like me? Do you mean someone who can't change a lightbulb or hold a hammer? Why in the world would Todd want to be a half-man like me?"

I absolutely loved Hugh for that. Loved him.

And, though Todd would never have admitted it in a million years, I think he liked him for that, too. In fact, I think Todd likes Hugh a lot.

This morning, however, he's back to being grouchy and sour, claiming that Hugh and I haven't been dating long enough (four years!) to get married and worrying out loud that Hugh will have me "dressing in a ratty brown cardigan and typing out his manuscripts" for the rest of my life.

"What's your problem?" Patty says. "Why can't you be happy for your sister? Are you afraid of being knocked off her big brother pedestal?"

"Right. Like any man could. It's not that. It's not even what I think about Hugh. The reason why I'm not happier for Genie is because of the institution of marriage itself. It's anti-women."

Patty raises an eyebrow. "Oh, really? And when did you become the feminist?"

"I'm not a feminist. I'm observant. Marriage for men is great, aside from that annoying clause about

53

forsaking all others. But marriage for women is slavery. They have to take care of the kids, fill the refrigerator, keep the house in order, and, in most cases, hold a job. And, may I add, keep themselves sexually enticing."

Ouch!

He sips his coffee while Patty glares at him so fiercely I fear flames may pop out of his forehead.

"Where have you been for the past thirty years?" she practically screams. "This is the twenty-first century. Men and women can share equally. Men get paternity leave now. Hell, more women than ever out-earn their spouses. There's no reason men should bear the financial brunt while women are saddled with domestic duties. It can be a beautiful partnership."

Patty as the defender of matrimony. Todd the feminist. Clearly, the Earth has tilted too far on its axis.

"Yeah? If it's so great," Todd says, "then how come you're not the one getting married?"

"Maybe I haven't met the right guy."

We know this is an out-and-out lie as Patty has openly stated she dates in volume, not in quality, because she's looking for fun, not a lifetime commitment.

"You seem to have worked your way through Boston's Top Ten Singles list. I don't think it's a matter of not meeting your life mate. I think you don't want to get married for the reasons I said. Admit it."

She glances up at me doubtfully. "Not exactly." Though I know that's exactly why she doesn't want to get married—because of the Four *D*s: Diapers. Day care. Dinner. Depression. She's been there, done that, as oldest sister of the Pugliese brood.

Todd waves a red coffee stirrer. "Your problem is you're still suffering from ingrained sexism. You won't admit I'm right because you're afraid of being called selfish, whereas if I tell people—as I often explain to the women I date—that I have no intention of marrying, suddenly I'm the guy to catch."

Wait. I have to think about this. A woman who says she doesn't want to marry is a selfish shrew, whereas a man espousing the same philosophy is hot stuff.

Patty says, "You must have the biggest ego on Earth."

"That's not the only thing I got that's big, honey."

"Oh, yeah?"

"Yeah."

"Toothpicks do not yardsticks make, Todd."

Uh-oh. Patty's revving up. If I don't get them to change the subject soon, our Sunday morning coffee klatch could very well end with a nasty pantsing incident.

"Lookit, you two, I've got to take a shower and start my day, so unless you're here on a specific mission, Todd, I'm going to have to kick you out."

This does the trick because Todd says, "Yeah, I'm on a mission. I want you to stop by the Peabody Road house."

"What for?"

"To buy it." Todd says this matter-of-factly, as if

he's talking about a flat of geraniums instead of the prime piece of real estate he's been renovating for thousands and thousands of dollars.

"Buy it? Me?"

"Now that you're engaged, you and Hugh should buy a house—and this is the perfect place for you two."

That's impossible. The duplex Todd's been working on for six months is *wayyyy* out of my price range. A huge two-family Victorian in Watertown abutting a country club golf course in a working-class neighborhood recently gone absurdly upscale.

Not to mention that there is no Hugh to buy it with. Minor detail.

"I can't buy a house," I say, watching Todd watching Patty leave the room to get changed. "Especially not that house you've been working on. I mean, what's the asking price? Four hundred thousand?"

"Try half a million, and it's a bargain at that. The kitchen's not finished and the bathroom doesn't have a bathtub. Cecily Blake, the owner, told me she's running out of money for renovations and she wants to move to California and get the damned thing off her hands. I'm telling you, those are ideal conditions for a steal."

"I can't afford it. Not on my salary."

Todd gets up, thoughtlessly leaving his coffee cup on my table. "Sure you can. Hugh's a bestselling author raking in the dough."

"And he would rather be homeless than live in a

two-family," I add quickly. "He hates neighbors, especially ones right upstairs."

"So buy it for the investment potential. Meanwhile, you two can settle down in some mansion out in Concord. Or, you could be frugal, learn to deal with the upstairs noise, and move in. By renting the top apartment, the place will end up paying for itself."

Patty comes out of my so-called guest room pulling a shirt over her bra and flashing her flat abs, an act that does not go unnoticed by my brother. "Todd's right. Anything under six hundred on Peabody Road is a find. You and Hugh should at least consider it."

Me and Hugh? Is she on crack?

"Won't last long, Genie," Todd says. "I guarantee that once this goes on the market, it'll be snapped up in a day." He snaps his fingers to emphasize the snapping potential. "The difference is, those buyers don't have the advantage you and Hugh do—namely me, the inside contact. You could make Cecily an offer today before a Realtor ever gets her grubby hands on it."

Shoot. If only Hugh and I really were engaged, this situation would be unbelievably ideal. A gift dropped from heaven. I swear, my life is a seesaw. When one end is up, the other is down. This is why I need an equal partner.

"Okay. Let's say Hugh and I"—I fire a warning look at Patty—"*do* want to buy a house and this one's a total find. Hugh won't be seeing royalties on *Hopeful,*

Kansas for months, maybe a year. Either way, we're screwed."

"Simple. Mom and Dad."

"I can't ask them to buy me a half-million-dollar house."

"Why not? They bought a half-million-dollar house for Lucy and Jason."

It shouldn't irk me but it does—when Lucy and Jason got married Mom and Dad put the down payment on their monstrosity in New Hampshire, a huge colonial with a fireplace and media room and four bedrooms.

Yes, it was very generous of my parents and of course I was happy for Lucy and Jason, who happens to be one of those squeaky-clean born-again Christians and the nicest guy you'd ever want to meet. When they heard the good news, Lucy screamed for joy and Jason fell to his knees and started praying, thanking God for the nine splits of the Microsoft stock Dad had the foresight to buy at $28 a share back in the mid-1980s. We were all thrilled for them, even me.

Still, somewhere in the darkest part of my soul, the little green troll of envy poked at my heart. I couldn't help but feel slightly miffed. Here I was, the dutiful older sister, the one who, unlike Lucy, had worked every day since turning sixteen, still living with half a kitchen and a walk-in closet for a bedroom because no man had deemed me eligible for a lifetime commitment. Whereas Lucy—who had never held a job for more than six months—got her dream home handed to her simply because she happened to meet the right guy at the right time.

It wasn't fair. I know that makes me sound like a petulant kindergartener stamping her foot, but it's true. It wasn't fair. And the only way I've been able to move on is by mentally downplaying it and remembering that my relationship with my sister will always trump cash. Always.

Anyway, I've never been sure how much money Mom and Dad gave them, really.

"Oh, their gift wasn't that much," I say, casting my line into dangerous waters. "Twenty thousand at the most, right?"

Todd snickers. "Try two hundred."

Two hundred thousand? The words stick in my throat, though not in Patty's. She shouts, "Two hundred thousand! Holy shit, that's a lot of dough."

"You got that right, babycakes," Todd says.

"The only real estate my parents ever bought me was part of the Pugliese plot in Mount Hope. Which, let me tell you, does not exactly fill me with peace of mind. We Puglieses have never been known to coexist without incident for one night, let alone all of eternity. Not for nothing was Grandpa buried with his Glock."

"Yeah, well, Mom and Dad didn't want Lucy and Jason to be burdened by high monthly mortgage payments," Todd explains. "Not, you know, with them starting out and all."

I have to sit on the couch and absorb this. Two hundred thousand dollars. My parents gave Lucy two hundred thousand because she was "starting out." Yet, in their mind, I could make do with a hot, cramped tower until my prince came along to rescue me because I wasn't starting.

I was stagnating.

"Well," says Todd, "did that change your mind?"

Did it ever. "Give me an hour. Patty and I will meet you there."

Chapter Four

Hugh and I almost did buy a house about a year ago. An experience that nearly killed our relationship faster than Grandpa Pugliese's Glock.

The house was a bright blue Victorian in the Spring Hill section of Somerville with bay windows and inlaid pine floors and a cheerful yellow kitchen plus an airy room on the second story that would have been a perfect place for Hugh to write. I pegged that as the selling point, the office. Though, privately, I thought it made a much better nursery.

The problem was money. There was no way I could buy it alone, not on my salary as an admissions counselor. And since Hugh had yet to break out to the bestseller list with *Hopeful, Kansas*, he wasn't able to, either. But with Hugh's savings and mine there was a chance we could pull it off together. We could merge the assets, as my father likes to say.

The tour of the house was the clincher. Just one hour of meandering around and I could picture Hugh reading in the golden living room on a cold winter night, a pine garland wrapped around the carved wooden banister, a twinkling Christmas tree in the corner. We'd throw cozy dinner parties for our friends in the fall, plant our raised gardens in the spring, and spend lazy summer evenings on the porch, getting to know our neighbors. And someday, someday we might even hear the pitter-patter of little feet running down the stairs on their way to school.

I was so immersed in this fantasy that I could actually smell my roasting chicken in the oven, the one I was making while upstairs Hugh was banging out his latest novel on the computer. I could hear the rain on the roof, feel the garden dirt on my fingers.

That's when I had an epiphany: This house had to be mine, oh yes.

Hugh was at his laptop when I burst through his door, excited and pink-cheeked and brimming with hope after the showing. I can distinctly remember what he was wearing (a *Cool Runnings* T-shirt) and what he was drinking (chamomile iced tea in a pink glass, using that morning's *Boston Globe* as a coaster).

"So you like it, do you?" he said as I gushed about the yard, the living room, the office—can't forget the office—the garden, and the kitchen where on snowy days I would bake cinnamon cookies and drink hot cocoa with our children, Meg, Beth, and Amy. Slowly, gradually, Hugh's smile slipped into a frown.

"Genie," he said, using his professor voice to cut me off. "Stop."

"Why?" I didn't understand how he could not be as thrilled as I was. What was not to love? The house was adorable!

"I'm not there yet."

"What do you mean you're not there yet?" Though I knew exactly what he meant.

He pushed back his chair and tented his fingers as if I were one of his students and he was soberly discussing my failing grade. "To make that kind of commitment is impossible for me. I can't think of anything right now except this book. I'm up to my eyes in revisions."

"Then after revisions?"

His lips twitched. Looking back, it definitely was one of those body language things I should have paid attention to. "Possibly. But don't hold me to that."

The revisions were due in two weeks. All I had to do was hold on until then. Surely, Hugh would see the light after the book was off his back. Each night I prayed that the house would stay on the market, that it would wait for us. If only he'd get those damned revisions done, then I could give him the tour and he would fall in love with it as I had.

Hugh finished the revisions, turned in the manuscript, and promptly made a concerted effort to sleep, relax, read, exercise, go out with friends, catch an independent film in Harvard Square, learn how to brew true Turkish coffee—anything but check out the house.

"It's just as well," he said when, brokenhearted and

verging on tears, I angrily informed him that thanks to his foot-dragging, the house had been sold. "Don't take it too hard. It wasn't in our cards."

After that, we never discussed houses again. Though that didn't stop me from looking—constantly—and praying that Hugh would change his mind.

The familiar feelings of domestic longing come rushing back when I drive up to 25 Peabody Road. Though I've passed by this house and picked up Todd here a few times after work, I've never really stopped to appreciate the place. Twice as large as the adorable blue Spring Hill house in Somerville, it has a wrap-around front porch, shutters, real stained-glass windows, and unbelievable privacy.

Todd's right. It is a rare find.

Even Hugh would go for it, I think, immediately kicking myself for falling into the old habit of automatically asking myself what Hugh would do. I must get over him for my own sanity. I have to steam forward, forge the next stream, climb every mountain. Just because he won't be upstairs writing doesn't mean I can't bake cookies in the kitchen. Though it won't be half as much fun without our children, Meg, Beth, and Amy, the darlings.

"Hurry up. You're creeping along like a couple of old ladies." Todd is waiting for me on the front porch, showered and shaved, as eager as a kid on Christmas morning. "Until now, you've only seen the kitchen torn up, Genie. Wait 'til you see what we've done to the rest of the house. It'll blow your mind."

"Not too shabby," Patty says, slowly climbing the wide front steps. "I can't believe it's only half a mil. There must be mold."

"No mold, baby." Todd graciously opens the front door for us. "No kitchen. But that's okay since Genie's no cook."

"Ha, ha." I stick out my tongue at him as we enter the recently renovated living room, where, much to my delight, a fireplace with a gorgeous new marble mantel awaits.

"Can't you see Hugh here?" Todd positions himself by the mantel, pretending to puff on a pipe. "Yes, yes. But you're arguing from a strictly Hobbesian perspective. Consider if you will, old man, the Swiftian viewpoint. Blah, blah, blah. More hot air."

"Is that supposed to be British intellectual?" Patty asks. "Or Alistair Cooke with sleep apnea?"

"Like there's a difference."

One of Todd's workers, a tall tan man with dark curling hair, walks by with a long strip of white painted molding balanced on his shoulder. Nick the carpenter. Crap. The last man on Earth I should have to deal with this morning.

Not that I have anything against Nick personally. I'm sure he's nice enough; at least every other woman on the planet seems to think so. Todd told me that ever since he hired Nick to build some bookshelves and the kitchen cabinets and to install the trim, this house has taken on a magnetic quality, drawing to it love-smitten females of all shapes and ages, including the ninety-year-old next-door neighbor, Mrs. Ipilito, who trots over every afternoon with a pot of espresso and a basket of biscotti, just for an opportunity to stare into Nick's Mediterranean blue eyes and sigh over his Apollonian shoulders.

Nor does Nick do anything to dissuade them, apparently. According to Todd, he chats up all his female admirers, never failing to notice if the single mother down the street has had her nails done or changed the color of her hair. I've even witnessed this firsthand.

Two weeks ago, when I stopped by to take Todd out to dinner, I caught Nick flashing me his mesmerizing smile even though I had done absolutely nothing to encourage him.

"What?" I finally had to ask.

"Nothing." He kept stupidly grinning, almost laughing to himself before yanking a hammer out of the canvas tool belt that hung low on his hips. His very trim hips. Which was when, for no reason I've been able to fathom, my whole body kind of burst into flame. No, really. My face flushed and a wave of heat ran right up my neck. I'd say it was a hot flash except that I'm too young. (At least, I *hope* I'm too young.) And the worst part of it is, I think Nick knew I burst into flame, too.

After this thoroughly mortifying experience, I resolved that should he ever try to cast his spell on me again I would simply walk away. Today, however, I'm in a rare mood. With Hugh having just dumped me, I'm itching to take on any egotistical man who assumes he's God's gift to women. Just let him try his seductive powers. Let him try. The way I see it, men like Hugh, and, quite possibly, Nick, need to be stopped in their tracks so they don't bulldoze through life, razing the hearts of vulnerable women—like I used to be.

"You guys know Nick?" Todd asks us. "Nick is the best carpenter this side of the Charles River."

"That's not saying much, man." Nick laughs and climbs the ladder to nail in the molding. Despite my simmering irritation, I'm disappointed he didn't attempt to charm me with his special grin. Not that I wanted him to charm me with his grin, just that I was ready for it.

"You're making people work on Sunday?" Patty asks Todd, though her gaze is assuredly fixed on Nick's tight jeans. Patty's the type who wouldn't mind being under Nick's spell. She claims this is a perk of being a woman, that we get to sleep—or dream about sleeping—with men like Nick.

"We have to work on Sunday. Gotta get this house on the market," Todd tells her. "When I say Cecily's motivated, I mean motivated. Come on. We'll start with the kitchen, since it's the worst part of the house and you've already been in it."

We move from the dining room with its bay windows and built-in glassed bookshelf (spectacular!) to the kitchen, which is definitely too small and, aside from a sink, a dented Sub-Zero refrigerator, cabinets with no doors, and a standard gas stove, is largely unfinished.

Todd pounds the rough-in for the counter. "This is why you're getting a price break. I'm telling you, if this kitchen were done, the ticket would go up another hundred grand."

Fine by me, since if I had my druthers, I'd knock out the butler's pantry and design the kitchen from scratch. The cabinets would have to be white with maybe Italian tile on the backsplash. I'd put in rock maple counters for easy cutting, perhaps some granite or soapstone. A slab of marble for rolling out pastry dough. Though, what am I saying? To do all that would be *hugely* expensive.

Todd leads us around to the master bedroom and downstairs bath (no tub, only a modified shower) and second bedroom, all of which face the golf course for rare quiet—except for the occasional buzz of golf carts and whacking balls. In the rear is also a sun room, which is, Todd notes, a perfect office.

"Or baby room," Patty suggests.

"Don't make me think about my sister having sex. Please," Todd says, circling us back to the kitchen.

He's about to show us the upstairs apartment when his cell rings and he goes outside to take a call. Cecily Blake, probably. The woman can't seem to leave my brother alone.

"Well?" says Patty. "What do you think?"

"I think it's fabulous and way out of my price range."

"Your price range could buy you a closet in Roxbury. This is awesome. You definitely should get your parents to chip in."

Lowering my voice so Todd won't hear, I point out that, unless she's forgotten, I'm not really getting married.

"Yeah. But that's the whole point of pretending to be engaged. Fake it to make it, baby."

"Even if that means lying to my parents?"

"*Especially* if that means lying to your parents. In case you hadn't noticed, Genie, they've been operating on a two-tiered system with you definitely in the bottom tier. I mean, if you're not going to help your kids buy a house, that's one thing. But if you are, then don't discriminate based on whether they're married or not."

Patty, who cannot keep her voice to a whisper no matter how hard she tries, is working herself to the point where the next-door neighbors surely can hear. And by that I don't mean Mrs. Ipilito, I mean Connecticut.

"Plus, the quality of craftsmanship is stunning," she yells. "Twelve-foot ceilings. Crown molding. Custom-made cabinets. Your father's going to realize the investment potential long after he finds out your engagement is a crock of shit."

There is a crash in the other room followed by

Greek-sounding swearing. I have to remind Patty to keep it down. We're not the only ones here.

"Oh, he doesn't care," she says, waving off Nick. "But you have to admit I'm right."

"I don't know." I must search for reasons to disagree, otherwise when this house gets sold I'm going to sink into the same funk I sank into when I lost the Spring Hill place. "It's not so great. I mean, take the molding."

Patty looks up at the molding. "What about it?"

"It's clearly mass manufactured, probably bought at Home Depot. Quality molding would be hand carved, like those old homes in Back Bay. And the cabinets . . ." I tap the cabinet. "Glued. Quality cabinets have no glue. They're dovetailed together, like the Shakers built. This is just modern carpentry. As Hugh would say, totally without art."

"I'm not so sure it's *totally* without art." Nick is standing in the doorway, scowling at me. "I happen to put a lot of sweat and creativity in what I do."

Super. He's the carpenter and he's just heard me trash his work. Well, there's not much I can do about that now, can I? It's either stand my ground or apologize so he'll go away. But I can't apologize, because I'm right. Hugh taught me how to distinguish fine craftsmanship from its slapdash imitation. And believe me, Hugh knows quality—as he'd be the first to tell anyone.

"I don't think we've really met." Patty opens her purse and pulls out a business card. "I'm Patty. Call me if you need anything. I'm also a terrific lawyer."

Nick momentarily glances at the card and says, "Thanks. But I don't need a lawyer right now."

"The services I have in mind aren't necessarily legal in nature," she observes.

"Look. I'm sorry if you were offended by what I said," I begin, diplomatically. "I was only pointing out that in the old days they took more care. They didn't have modern conveniences like glue or machines that would turn out molding. As a result, the end product was more lasting."

"Really? You might be interested to know that carpenters have used glue for centuries, with or without dovetailing, and I'll tell you something else about your fancy Back Bay molding. It also was cut by machines, albeit crude machines. The rich folks on Beacon Hill might like to think their molding was hand-carved, but that's because they're paying six million dollars a unit. Whoever told you otherwise doesn't know his ass from first base."

Instinctively, I bristle. This is exactly what I suspected, that Nick is a know-it-all like Hugh, another handsome man eager to put me in my place. Well, not today. Not after what I've been through.

"I'll tell you who told me," I say crisply. "Hugh Spencer. That's who."

Nick squints. "Hugh who?"

"Spencer. He's one of the foremost authorities on pure-method house building." I have no idea what the heck pure-method house building is.

lie, to wrap it around a kernel of truth.) Hugh really did build a post-and-beam house—just not *all* of it, only a little part. And that part he ended up having to supervise—albeit against his will—because his doctor warned him in no uncertain terms that one wrong move while heavy lifting and his bad back would be out of commission like that. Hugh was devastated. He really looked forward to hammering and mitering and stuff.

On the bright side, he did get in a lot of journaling.

Now Nick is grinning like he did the other day. It's that same I-know-something-you-don't-know grin and it requires every ounce of my will not to self-combust.

"You know," he says, putting one hand up against the doorjamb and sticking his other thumb in his belt, thereby striking the ultimate beefcake pose, "I think I may have heard of this Hugh Spencer."

"Really?" I say with shock, before I can catch myself.

"Really."

"Interesting." I am trying very hard not to admire the way his shirt hugs his abs or how his bicep is flexed or how the strong slope of his thigh looks under his worn jeans. He is attempting to cast his spell and I must not be tempted like Patty, the million-dollar litigator, who is transfixed, mouth agape.

"I figured you would," I say. "He's famous."

"Oh, I have no doubt. I'd like to meet him and ask him for some . . . pointers. Is he around?"

"England," I reply, my mouth suddenly parched. "Won't be back for the whole summer."

Patty blurts, "We hope."

Cripes. Her brain really does go south in the presence of a good-looking man. Thank heavens most of the Massachusetts Bar is ugly or this woman wouldn't have a career to speak of.

Luckily, before Nick can grill me anymore, Todd stomps in, red-faced and out of sorts from his phone call with Cecily. "The day I never speak to that woman again can't come soon enough. She must call me every hour, on the hour. Talk about the owner from hell."

"Have you ever heard of this famous Hugh Spencer?" Nick asks.

"Sure." Todd gestures to me dismissively. "He's Genie's fiancé. Finally asked her to marry him last night after shacking up with her for four years."

A kind of dawning realization sweeps across Nick's face, as if he has just put into place the last pieces of a confounding puzzle. "I see."

His expression raises my concern that perhaps he overheard Patty and me talking about my fake engagement. And, if so, then I've got a potential problem on my hands. Instead of feeling hot, now I'm feeling nervous. Really nervous.

"Then, may I congratulate you on your upcoming nuptials," Nick says, extending his hand. "I apologize for accusing your future husband of never really building a house. I was totally out of line."

I take his hand and shake it, Nick's pulse strangely beating against mine. Oddly, he doesn't let go. I'm not sure I can, either.

"Don't feel bad," Todd says. "Hugh's always telling me how to maintain my car when he's never once done an oil change himself. Too many carcinogens, he says. Can't risk getting cancer every four thousand miles or something. He's just book learning. Lots of tweed and elbow patches, if you catch my drift."

I don't care if Todd's losing my argument for me. Because right now I have bigger worries—like whether Nick knows I'm not really engaged to Hugh and, worse, whether he's going to reveal my precious secret to Todd.

Chapter Five

I don't want to pretend that I'm engaged anymore.

This has absolutely nothing to do with Nick and how he looked leaning against the doorjamb. It might *seem* as if my desire not to be engaged might have something to do with Nick and my curiosity about how he looks with those jeans off, but, really, nothing could be further from the truth.

Nor do I want to sleep around as a free woman—Patty's theory. It is just like Patty to distill the most noble of human actions, whether rocketing to the moon or unraveling our DNA, into two basic drives: greed and sex.

Sex is fine for some women, women who excel at

the physical gymnastics of love. But as I've been disqualified from the sex kitten club (thanks to Hugh), I will have to hope that eventually some kind and decent man will appreciate me for my mind. I will take up knitting and he will wear slippers and together we will watch PBS before retiring to our separate beds.

I'm sure we'll be very happy. In a way.

Honestly, there is one simple, fundamental, and honorable reason why I want to stop this charade and that is this: If Nick overheard Patty call my engagement a crock of shit, then it is just a matter of time before Nick lets my secret slip to Todd. I would much rather tell Todd the truth myself than have him hear it from his carpenter over a beer at the Cambridge Grill.

But first, I need to come clean to my parents. Starting tonight.

The weekly Sunday dinner with my parents is my mother's single-handed attempt to delay the unraveling of her matrilineal dominance over our family.

For years she reigned supreme, withholding allowances or the family car from those of her children who misbehaved, bestowing her mad money on and extending curfew for those who bent to her will. (Notice I did not say "behaved.")

Then we drifted off like dandelion seeds in a summer breeze. First, Todd left to go to school, and when he refused to come home—though he lived right down the road in Cambridge—my mother saw the writing on the wall.

She was not happy about her waning power. She threw fits. She threatened. She cajoled, and, at her most evil, she baked sour cream apple pie and deposited it outside Todd's dorm room with a note: "See what you missed?" The plate was empty, aside from a puny sliver, just enough to fan the flames of apple-pie addiction.

Don't even ask about her late-night calls to him about Leroy, Todd's beloved Jack Russell terrier, whom she hysterically claimed was wasting away from "Boy Abandonment Syndrome." Thank God Todd was smart enough to call the vet, who—after collapsing on the floor in a fit of laughter—confirmed there was, in fact, no such disease, though Leroy's diarrhea might disappear if our mother quit feeding him leftover sour cream apple pie.

I was the next to fly the nest and, warned in advance by Todd, would not acquiesce to her absurd demand that I return *every weekend* "to rest"—no matter how enticing her offers of clean bedding, washed laundry, a quiet house, free meals, HBO, and endless hot showers might be. Lucy, the youngest, was smarter. She fled to Charlottesville to attend the University of Virginia. With her my mother didn't try so hard. By then, I think, she was exhausted anyway. Plus, she had run out of tricks. Lucy didn't even have a dog.

All was going fine until we made our fatal mistake: Todd returned home after traveling the world for two years, Lucy married Jason and moved to nearby Concord, New Hampshire, to run Jason's family business, and I, well, I never went anywhere. I just stayed. For the first time in years, all of us were within my mother's reach. And that's when she bared her claws.

We didn't stand a chance. Before we knew what was happening, Mom's Sunday dinners were required attendance. Only Hugh managed to weasel out of them and that was largely due to his ability to stutter his way out of anything.

Though I love my sister and can, usually, tolerate her goody-two-shoes husband, I am extremely disappointed to see their Windstar in my parents' driveway when I arrive. Telling my parents that I made up my engagement with Hugh will be painful all by itself; having perfect Jason and Lucy there to witness my shame will be intolerable.

I park at the curb, apply a modest coat of Honey Blush lipstick, grab the plate of brownies I made, and set my shoulders back. I march past my mother's roses to the patio, where my family, a smoldering charcoal fire, and certain damnation await.

"There she is! There's the bride-to-be!" My father throws down his Sunday newspaper and stands to greet me with open arms. "Nance! Lucy! Come on. Our Eugenia's here."

If he's calling me "our Eugenia," then this is going to be worse than I expected. My father is in a cheerful, short-sleeve madras shirt that only a sinister wife like Nancy Michaels would order from Sears.com for her husband. I have barely put down the plate of brownies when he smushes me against him and starts mumbling something about me being such a great daughter. He smells of barbeque and vodka.

Darn. They've started already.

"She's here. She's here!" This is my mother screaming as she whips back the sliding screen door and dashes to the patio. She practically flings a Saran Wrap–covered plate of marinated chicken (from Whole Foods—my mother never cooks if she can help it) onto the glass table and rips me from Dad's arms. "My baby girl's getting married. At last, at last."

I sniff for the telltale vodka and find it under a layer of Trident cinnamon gum and another layer of Chanel No. 5. This could ruin all my plans. If Mom and Dad are truly on the road to Tanktown, there's no way I can drop the bomb. Dad will go ballistic and Mom will start sobbing. It'll be a mess.

"We never thought this day would come," she blathers. "Four years. Four long years. Who knew?"

Not Hugh, that's for sure.

Dad puts his hand on my shoulder, paternally. "We figured you'd die a spinster. A dried-up old thing in lace. Just like your crazy old aunt Tilley."

"Thanks, Pop. I appreciate that." I must maintain my good humor.

Mom appraises me at arm's length as if I've just returned from a tour of duty overseas. As always, she is impeccably dressed in a Carolina Herrera white shirt. (The only shirt she wears. She's got, like, fifty.)

And a pink and green Lilly Pulitzer wrap skirt. Her silver highlighted hair is pushed back from her face with her standard headband, thereby showcasing her famous Howland cheekbones. (Mom openly brags that she can trace her ancestry back to *Mayflower* passenger John Howland—a claim to which my father responds, "You and half of America.")

Tears spring to her eyes. "We're so glad it's Hugh. I can't tell you how glad."

"And not that loser who sold T-shirts. What's his name . . ." My father looks off, trying to remember. "Tommy."

"Toby," I correct. "He wasn't a loser. He was an assistant political science professor who printed T-shirts protesting the war and donated his profits to Amnesty International."

Dad rolls his eyes as if there couldn't be a bigger waste of time than the pursuit of world peace.

Mom says, "At least Toby wasn't as bad as Kent. Honey, if you had married him, your father and I were prepared to abduct you and take you to one of those deprogrammers."

She needn't have worried. Kent, like Hugh, had no intention of marrying me. Not because of my sexual inadequacy (though, you never know) but because I wouldn't go into therapy and admit my parents were self-centered social alcoholics who had never reaffirmed my validity as a person. As if I needed to shell out $200 an hour to learn that.

"Taken that boy out to the woodshed and strapped

his behind is what I should have done," Dad is saying, his hand balling into a fist.

"We don't have a woodshed," I point out. "And Kent was six-three and outweighed you by thirty pounds. You wouldn't have stood a chance."

"Oh, well. All's well that ends well." This is Mom's standard line for changing the subject. "The point is we need to plan, plan, plan. Your wedding's in September. That doesn't give us much time. Are you sure you don't want to put it off a bit?"

Here, suddenly, is my out. Handed to me like dessert on a platter. A delay. What a brilliant idea. "Actually, Mom . . ."

She lets out a screech. "What am I talking about? You don't want to put it off. You've waited all this time—of course you want to get him to the altar before he changes his mind!"

With this my mother—whom I've just concluded is perhaps more soused than I initially assessed—sweeps her arm so wide it hits the umbrella at the center of the glass picnic table and the whole thing wobbles.

Fortunately, Lucy's there to catch it. As always, she is smashingly coiffed and composed, in a yellow halter top and white shorts that emphasize her toned physique. This comes from her daily schedule of working out, doing yoga, and assiduously avoiding any task smacking of actual employment.

Somewhere along the line, Lucy went from being my snotty kid sister, younger by a whopping eight years, who blew off her bills and nicked her car on fire hydrants (she is the worst parallel parker *ever!*), to being a responsible, prudent hausfrau. It was as though the moment she said those marriage vows, people decided she was mature and stable while I, in my singleness, was reduced to the family baby.

"Guess what I found in the attic?" Lucy holds up a sage green book. "Don't you want to scream?!"

Stuffed to the gills with brochures, fabric swatches, sample invitations, and even a few dead flowers is Lucy's old *Martha Stewart's Keepsake Wedding Planner.* The very sight of its torn binding brings back bad memories of hours and hours spent tasting dry, oversweet cake, trying on endless dresses, and debating every detail down to whether the ribbon on the ring bearer's pillow should be narrow or wide.

"I saved it for you. I knew this day would come!" She lets out a squeal and wraps her bony arms around my neck. Whispering in my ear, she adds conspiratorially, "Now you can kiss that admissions job goodbye and we can hang out together at the Arsenal Mall all day!"

Yippee.

We spring apart and Lucy shoves the book into my arms. I nearly keel over with its weight. "I have done so much bushwhacking for you. You'll have it easy peasy. I've written down all the right florists, the right caterers, everything."

"Though maybe Genie will want to get married in

England," my mother adds, batting her eyes hopefully. "That is a possibility, isn't it?"

This, of course, would elevate my mother to a celestial realm among her girlfriends, to have a daughter marrying in Old Blighty.

"I'm not sure there will be a wedding, Mom . . ."

Lucy jerks my arm. "No way. You have to marry here. I've already contacted Bea Cummings."

I search my personal data bank for a Bea Cummings and come up with the chain-smoking, coughing hag Lucy hired to do her wedding.

Oh, no. She didn't. A wedding planner already?

"This is awful," my mother exclaims.

"Too soon," I agree. "Much too soon."

"No," Mom disagrees. "Too late. This morning I called Elise."

Elise?

"Mom, that's awesome!" Lucy again squeals so loudly my father covers his ears. "Elise DuPont is in *such* demand. How did you do it?"

Mom opens her mouth to answer, sees my father frowning, and snaps her trap. "Tell you later. Right now we have to figure out what to do. Elise or Bea."

Suddenly, both of them are staring at me. "Well?" Mom asks. "Which is it, Genie? Elise or Bea?"

I am speechless. I couldn't pick out either in a lineup.

Lucy says knowledgeably, "Get used to it, Genie. This is the first of many, many decisions you're going to have to make between now and September fifteenth. Frankly, you can't go wrong with either. Bea is kind of sarcastic and cold, but she's a pro who's been in the business forever. Your wedding will run like clockwork. Elise is more flighty and younger, but much more creative. She'll make it magical."

I am frozen in place. When I signed up for this faux marriage thing, I never imagined I'd be hiring wedding planners within twenty-four hours. Come to think of it, I have no idea what I imagined.

"Hold on," my mother says, stepping back. "We're getting ahead of ourselves, choosing wedding planners when we haven't even covered the basics."

Whew! My shoulders sag in relief and I realize my muscles are throbbing, I've been at such rigid attention. "You're right, Mom. We should slow down."

"Absolutely. I'm sure Hugh will want input. Don? Where did you put that number for Hugh's parents, the one that came on their Christmas card last year?"

My hand shoots out to avert a crisis. "You are not calling Hugh's parents."

"Of course we called them. That's what one does when one's daughter gets engaged. The parents of the bride immediately call the parents of the groom to congratulate them." She shakes off my hand. "Don't be so dense, Eugenia."

I calculate the grammar in my head. There's a past tense there. "You mean you already called?"

"Last night. Though we totally forgot about the time difference, didn't we, Don? They must have been in bed because they didn't pick up."

Suddenly, I'm overcome by a violent urge to jump out of my own skin.

"So, we'll try again now. It's better you're here, anyway, Genie." Mom takes the portable from Lucy, who's thoughtfully fetched it from the family room. (Thanks, Lucy.) "And if Hugh's there, we'll talk to him, too. I can't wait to tell him how happy we are that he finally asked you to marry him, and in such a dramatic way, too."

No, no, no. They cannot call Trevor and Susanna Spencer. They cannot call Hugh. That would ruin everything.

I reach for the phone. "You can't. It's too late."

"It is not. It's only ten there."

"You forget about their daylight saving time," I argue, winging it. "They're seven hours ahead of us in the summer."

Mom holds the phone out of my reach. "Don't be ridiculous. They're only five. Now do I have to dial a one first, Donald, or a zero?"

In desperation, I turn to Lucy, who is smiling from ear to ear. Of course. Why wouldn't she be? She thinks I'm really getting married. She has no idea that we are about to call two near strangers in another country, on another continent, and welcome them to our family for no reason other than I am pretending to be engaged to their son.

"Put it on speakerphone, Nance," Dad says.

"Right." Mom presses a button and props the phone on the glass table, while we gather around listening to the foreign farting ring of Trevor and Susanna Spencer's London phone. My heart is pounding so hard everyone must hear it. I have got to get out of here. I cannot stand here while my whole family listens to Susanna proclaim me insane.

Dad slaps an arm around my shoulder and holds me tight. "We are so proud of you, do you know that, Toodles?"

Not Toodles. Anything but Toodles.

"Hellooo?" The woman answering is ultimately British. Upper crust. Refined. I cringe, anticipating what will come next.

"Well, HELLO!" Mom shouts, completely forgetting that satellites and digital technology means you no longer have to holler at the foreigners. "This is Nancy Michaels calling from America."

There is a pause, an awful, dreadful pause. "Who?"

"NANCY MICHAELS," my mother shouts. "GENIE'S MOTHER."

Oh, God. I can't take this. Any minute now and my cover will be blown.

"I'm afraid I don't know what you're talking about? Have you rung up the wrong number?"

Mom gives Dad a questioning look. "Is she daft? Genie, has Hugh's mother gone dotty?"

"Just forget it, Mom," I urge. "Call back later. I told you it was late."

"Nonsense. Donald, you talk to her."

Dad lets go of me and in an even louder voice bellows, "THIS IS DONALD MICHAELS, FATHER OF GENIE MICHAELS. HUGH'S FIANCÉE."

Oh, crap. He told her. *Hugh's fiancée.*

"I had no idea," the woman says, clearly confused. "Let me go find Hugh." With a clunk, she puts down the phone and goes off.

That's it. I need to escape so that I'm not here when Hugh returns and the hail of shame rains down.

And then I see my savior. Jason, touchstone of all that is right and proper, is carrying out a salad and regarding my mother's empty martini glass with dismay.

Jason doesn't look like your run-of-the-mill super Christian. His brownish hair's not short. In fact, it's kind of long and shaggy. He doesn't wear Dockers or a cross or anything. Right now he's in a white button-down shirt and wearing his customary hemp necklace. If they'd made born-again Christians like him when I was in my twenties, I might have gone to a few revivals.

"Congratulations, Genie," he says, giving me a quick, brotherly hug.

"We're talking to Hugh's parents now," Mom says excitedly. "Having a bit of a communication problem, though. They can't seem to find Hugh. They're taking forever."

Praise the Lord for small miracles. "Mom. Don't you need another drink?"

Mom looks doubtful, all part of her act. "Maybe just one more martini. No, a pitcher for all of us. It is, after all, a special occasion."

A pitcher of martinis? Gag. She really is going over-board.

"I'll make it," I say, trying to move past her.

"But you can't. You have to be here when Hugh gets on."

"Let Jason make them," Dad says.

"Yes," Mom agrees, "let the Christian boy make them."

"Those who don't drink, mix, you know," adds my father heartily, handing Jason his own empty glass. "Make 'em in the spirit of FDR, son."

Jason exchanges wordless signals with Lucy, whose plan, I'm guessing, is to have him mix them weak. I'm not sure it is possible to mix a weak martini, but I'm willing to help. Anything to flee the prospect of hearing Hugh's shocked and angry reaction.

"I'll go with him," I say, "to make sure he can find the vodka. Call me when Hugh gets back on. I've got to go to the bathroom anyway."

Mom waves me off. "Very well. Make yourself one, too."

"No, thanks. I'm not drinking."

She shoots a stricken look at Dad. "Not drinking?"

"Nope. I'll just have a 7UP."

I turn my back and follow Jason to the kitchen as Mom, Dad, and Lucy clump into a huddle. In any other family not drinking would be barely noticed, totally accepted, or even applauded. In mine, it's cause for immediate discussion.

Chapter Six

Jason is examining a shelf of my mother's cookbooks when I enter the kitchen. Poor kid. He has no idea that martinis are not food.

"Let me help. I think the vodka's in the freezer."

"I know what a martini is. I just need to know the proportions." He picks out a slim red book of drink recipes circa 1955 and begins flipping through it. "What was that about FDR?"

The huge bottle of vodka's lying on top of the frozen vegetables and ice-cream sandwiches like the bully of a frozen underworld. I pull it out, one ear cocked toward the patio for the inevitable cry of disbelief when Hugh tells them the truth.

"It means to make them dirty. FDR liked his martinis dirty."

"Dirty?"

"Lots of olive brine."

"Oh." He goes back to studying the book as if he's cramming for a chemistry exam.

"I'm sorry my parents do this to you. I mean, you shouldn't have to . . . 'cause of your"—oh, God—"beliefs and all."

"That's what you get, being a Christian," he quips, flattening out the pages. "First, we're thrown to the lions, and then we're forced to mix martinis for Episcopalians."

My mother would argue that as Episcopalians we

are Christians, too, but I'm not in the mood for religious debate. Instead, I search the refrigerator for olives while Jason tries to find the vermouth.

"So, you and Hugh are going to buck the trend and get married," he says, pouring vodka into a measuring cup.

I pull out a tray of ice. My parents' automated ice maker broke one week after they bought the new refrigerator and they never bothered to fix it. "Yup."

"Excited?"

"Kind of."

"You, um, don't seem thrilled." He pauses. "Is it Hugh?"

Crack! The ice cubes pop out of their plastic tray. "You might say that."

"Because he's not here?"

"More like because he doesn't know."

"Doesn't know you're here?"

"Doesn't know we're engaged." I cannot believe I just said that. "Hugh never asked me to marry him. I made it up."

There is silence. My back is to Jason and I don't dare turn around, though I hear him pour in something else and then the clank of a spoon against glass. All I can think is *Don't stir, you idiot!*

The stirring stops and Jason asks, "You're kidding me, right?"

"Nope." Grasping a handful of ice, I dump it into the glass pitcher. "You're not supposed to stir the martini. It bruises the vodka."

"You can't bruise vodka. It's diluted ethyl alcohol. I don't know how you people can drink it." He removes the spoon and carefully lays it on a dishcloth. Then he reaches out, takes my hand, and says, "Why?"

"Because it loosens all your joints and makes you feel relaxed."

A minute passes while he processes this. "I'm not asking why you drink. I'm asking why you're lying about getting married to Hugh."

The only reply I can think of is, "It's a long, complicated story. The bottom line is that Hugh apparently has been having an affair and she's the woman he proposed to on television, not me."

"Ahh."

"You've got to take out that ice or it'll be watery. My father hates that."

Jason holds up the spoon. "With this?"

"I dunno."

"It'll get stirred."

"That's a risk I'm willing to take."

I watch as Jason carefully lifts out each ice cube and am reminded of *The Gods Must Be Crazy*, when the bushman studies the Coke bottle. What an odd ritual this must be to him, the act of preparing and ingesting poison.

"Do you think I'm going to hell?"

Jason gives me a look. "Why do you ask me questions like that?"

"Because you're an authority on what's in and what's out as far as hell is concerned."

Lifting out the last ice cube, he chucks it into the sink and says, "You ever want to sit down and talk about God's eternal plans for each of us, I'm here for you, Genie, but right now I think you've got other stuff to worry about."

"Like the fact that my parents are talking to Hugh's parents, who have no idea that their son is fake engaged to me?"

"For starters," he says. "It'd be better if you were honest with them now so they wouldn't have to find out from other people, don't you think?"

I open the olive jar and dump in its brine, holding my fingers against the glass so the olives don't fall in.

"Might be too late. I may have passed that point." Still no whooping or crying from the patio. My mother is not flinging back the screen door, demanding to know if I took her for a fool. What's going on?

Jason is washing glasses and setting them on a tray very neatly. I think about how tidy and uncomplicated his life with Lucy is, how they entered adulthood taking all the appropriate steps—a suitable courtship period, a proper engagement, and a religious wedding. They didn't move in together before they married. They bought a brand-new house and decorated it in coordinating colors so that it was ready and waiting for them, new sheets and all, when they stepped off the plane from their Jamaican honeymoon.

"Is it true Mom and Dad gave you guys two hundred thousand to buy your house?" Yes, it was rude to ask. It just slipped out.

"Three hundred." Jason looks up. "Is that why you're faking your engagement?"

For some reason I feel busted, even though I didn't fake my engagement to get money. "No. I didn't find out Mom and Dad gave you that much until Todd told me today. I thought it was more like twenty or something."

Jason reddens slightly. "It was way too generous of them. I wouldn't have taken it if Lucy hadn't had her heart set on the house. I mean, don't get me wrong. I was really relieved and grateful. Just that, sometimes I feel guilty."

Welcome to the club.

Still no sound from the patio and I'm not about to go outside and find out, either.

I pop a green olive into my mouth and suck out the pimiento. It tastes like salty tears as I do a mental tour of Jason and Lucy's brand-new house with its downstairs master suite, its media room with the plasma TV over the fireplace, and its upstairs "children's playroom" with four dormers and interconnecting bedrooms and bathrooms.

Three hundred thousand dollars. Whew. If I'd had one-third of that, I could have bought the Somerville house already.

"You know, Lucy wasn't the only one," Jason adds, after thinking about it. "Your parents also gave Todd a chunk of change when he started his business."

I nearly swallow my olive whole. "Todd got money? How much?"

Again, Jason reddens. "I don't know. I just didn't want you to get all mad at Lucy."

"Was it three hundred thousand?"

"*Shhh.* We shouldn't be discussing this."

"Why the hell not?"

"It's none of our business."

It is too my business. Each sibling gets cash for neatly fitting into their assigned, gender-specific roles, whereas I'm left to ride the subway every morning, punch a clock, clip coupons, and live in a cramped apartment. I mean, I don't want to come off as a pig, but fair is fair.

"What if I never marry?" I ask.

Jason cocks his head thoughtfully. "I don't know. The way Nancy and Don put it, they were happy to pay for the house for Lucy and me so we could start off on the right foot."

"Are you telling me life doesn't start until you get married?"

"That's the way your parents think. Me, too, I suppose. I mean, isn't that why two people get married? It's a foundation on which you build your family. People our age, the ones who are living together and hooking up and claiming marriage is dead, they're missing out on the best gift God ever gave to man, aside from life. Check out Genesis 2:24."

Genesis, ha! Don't start throwing the Old Testament at me, buddy, I want to say. Trying to hide my hurt, I reach for my purse. "I need to call Todd."

"Don't be mad at him. Darn. I knew I shouldn't have told you."

94

but he just purses his lips in disapproval. I can't believe Jason spilled my secret so fast. That fink!

"Jason told you?"

"No," Mom says. "Lucy and I figured it out. Your paleness. Your utter panic at us calling Hugh's parents."

"Your not drinking," Lucy adds.

"What?" I shrug, clueless. "What are you talking about?"

"That you're pregnant." Lucy throws up her hands. "There. I said it."

For one brilliant moment I feel a breeze of bliss. An out-of-body snapshot of how ridiculous we all are.

"I'm not pregnant."

"You're not?" Mom blinks and reaches for my hand. "Then what were you talking about in the kitchen with Jason for so long? We were sure there was some crisis."

Jason gives me a thumbs-up of encouragement.

"No crisis. I was just hashing over the wedding." I smile at Lucy. "After much thought and consideration, I've decided not to go with a wedding planner. I'll make all the arrangements myself, though Mom, I'm going to let you do most of the planning since you're so good at it. Also, I think we should move the wedding up to August. After all, what's the point of waiting? Seems to me I've waited long enough for what I should have done long, long ago."

And with that, I help myself to one of Jason's martinis, a certain risk if there ever was one.

Chapter Seven

So, that's it. I guess I'm officially on the road to marriage. Let the chips fall where they will.

This is my new attitude as I leave my apartment Monday morning for the hike down Trapelo Road to pick up the number 73 bus. Now that I've given over to this concept of being engaged, of taking a risk, I feel different, free, as if anything is possible, good or bad. Though I'm not expecting bad. I'm betting on good. Absolutely good all the way.

Possibly, my spirit of optimism is due to the day itself, a sparkling warm June morning bursting with rebirth. The trees are now leafy and green, the daffodils have given way to rosebuds, wet wash is already on the lines, sprinklers are starting up, and, better yet, the kids are out of school. No more hordes of shouting, pushing teenagers deafened by white iPod buds to battle at the bus stop.

The air smells fresh and new, earthy. I could sprint to the bus, I'm so charged. I'm more than charged. I'm electric!

Really electric. This morning I bounded out of bed, fed and watered Jorge, shot him up with insulin, and deposited him outside to sit in the exact same spot until I came home from work to take him inside. After that I made my bed with dime-tight hospital corners, executed fifty sit-ups and fifty leg lifts while watching a rerun of *The Daily Show*, and did not stop once to think about being alone in a coat closet with Jon Stewart.

Showered with almond soap, exfoliated, shaved my legs and other parts. Chose a nice flowered sundress—the first of the season—and strappy sandals since we're allowed to "dress alternatively" during the summer. Blow-dried my hair and contemplated for the umpteenth time turning up the blond in my highlights. (Hugh was aghast at this suggestion since bleached blondes reminded him of scary German girls who used to sit on him at Turkish resorts. He much preferred my subtle honey brown. So much less threatening.)

Yes. I definitely should get highlights.

Then it was coffee with cream, no sugar (a holdover from my Atkins days), oatmeal, half a banana, and a review of my scheduled interviews: a Phoebe Shambo from Hanover, New Hampshire, and a Kara Weeks from Chicago. I hardly ever get the boys. They're too coveted. Those go to Bill, my boss, or his right-hand man, Kevin, the prodigy.

Yet, this morning not even my office's sexism can get me down. I am too . . . Zen. This is my new philosophy. From now on, I am not going to worry about pretending to be engaged or the resulting consequences down the road (outrageous, expensive wedding being planned by mother/sister, Hugh finding out and going ballistic).

No.

I have resolved that life's troubles will henceforth be

nothing but a tangent touching me at one infinitesimal point. Worrying is banished from my personal vocabulary, having served no purpose in the first place. (Worrying, that is, not a personal vocabulary.)

In fact, a case could be made that worrying about a problem actually *prevents* you from resolving it, because it deceives your mind into thinking that you're doing something when really you're not. Not only that, but worrying is super bad for your skin. Yes, I refuse to worry from here on out.

Take this latest crisis over Hugh. Naturally, I could wring my hands over him. I could stay up all night and call my friends and drown my woes in mint chip ice cream as I privately hash and rehash that line about him not being attracted to me sexually. (It still stabs me to the core. I'm not sure I'll ever recover.)

But I've done the ice-cream-and-whining routine with other breakups in the past and *nothing changed.* The guy who dumped me did not come back begging for forgiveness. He did not see the folly of his ways and prostrate himself at my feet. Instead, the sun set and rose again, day after day, the wounds healed, and eventually the man who had previously been the sunshine of my existence faded into a dim and dusty memory.

This is the gift of thirtysomething heartbreak, I think. It's not so life and death, unlike when I was twenty-two and I went to pieces because the man I'd slept with on Saturday hadn't called me by Sunday night. Back then I had to cook up all sorts of justifications for his silence (or, rather, rudeness): Work had piled up, his dog had died, his phone had been disconnected. Okay, so that last one made him sound a bit slack-jawed. Still, it could happen. Phones get disconnected every day for the oddest of reasons.

With Hugh, it's different. Already, I have put him behind me like a childhood best friend from summer camp or a freshman roommate. I'm even having trouble remembering what he looks like or what we did together for four years.

Though, I have to admit, I am kind of curious why he hasn't at least e-mailed, especially with my parents calling Pippa and all.

Not that I miss him. I *don't*. It's just that I would think he'd want to check how I was, at least to see if I'd recovered from the breakup. Or to inquire about Jorge and what I've done with the small collection of Hugh's winter clothes I stored under my bed in a zipper bag and if I still have his great-grandfather's gold cuff links in my bedside drawer.

Certainly, he must have been alarmed to find that my parents were calling his parents to congratulate them on our upcoming nuptials.

"Quite startling, really," is something I can imagine Susanna Spencer saying about Mom. "Such a brazen woman, claiming her daughter was marrying you, Hugh. Do you suppose she was just completely blotto?"

If I'd been in his shoes, I'd have been on the phone *tout de suite.*

Then again, these are Hugh's parents we're talking about and they are—let's see, how to put this—*completely bizarre.*

Who sends a six-year-old miles away to boarding school in Scotland? If your answer is the British, you'd be correct. But not all British. Certain types of British, like Susanna and Trevor Spencer. People who "hunt" in tweed clothing nice enough for church, people who travel to estates for weekend-long parties and ski on Alps that are French. I don't even think Trevor works. He does have an office in London, but from what I've been able to discern, it's more like a base station for tête-à-têtes in Knightsbridge.

It always broke my heart to think of little Hugh in his little navy short pants and little beanie waving, "Good-bye, Mummie," as his nanny—yes, his nanny—led him to the train.

"It was all very jolly," he explained to me one night. "Rather good for the fortification of one's upper lip." Here's a tip: No six-year-old should need a stiff upper lip.

Then he told the story of how, suffering from chicken pox at age seven and slightly delirious, he lay in the boarding school infirmary and tried to think pleasant thoughts about what Mummie smelled like. ("Couldn't quite get it right, unfortunately. Kept wanting her to smell like cinnamon and kept coming up Dunhills.")

That pitiful Victorian tale was so sad, I wished for a time machine so I could turn back the clock and

102

rescue the *enfant* Hugh alone in the St. Bart's Nasty School for Unfortunate Rich Boys. But when I dangled it out there that perhaps his mother might have been a tad neglectful, Hugh immediately rose to her defense, claiming she hadn't neglected him in the slightest because she'd had Nanny send up a box of special tea and lemon drops that the St. Bart's nursing staff took for themselves, arguing candy wasn't good for sick children.

I apologized and assured him this did mean his mum loved him desperately. Secretly, however, I vowed that if I ever were in the position of being in charge of Susanna Spencer's care, I would see to it that she lay alone in an infirmary and tried to recall what someone dear to her smelled like, too.

Okay. So I might have gone a bit overboard with that one.

Anyway, no use sweating the St. Bart's chicken pox drama. There's some other woman to look after Hugh now, to hold him in the middle of the night and be the Mummie he never had.

To be fair, Hugh never did treat me like his mother. Far from it. The first night we ever slept together was perhaps one of the most erotic nights of my life. It happened entirely by accident, which, I'm afraid to say, is always the best way. (Sorry, Planned Parenthood.)

We'd been dating for about a month when a freak November snowstorm blanketed Boston and we were stranded in his apartment, which, granted, was above a funeral home, but which also had a spectacular, working fireplace.

There were a few sticks of wood, enough for a small fire. However, we had no food aside from some grapes, crackers, two cans of Progresso clam chowder, and a superb cabernet. To us it was a feast. We drank and ate and talked until the fire died down and snow knocked the power out, and suddenly Hugh was kissing me on the couch in a way I'd never been kissed, ever.

Before I could say "Wait, hold on, not quite ready," he had nuzzled down the collar of my sweater and his lips were exploring my neck. After that, all I remember is sinking into that deep bed of his with the cream duvet and the 1,000-thread-count sheets. We stayed there for two days until New England Power turned on the lights and the heat cranked up.

I used to think our decadent weekend in bed was because I drove Hugh mad with desire, that he couldn't help making long, slow, passionate love to me over and over and over.

Now, in light of his latest revelation, I realize he was just trying to stay warm.

"Genie?"

It's Frank, the bearded driver of the number 73 who smells like bagels and lox and garlic. "Monday morning daydream?"

"Something like that." I flip him my pass and get on.

"Don't worry. Friday's just around the corner. See if you can hang on 'til then."

・ ・ ・

I like Thoreau best in the summer when the campus is quiet and lush. Aside from some lingering students and the occasional conference attendees, it's practically empty.

That's not counting the tours. The tours and tours of prospective freshmen and anxious parents being led around by various admissions interns to Billings Hall (where Admissions is located), Fillmore Library, the Student Center, and the pièce de résistance—the Sports Complex (heated Olympic-size swimming pool, sixteen tennis courts, racquetball, squash, weight room, Jacuzzi, sauna, and even, I am told, massage by appointment).

Not for nothing was Thoreau voted by *Rolling Stone* magazine as the finest four-year, four-season resort east of Las Vegas.

Alice, our secretary, is fiddling with a window air conditioner when I enter her first-floor office to get my mail. She has leaped into the summer season with both feet by donning a short, short white miniskirt. Her subdued navy cap-sleeve sweater and faux pearls are for the parents who will never see the tattoo of Chinese characters over her left breast or her tiny silver ankle bracelet with its not-so-innocent charms.

I attempt ultimate nonchalance. "Hey, Alice. Have a good weekend?"

Usually, this sets her off as Alice is obsessed with Fridays and Saturdays and can discuss them endlessly. From Monday until Wednesday at noon she can run a nonstop monologue about what she did the previous weekend. At some point on Wednesday, usually during lunch, this train of thought abruptly switches to what she *will* do the upcoming weekend, reaching a crescendo of planning around three on Friday, when she knocks off early.

"The better question is, how was *your* weekend?" she says provocatively.

"Um, okay."

I can feel her gaze boring into me as I check my box for Saturday's mail and flip through various meaningless Bill Gladstone memos about upcoming meetings and retreat dates, memos that I will round-file in the privacy of my own office. Then I take a deep breath, tuck my mail under my arm, and say with exasperation, "Mondays. What a drag!"

"Not so fast." Alice snags my left hand. "Where's the ring?"

"What ring?"

"Don't play dumb. We all know what happened. Donna in English practically sent out a newsletter."

Instantly, my armpits go damp. Though I had an inkling that gossip about Hugh's appearance on TV might be circulating around the English Department, I had not expected it to hit my neck of the woods so soon. If Donna knows, then everyone will.

"What's going on?" asks a male voice from the other side of the window.

Brandon, our building's handyman, is holding the air conditioner from his side.

"She got engaged," Alice says. "On television. Hugh Spencer asked her to marry him. Colleen Hirst, the dean's secretary, TiVoed it."

That's how hot Hugh is on campus. Women like Colleen actually TiVo his TV appearances.

Brandon frowns at me in disappointment as though my engagement is a personal affront to his own credentials. "Thought you weren't looking for a serious nonplatonic relationship."

Oh, dear. Is that what I told him?

Years ago, shortly before I met Hugh, Brandon asked me—in a carefully worded and clearly rehearsed speech—if I would like to see the Boston Pops. This was particularly painful because he'd probably thought and thought about what I might consider a fancy date and he came up with the Pops. (Note to men: No woman under seventy likes the Pops.)

Because he'd gone through such agony and because I knew turning him down would devastate him, I went with him to see the Pops and, prior to that, a way-too-expensive dinner at Pier 4, during which he kept rubbing his sweaty palms on his pants and talking about his ex-wife getting the kids and how that was so unfair. The worst was the awkward fumbling kiss in the car at the end. I cringe recalling his eager lips zeroing in on mine.

Since then, we've never been truly at ease around each other. I rarely ask him for help with the copier or changing the fluorescent light fixture, unless I absolutely have to. And then, I never bring up our personal lives. I just assumed he knew Hugh and I were together. Guess not.

"Alice doesn't know what she's talking about," I bluff. "She's smoking dope as usual."

"Not this early in the morning I'm not!"

Gotta love Alice.

"Look, Brandon," she says, fed up. "Hugh and Genie have been dating for four years, as long as Trey Ray and I have. What would you expect? That he'd dump her?"

Cough.

"I'll tell you what, if Trey doesn't end up marrying me after all his shit I've put up with, that man will never walk straight again. Kick and twist. Learned it in self-defense."

Brandon winces and wobbles a bit with the air conditioner.

"I've gotta go," I say, before Alice kicks and twists me for details. "Bill's swamping me with memos."

"He called, you know," Alice says, as I turn the corner.

"Bill?"

"Hugh."

I freeze with my hand on the banister. Why would Hugh have called the office and not my home? Why didn't he just leave a message on my machine?

"How long ago?"

"Ten minutes or so. Brandon was here, weren't you?"

As if that mattered. "Great. I'll call back." I do not

ask if she mentioned our engagement because that's not a question real brides-to-be would ask.

I manage to climb all of two steps, my heart beating like I'm about to have a coronary, when Alice again shouts, "He wanted to know what the insanity was all about."

Five. Four. Three. Two. One. Deep breath. "Did he? That joker."

"I told him to leave a message on your machine. You might want to check."

I cannot dash to my office fast enough. An eternity passes as I fumble with the lock, open the door, and slam it behind me. Finally, I am safe in my small office with its one window and posters of Athens and Rome, places I'd planned to visit on my honeymoon. Or, like, whenever.

Okay. I cannot panic. We are letting the chips fall where they may, right? I am Zen, problems are a tangent line touching me at one infinitesimal spot.

Besides, what's the worst that can happen? I will not lose my job over this. I mean, it's a personal matter, not a professional one. Sure, the department is super-sensitive about honesty after that *Opal Mehta* fiasco, which Connie claims will change admissions policies nationwide forever. But Connie . . .

Wait a second. Where *is* Connie?

Connie's office is across from mine and the door is closed, the light underneath off. It's after nine and she's not here. That's funny because Connie's *always* here. That's what you do when your one aspiration in life is to become assistant director of admissions with the "big office" downstairs next to Bill Gladstone's.

And her car. I hadn't noticed it when I came in.

I rush to my one dinky window, which looks out onto the parking lot.

Her parking spot, the one with the sign that reads CONNIE ROBESON, ADMISSIONS COUNSELOR, is empty. (The designated spot was a concession to Connie after she was passed over—again—for the assistant admissions director job that Kevin the Wunderkind now has.) Her leased Saab convertible is not there.

Oh, happy day. Is it too much to dream that Connie the big-mouth busybody is not here to torture me with endless questions about my betrothal?

I pick up my phone, ignore the blinking message light that no doubt is Hugh inquiring what all the insanity is about, and call down to Alice, who answers with her standard "Thoreau College Admissions. Alice speaking. How may I help you?" Even though she knows full well it is just me from room 201.

"Is Connie here?"

"Nooooo, she's not, Genie." Alice pauses and I hear Brandon crack a joke. His hanging around gives further credence to Connie's theory that when Alice helps Brandon in the basement, the only fuse she's flipping is his. "And I can say no more, especially . . . to you."

To me? This is very strange. Of all the admissions counselors, I am Alice's closest friend. Connie is a user who only sucks up to Alice when there's a paper jam or when she needs a huge file photocopied right away.

"Oh," I say. "Sure. Just wanted to know if she'll be back later today is all."

"Don't you want to know where she is?"

"No. That's all right." I fake a yawn.

"She's . . ." Alice pauses again. *". . . out of the country."*

It is heavy, important, the way Alice says "out of the country," as if my expected reply is supposed to be, "Oh, *really.*"

But I have no idea what my correct response should be except to say that I didn't know she was planning to go on vacation this week.

"She wasn't. She left yesterday on the spur of the moment. *Hint. Hint.*"

Hint, hint?

"You mean, she's not traveling for work?"

"Nooooo. Guess again."

"You're crazy, you know that, Alice? I'll catch you later." And I hang up.

Hint, hint, indeed. Here's a hint: Alice needs more work to occupy her day. She could start by cleaning up my desk, which is a mishmash of memos, Post-its, clipped magazine articles, and files. All stuff I'd left in disarray to meet Steve for drinks and a game of pool on Friday.

Friday seems so faraway now, such a sweeter, simpler time in my life. On Friday, I hadn't yet lied to my family and friends. On Friday, I was still under the impression Hugh and I were a couple never to be split. Look. There's my calendar. "Hugh's back!" excitedly written in red ink on the day he is to return from England.

I twirl my chair around to survey my framed photos. And there Hugh and I are behind glass, blissful and in love.

I keep a select group of photos on a low bookshelf so students being interviewed will glean that I am a human being and not an automaton. There's a deceptively normal group shot of my family, windblown and tan on Cape Cod, that does not display the beers my parents are clutching behind their backs. Another of Jorge in someone's lap, before he became clinically obese. A picture, for some reason, of just Jason and Lucy (probably because they frame and send so many photos of themselves, I'm overloaded at home). And exactly two pictures of Hugh and me.

One is of us at Thanksgiving, still glowing from our nor'easter snowbound lovemaking weekend in Hugh's apartment. He is kissing my red cheek and I am smiling broader than I think is possible for my mouth.

The other is of the two of us on a ski slope in Vermont. Hugh is wearing a totally ridiculous yellow and chartreuse cap that he refused to take off. And I am looking positively terrified at the prospect of heading down that mountain. My eyes are bugging out, my jaw is to my feet, and I am clutching Hugh, the expert skier, who is laughing good-naturedly.

Applicants love that photo. They can relate to abject terror.

Applicants. Yes. Must get to work. I cannot sit in my office all morning mooning over what might have been. I suppose I *could* check my messages, but that would involve facing the possibility of hearing Hugh scold me. And scolding would interrupt my Zen tangents.

I open the file that Cory, one of our zillion admissions clerks, prepares for us every Monday. It is filled with the latest statistics about how various "indicator" high schools across the country scored on a bunch of tests, including subsections like AP math and AP history and AP biology. There's a bit about the incoming class at Swarthmore (another alleged rival school), an article about Harvard doing away with early admissions, and then a memo from the dean—another—in a series I like to entitle Calling All Dicks.

Because boys, boys who score high and play sports and participate in civil projects and don't run their cars into telephone poles, are akin to holy grails for small liberal arts colleges. We have a crisis in this country of under-performing, verbally challenged men and this does not bode well for all the over-performing, verbally superior women I see coming through my door. Unless these smart gals don't mind hanging out with guys who are stumped by instructions on how to wash their hands before returning to the Burger King fryer, they are going to have a hard go of it.

I have a theory, like everyone else, about the dumbing down of men, and that's this: Most video games are geared toward males. There are precious few written for females. So while the video game industry has taken off (taking our boys with it), the girls are outpacing them on grades, tests, and extracurricular activities, though their skills at *Halo 2* suck.

Coincidence? Don't think so.

Knock, knock. My door opens before I can say "Come in," which means it's Alice. And she still has that stupid smirk on her face as if she knows something I don't. "Busy?"

There's nothing I love more than gossiping with Alice—unless I'm currently faking my engagement. "I kind of have a lot of work to do."

"'Cause I've got a kid downstairs, Adam Crawler from the Bronx, New York, who has a nine thirty appointment with Kevin. Kevin was really eager to meet him, only he's stuck in a conference with Bill in Boston. I'd pass him off to Connie, but, you know she's . . ." Alice wiggles her penciled eyebrows suggestively.

"Out of the country. You told me." Well, at least Adam Crawler won't be asking me questions about where she went. "I'll see him."

"You're a star. Here's his file. I'll give you five so you can act like you're prepared. And I'll get you some coffee. This kid is high-test. You'll need it."

Quickly, I flip through Adam Crawler's file looking for the pertinents: SAT score—2380.

Almost perfect score. Grades? Pulling a 3.9 average. I scan for where he "screwed up" and see a B in Domestic Science. Couldn't flip a pancake, huh? Extracurriculars: tennis, chess, and bowling. That's brave. Organizations: Math Club; Debate Club; president, *Star Trek: The Next Generation* Official Fan Club, Mid-Atlantic Chapter.

That he had either the guts or the naïveté to include that last one says volumes. Oh, what about his essay: "Why Thoreau College?" Good. He personalized it. That's a check in his corner. Admissions counselors everywhere despise mass essays prepared by professional college counseling services. So, what does our friend Adam have to say about Thoreau?

Why Thoreau?
Why not?

At the end of the day, what does it matter which college I get into? Sure, there might be a difference between MIT and Cedar Crest School for Girls, but both can teach the complete works of Shakespeare, right?

It's not financial aid that will drive my decision—though I wouldn't reject a nice package, if you get my drift. Nor is it the teacher/student ratio or how many undergraduates go on to pursue advanced degrees.

For me, where I go to school for the next four years all comes down to one issue: What are my chances of getting laid?

This job never ceases to surprise me.

For that reason, Thoreau is my first choice.
Ratio of females to males: 3:1.
Percentage of incoming class that are virgins—
72.2%—as gleaned by anonymous sources on the
Internet.

Really? Where's he getting his information?

Moreover, for a New England college, a notable
number of your female student body comes from
rural areas in the Midwest. While most prospec-
tive students would find that a turn-off (who wants
to be in a class with a bunch of cow tippers?), my
analysis suggests that girls from, say, an Indiana
farm might find a guy from the Bronx to be exotic.
I even plan on purchasing several pairs of tight-
fitting sleeveless white T-shirts (I believe the ver-
nacular term for them is "wife beaters") and some
of that hideous "man" jewelry, also known com-
monly as "bling."
What does Thoreau get in accepting me?
A much-desired male student who will not only
excel off campus, but also on. A future alumnus
who will be a millionaire by age 25 and a multi-
millionaire by age 30 looking for a nice nonprofit
institution in which to sink some of his tax-
deductible wealth. (The Adam J. Crawler Institute
for Advanced Sexual Studies has a ring.)

Also, I am short of stature and do not take up much space.

I look forward to meeting with members of the admissions staff and discussing that financial aid package further.

Until then, Adam Crawler.

Unreal. I toss the essay aside. If it were my call, I'd accept him early admin sight unseen. No wonder Kevin was eager to meet him.

Alice enters with a boy in an ill-fitting blue suit and yellow tie that only a geek like the kid who wrote this essay would have chosen. He's right. He is short. As Alice places a cup of coffee on my desk, she points at my blinking phone.

"You have a message."

"I know."

"It might be Hugh."

I nod at Adam to take the leather chair opposite.

"Yes. Well, then . . ."

"It might be important. He said it was. You know, that insanity business."

I give her a meaningful look, the kind someone as smart as Alice would easily understand as *time to go.*

"All right, Alice," I say. "Don't worry. I'll handle it."

"Either that or it could be the Publicity Department. They're writing up a press release about Hugh and they want you to call extension 504."

I smile at Adam, who is surveying my small office

with disdain, as if trying to figure out if he's been passed off to a lesser admissions officer. "Right. I'll give them a call as soon as I'm done here."

At last Alice leaves and I sit down to face the already infamous Adam Crawler.

"Sorry about that," I say, retrieving his essay from the edge of my desk. "So, let's talk about this essay and your reasons for choosing Thoreau. Very unorthodox, wouldn't you say?"

Adam pushes up his glasses. "Who's Hugh?"

Ah, yes, the old let's-create-a-personal-relationship interview technique. Seen it many times before. "Hugh is my boyfriend. There." I point to the pictures behind me and turn back to his file. "Aside from getting laid, as you put it, do you have any idea what other academic activities you'd like to pursue if you are accepted here?"

Adam is squinting at the one of us at Thanksgiving. "That's Hugh Spencer, the writer. Mom's all thrilled that he teaches here."

"Yes." I smile politely. What were the chances? "Did you read *Hopeful, Kansas*?"

"God, no. But Mom did. Cried all the way through and made me watch him on TV Saturday night. I was stuck in a hotel room with her so I had no choice."

A hotel room? "Then I assume you're going on a tour of colleges. Any others that have caught your fancy?" I take a bogus note and pray Adam went to the lobby to swim or play arcade games before Barbara Walters signed off.

"Didn't he . . . ?"

Oh, brother. Here it comes.

"Didn't he ask his girlfriend to marry him?"

Just my luck. First applicant of the day and he's a total loser who watches bedtime TV with Mother.

"Did he ask her to marry him? I'm not sure that's *exactly* what he did."

"You mean that was bull? It was all staged? I knew it. You could tell. I told Mom that he did that just to sell books and she said I didn't know what I was talking about. I knew he was a complete phony."

"No, no. Hugh's not a phony." Cripes. This kid is smarter than I thought. "That was a genuine proposal. He asked her to marry him."

"He asked *her* to marry him." He sits back and grins. "You mean he asked *someone else* and that's why you're not returning his messages. You got served, cold, on national TV."

My hand under my desk involuntarily balls into a fist. Adam Crawler I'm not liking so much now, even if he is a precocious genius. Of course the guy can't get laid. Tossing aside his essay, I turn to his file and run my finger down to the B on his transcript.

"Now, Adam, your parents didn't drive you all the way here from New York to talk about me. We're here to talk about you. So, how do you explain this B in Domestic Science?"

"You must have wanted to punch his lights out. I mean, I've been served by girls lots of times, but not on national television. Whew. That's gotta be, what? Two million people."

Four point one.

"Or is it that he dumped you long ago? And you can't let go and you keep his picture there, which, you know, is megapathetic. You should get help, man."

I hear a *snap* and look down at the two pieces of yellow Ticonderoga number 2 in my hand. Adam should be glad it wasn't his neck.

To hell with it. "Okay, Adam. Here's the skinny. Hugh and I are getting married. I said yes and that's that. Now, we've wasted a lot of time discussing my life, which happens to be none of your business. Let's try to fit in yours, starting with this transcript." I tap his transcript so hard I make a dent in the paper. "An A in Algebra II. Not an A plus? What, were you slacking off that semester?"

"Then where's your ring?" He absolutely will not let this go.

"We haven't picked it out yet."

"Right. I believe that." He shakes his head. "What does it say about our society when an aging spinster has to invent a fiancé?"

Aging spinster!

"What happened to individual self-fulfillment, women's liberation?"

I check my watch as my temper is about to explode the top off Billings Hall. "Whoops. That's it. I've got another appointment waiting." And before Adam can so much as argue that the standard admissions interview lasts twenty minutes, not five, I have buzzed Alice to retrieve him.

"I hope you won't hold our conversation against me," he says cockily as Alice leads him out the door.

"Not at all." And, in fact, I mark up his folder with incredibly flowery praise. Far be it from me to be accused of bias. I've been an admissions counselor long enough to know that backing me into a corner was likely his strategy all along. Lucky for him the corner was so ready and waiting.

"How did it go?" Alice asks, getting Adam's folder.

"Fine. Fine young man."

"Really? 'Cause he seemed like a snot to me. You gonna pick up that message? If it's bad news, you might as well get it over with."

Alice is right as usual. I should just get it over with.

I wait until she leaves to press the message button and type in my code. Five messages. The first is from my mother, who is in some sort of fluster about ordering invitations and registering and securing a church and then a club for the reception. I have no idea what I was thinking, letting her get involved with planning this bogus wedding. Talk about enabling!

The second is from Todd, apologizing for being so hard on me the night before and hoping I'm not mad at him for what he said about my loser life. (Right. Will do, Todd.)

In a weak attempt to make amends, he ends the message by inviting me to the Bob Dylan contest he enters every year that is hosted by my friend, Steve, who, in addition to being the lead singer of the Wily Coyotes, is also an absurdly popular disc jockey at FM 107.

"A whole bunch of people are stopping by to see me do 'Rainy Day Women,' " Todd says, proceeding to list a whole bunch of people I've never heard of until he gets to Nick. "He specifically wanted to know if you were coming. Said he had to ask you about this information he found about something called pure-method house building, whatever the hell that is."

This gives me pause. Maybe there really is such a thing as pure-method house building? Maybe Hugh told me about it and I filed it deep in my subconscious. Either that or Nick knows I was bullshitting and he has plans of embarrassing me at the Dylan contest.

Ha! Let him try. I'm not giving up that easily to a man who refuses to let himself be bested by a woman.

Steve has left the third message, also an invitation to the "It Ain't Me, Babe" Fifth Annual Bob Dylan Be-Alike Contest. Poor Steve is constantly inviting me to his "gigs," as he calls them, though I rarely accept. I hate to disappoint him again by not showing up.

Also, I need to support Todd, even if that means facing off against Nick. Oh, well. Such is the sacrifice I am called to make in the name of sisterhood. If I have to spar with a mortal Greek god, then spar I must.

The fourth message is from Giles in Thoreau Publicity, looking for an interview.

And, finally, Hugh. I breathe deep, preparing myself.

"Genie." He is crisp, efficient. "I've just received some alarming news from Pippa, who's house-sitting for my parents while they're in Italy for the summer, something about a Mr. and Mrs. Michaels calling up from the States claiming that you and I are getting married.

"Now, lookit, Genie. I appreciate your support. I always have and I can't tell you what this Barbara Walters interview has done. My publisher expects another good run on all the bestseller lists and Miramax is speeding up the film production. I'm sure you're as thrilled as I am."

I'm thrilled all right.

"Still . . ."

Here it comes. The big warning.

"If your family is confused about whether I've actually asked you to marry me, I believe it is your responsibility to disabuse them of this notion immediately."

You do, do you?

"I mean, having to explain the whole mess to Pippa, a dear old friend, was humiliating enough. Especially with *you know who* there."

No. Who? I have no idea who *you know who* is.

"Because by now I'm assuming you've found out who *she* is and I would—*we* would—vastly appreciate your tact at the office. I'm sure you can understand, even if you are hurt. Really, Genie, it's better this way. Years from now we'll look back and—"

"Oh, bugger off," I say out loud, before hanging up. If there's one advantage to this breakup, it's that I no longer need to obey Hugh's constant and frequent "corrections." Life is too short to listen to a man tell me how to live it.

That's when it occurs to me that maybe being dumped by Hugh might not have been the worst thing in the world.

In fact, it might have been the loveliest parting gift ever.

Chapter Eight

Okay. I'm pretty sure there is no such thing as pure-method house building. I've searched the Internet and even asked my father and the guys down at Coolidge Hardware (who gaped at me like I was an alien invader). No one's ever heard of it.

I am screwed.

Then again, I do have the advantage over Nick in that I'm a woman. Most men, I've learned, can be easily distracted by a flash of leg, a bit of cleavage. They're like apes, really, a half a notch up the evolutionary scale when it comes to all things sexual. Show them the merest hint of a nipple and their brains instantaneously go to mush. It's not very feminist of me to say, but I seriously think Condoleezza Rice could solve the Middle East crisis with a decent boob job and a quality Wonderbra.

Which is also how I have come to justify my rather impulsive purchase of a Charlotte Tarantola mocha tank with its figure-hugging ribs for a whopping $65 from Neiman Marcus. Pair that with a 7 For All Mankind miniskirt and my guess is he won't stand a chance.

Not that my goal is to achieve anything more than to throw Nick off guard. Certainly, I am not trying to impress him, much less seduce him, despite the glowing bronzer I applied in places sure to catch his eye and, therefore, initiate the brain-mushing process.

In my opinion, this is nothing more than war. A war against all egotistical men who are used to having their way (like Hugh) or who assume every woman will fall in love with them (like Nick). In my opinion, if Nick is bound to pick away at my pure-method-house-building story, trying to trip me up, then he will have to defend himself against my newly shaven and baby-oiled legs in Cole Haan slides. (A steal at $100.)

Catching a glimpse of my reflection as I pass by the store windows in Harvard Square on my way to Club Mercury, it strikes me that I have never dressed this way before. Never. My usual summer outfit, even for club hopping, is the typical Bostonian student fare of a T-shirt and shorts with Teva sandals or, for fancy occasions, a gauzy, hippie skirt imported from Tibet.

I have to admit I feel a bit brazen these days. Confident. Reckless. There's a new swish to my hips, a smile on my lips. Fake it to make it, Patty says, a phrase that, until now, I've considered Amway hoo-ha.

However, that was before I faked my engagement and began appreciating Amway in a whole new light.

"Wow. Look at you!" Steve gets up from a table on the dais to plant a friendly kiss on my cheek. "Is this all for me?"

"Why not?" I say with a laugh, as my gaze sweeps the room searching for any sign of Nick and, of course, Todd.

"Let me get you a beer. We're still setting up." He takes me by the hand and deposits me at a small round table that is way too close to a set of huge amplifiers. "Genie," he adds, giving me another kiss. "I'm really glad you came."

Yet another moment when it seems as if Steve hopes to romanticize our relationship. He's tried this in the past, mostly when he's had too much to drink. A confession of attraction here. A declaration of love there. My usual tactic has been to call him up the next day and josh him back to normalcy. His is one friendship I don't want to lose after seventeen years. It's a treasure.

At least, that's what I tell myself.

Now, in light of the number Hugh pulled on me, I'm rethinking this. Maybe sexual attraction is merely chemistry like Hugh said. Because I've tried to be sexually attracted to Steve, really. I mean, what could be better than falling in love with your best friend?

Unless you can't.

Steve is the guy who taught me how to drive in reverse around the Fresh Pond rotary, who took me out to Howard Johnson's all-you-can-eat fried clam nights and challenged me to finish more plates than he

126

"when he called Sunday night to ask if I would talk you into showing up tonight. Said he felt guilty about some fight you two had and then he dropped the bomb about your engagement."

Whoa. Back up. I can't decide which is more mind-blowing—that Steve thinks I'm actually engaged to Hugh or that my brother actually feels guilty about fighting with me.

"So, what's the answer?" Steve asks. "Did Hugh say this before or after you got engaged? Either way, why in the hell would you still be engaged to a man who doesn't deserve you and doesn't treat you like you deserve?"

Steve's nostrils are flaring, a sure sign he's getting angry, and I can't say I blame him. It appears to him like I'm throwing myself at a man who abhors my body when Steve has been waiting in the wings, ready to love me warts and all.

Unfortunately, the room is getting crowded so it's difficult to discuss my sex life discreetly. Contestants have arrived in beards and wigs, microphones slung around their necks. We are in a sea of fat and tall, black and Hispanic, and even a few female Dylans. Not the ideal atmosphere for sorting through feelings of intimate inadequacy.

"Let's talk later," I shout, trying to be heard above the "one-two-three" sound check. "Give me some credit, Steve. You might be surprised."

"Why should I?" Steve is leaning over half the table, practically in my face. "I'd never say anything like that to you. I just told you you're hot. But would you ever consider going out with me? Hell, no."

"Please, Steve."

"Lots of women love me. I've got groupies. Seriously, I do. Women who follow the Wily Coyotes from gig to gig. So clearly I'm not some freak."

"I never said you were a freak."

"Yeah, but you act like I'm a freak. When I kissed you on the cheek, you flinched."

That's a lie. "I did not."

"What if I kissed you now? Would you push me away?"

"Of course not." What's gotten into him?

Before I can figure out the answer, Steve curves his arm around the back of my head and pulls me to him, kissing me not on the cheek, but full on the lips. I don't dare pull away or, heaven forbid, flinch. I don't dare give him any indication that he is even the slightest bit unappealing. I am so supersensitive to the issue of sexual self-esteem now that I even kiss him back.

"Hi, kids."

Steve lifts his lips off mine and says, "Hi, Todd. Excuse me while I kiss your sister."

"By all means." Todd waves his approval. "Nick and I will step aside until you're done."

Nick?

I shove Steve so hard he nearly flies backward over his chair, banging his head against a pillar.

"What did you do that for?" he asks, righting himself.

"Sorry." Keeping my eyes focused on the table so I won't have to see Nick's reaction, I say, "It was enough. You proved your point."

"And I guess you proved yours."

"Don't be so dramatic."

"This is Steve Taylor," Todd says to Nick. "Genie's friend from college. Lead singer of the Wily Coyotes, that band we saw on the pier last spring."

Nick shakes Steve's hand and then spins around a chair to straddle it. He's so close, his thigh brushes mine. "Hi, Genie," he says.

"Hi." I quickly glance at him and then, seeing his dark blue eyes twinkling, look away. Oh, God. He's in a black T-shirt. I'm a sucker for men in black T-shirts.

"You look very nice," he says softly. "That's a good color on you. Goes very well with your skin."

The words are innocent enough, but his tone is not. "Thanks." I pretend to search the crowded club for a waitress. "The service around here is lousy, isn't it?"

"No wonder he made a pass," Nick adds, nodding good-naturedly at Steve.

My neck goes hot again.

"No. You don't understand Genie and Steve," Todd shouts. "They have a totally fucked-up relationship. Like *When Harry Met Sally* only without the imitation orgasm."

The word *orgasm* hangs over our table until Steve says, "You mean you actually watched that movie?"

"All part of getting laid, buddy, all part of getting

laid. You're right, Genie. The service here sucks," he says, watching a waitress buzz right past us.

"Excuse me, miss." Nick does nothing more than flick his index finger and—presto—the prettiest waitress suddenly appears. "Could we get another round?"

She takes a moment to wiggle for his benefit. "Four Heinekens?"

"Three," I correct, demurely. "I'm fine."

"Four," Nick says. "Save you the extra trip. If that's okay with you, Genie?"

I'm busted. Nick can probably tell I'm the type of girl who can keep up with the boys.

"Why not? It's Wednesday night," I say, thinking that Hugh would have cleared his throat, a nonverbal reminder that I have to watch it because of my alcoholic family. Also, that beer is loaded with carbs and calories—Hugh's most fearsome enemies.

"How come I never get that treatment?" Steve asks. "I could lift my fingers all day until I was only left with the middle one and a waitress still wouldn't show."

"Mediterranean magnetism." Todd rests his arms on the table authoritatively. "It's a handicap of Nick's I gotta deal with in the workplace constantly. Yesterday, the meter maid came by to show him that she'd ripped up the ticket he got on Mass Ave. No shit. A twenty-dollar ticket, gone, in return for five minutes of his Mediterranean magnetism."

"That's high treason in Boston, isn't it?" Steve asks. "Ripping up a ticket."

"So, you two have known each other since college?" Nick says, moving the subject off him.

Steve answers, "Met at the college radio station. Been best friends ever since."

I tense, hoping we'll leave it at that. "Are you doing 'Rainy Day Women' again, Todd? It cracks me up whenever you whine onstage."

"Glad to see we're back on speaking terms, Eugenia. And no, I'm not doing 'Rainy Day Women.' Not number twelve or number thirty-five. My song is a surprise that I can't reveal, seeing as we have an esteemed judge at the table."

Nick says, "You mean you've known Genie all this time, Steve, and you've never been more than just *friends?*"

"Ha!" Todd claps his hands. "Ha! If you only knew. 'Just friends' my ass."

Oh, please, I pray, as the waitress returns with our beers. Please let it stop here.

I turn to Steve. "Don't you have to go? The other judges are already on the panel."

He checks his watch. "I got at least ten minutes. Besides, my beer just got here. Priorities, woman."

The men go through the pretense of reaching for their wallets. I don't even bother. Finally, Nick pays and they spend an inordinate amount of time commenting on a slim blonde dressed as "early Bob." Just when I think she might entertain them for a little longer, Todd does a big brother and asks Steve to tell the story of the time he and I "hooked up."

"Ah. I never kiss and tell." Steve picks at his beer label. "Wouldn't be gentlemanly."

"I'm not interested in an etiquette lesson, I'm interested in having a laugh."

I know what Todd's about to say and I'm pissed. I would slap my hand over his mouth if I thought it would do any good. But once Todd thinks he's on a roll, there's no stopping him. My brother craves being the center of attention—even if that means it's at my expense.

"Check this out," he says, nudging Nick. "The whole four years Genie was at Thoreau she never left the library. All she did was study. I partied, she studied. We're opposites, right?"

"Sure," Nick says.

"Then, the night before graduation, she shows up on Steve's doorstep with half of Patty's condom supply and a request that he take her virginity. Honest to God. Like she was selling encyclopedias."

"It wasn't *half* of Patty's condom supply—it was more like a quarter," I say, trying to be a sport, even though I'd rather die than have him relate this to Nick, a total stranger. "Patty used to buy in bulk. We all know this stupid story, Todd. Can't we talk about something else?"

"You told him?" Steve grimaces. "Why did you tell him?"

I have no idea. Why *did* I tell him?

"She was twenty-one!" Todd pounds the table. "Twenty-fucking-one. That's why I call her Sister

Eugenia. And Hugh's probably Father Spencer because I bet the two of them never do it. They're all brain, no body."

Okay. He has hit way too close to home. I am ready to strangle my brother with my bare hands when I feel someone patting my hand under the table. It's Nick, who, above the table, is tolerating Todd with a stiff smile.

"Watch it, Todd," Steve says protectively. "You might want to get off this subject while you still have your testicles."

"Why?" Todd acts baffled that I would find this objectionable. "It's funny. And it happened fifteen years ago. What's the big deal?"

"Hugh's being a shit to her, that's the big deal. They're having problems and they're not even married."

"Enough." Carefully, I remove my hand from under Nick's. "So, who's the best Dylan here, do you think?"

Too late. Todd's on his muscle. "What did Hugh say now? I swear, I know he's my future brother-in-law and all, but that guy has his nerve. He's always telling Genie to do this or that. He steps over the line."

"And you don't?" I ask, laughing, still trying to keep the night upbeat.

Todd points his bottle at me. "Listen. If he has problems with our family, I'll set him straight. Mom and Dad may be a trip, but he has no business ragging on us."

"It's not about your family," Steve says. "Hugh told Genie she doesn't turn him on, that's all."

Silence. Dead silence falls over us. It is all I can do not to scream and then burst into tears.

"You fink!" Getting up, I push back my chair with a loud scrape. "You know, Steve, I know quite a few secrets about you, too, that I could spill here. But I'm not going to because I'm a friend."

Steve is truly stunned. "I was only trying to help. I didn't want Todd getting mad at Hugh for the wrong thing."

I will never be able to comprehend the bizarre logic of men. "Good riddance to the lot of you," I declare, managing to flash a grateful smile at Nick before plowing toward the door.

With sheer determination and rudeness, I elbow my way through the throng of stupid college kids until I'm safely outside in the refreshing June evening. My head is spinning from the noise and Todd and utter humiliation from which I'll never recover. Forget ever talking to Nick again. That's out of the question.

The worst of it is that for all of Todd's teasing, he's right. I am a frigid, puritanical prude. No wonder I don't turn Hugh on. I don't turn any man on. I never have. I never will.

Like in college, where everyone—even my hulking suite mate Claudia, the hockey player from Canada—was having sex except me. Whole weekends they'd spend in bed with their boyfriends. Meanwhile, there I was, uptight Genie Michaels, a sexual retard, bent over her books on a Saturday night, going to the campus theater to see *Casablanca* alone as a reward for an evening's hard work.

Tears spring to the corners of my eyes as I lean against the bus stop, hiding my face so no one will see that I'm crying. That's how pathetic I am, an adult at a bus stop that reeks of urine and smoke, bemoaning her pathetic sex life.

"Hey." There is a light touch on my shoulder and I spin around ready to lash out at Steve when I see it's not Steve, but Nick regarding me sympathetically. A breeze blows back his hair, revealing an alluring five o'clock shadow. He might be one of those men who has to shave twice a day.

"I'm really sorry Todd got carried away in there. He was completely out of line."

Quickly, I wipe the back of my hand across my eyes. "No big deal. I overreacted."

"You didn't overreact." From nowhere he produces a red handkerchief, a gesture I find heartbreaking. I've never known any man outside of my father to carry a handkerchief. "Personally, I think it's kind of sweet you went to a friend for, um, that. I know plenty of women who've done a lot worse. Anyway, if I hadn't pried, the subject wouldn't have come up. So, it's kinda my fault."

That's true, I think, indelicately blowing my nose with a *honk*. "It actually ended up fine with Steve. Not great. It wasn't earth-shattering sex or anything. But at least I wasn't a virgin under my mortarboard."

Nick smiles. "It takes time learning to like sex. At least, that's what women have told me. Doesn't appear to be anything close to a learning curve for men."

"Yes." I concentrate on folding the handkerchief like it's the American flag and not thinking of the numerous women lying next to Nick in bed, confessing that they never liked sex until him.

"And I'm sure it's been earth-shattering for you since then, especially with Hugh."

"Absolutely! And Todd's right. It was fifteen years ago. I'm all grown up."

"So I've noticed."

"By the way, you were really nice to take my hand in there. It helped," I say, handing him the folded handkerchief.

"Anytime." He looks at his feet, stalling. "Listen, Genie, I know we've just met and, really, I have no business saying this. But if Hugh said—"

"Steve was exaggerating." I wave him off before he can go any further. "Hugh and I have a terrific sex life. We can't keep our hands off each other."

"Right. Of course." Nick shoves his hands in his pockets and shivers as if it's cold, even though it's almost tropical out here. "Going back? Todd claims he's planned a kick-ass rendition of 'Subterranean Homesick Blues.' "

I roll my eyes. "Tell me he didn't bring cue cards."

"Stayed up all night making them. Sixty-four in total."

"And he spelled *success* the way Dylan did?"

"S-u-c-k-c-e-s-s."

"That Dylan was a lousy speller. Probably still is. No, I'll have to pass, I'm afraid. I hate to watch my brother's ego grow any larger than it already is."

Nick grins and, instantly, I feel a true blush coming on again. "See you around, then," he says, turning back to the club. "Glad you're okay. I'll let Todd and Steve know."

"Tell 'em I'm fine," I holler back. "Never better!"

As he walks away, the women waiting in line stare in approval while the men bristle and try to make themselves taller, broader.

What did Todd call it? Mediterranean magnetism.

Mediterranean magnetism. Animal magnetism. No matter its name, there's a definite possibility I could become positively charged.

Chapter Nine

It is impossible to get any work done as a bogusly betrothed person. I don't know how real brides-to-be do it.

Just when I'm about to delve into an essay or analyze a spreadsheet of scores, someone from my family calls with something wedding-ish.

"And then this Pippa person said the strangest thing," my mother is saying, relating again (it is her third call today) the jarring experience of calling Hugh's parents and finding them on holiday. "She said Hugh had told her he'd broken up with you, not asked you to marry him. Now why do you suppose she'd say something like that?"

This is one of my mother's classic rhetorical questions. I don't even consider answering it. Instead, I look up Lateka Swambi's math scores. Impressive. Those Bergen County schools can prep kids like no place else.

"I'll tell you why. Drugs. Don't you think Trevor and Susanna should know what their house sitter is up to? Shooting heroin and blowing cocaine, so doped up this Pippa person can't even be civil to the soon-to-be in-laws of their own son."

I lie that British house sitters are often drug addicts, part of the United Kingdom's efforts to cut rehab costs by farming out addicts to foster families. I am getting *sooo* good at lying because she actually says, "Interesting," and hangs up.

One hour later. *Ring!* "Guess who's throwing you and Hugh an engagement party? Tula Abernathy!"

"What is a Tula Abernathy?"

Mom is appalled I have to ask. "You know Tula. She was married to Bucky Abernathy for years until he drowned in his swimming pool while strapped to his wheelchair and then, after that silly, stupid police investigation, she moved to Palm Beach for the winters."

I say, "Police investigation?"

"It was only a technicality. No proof at all, aside from the missing brakes on Bucky's chair, though, really, Tula couldn't be blamed for that, not with her arthritis. Can't so much as twist a screwdriver, poor thing. Anyway, Tula's a *huge* fan of *Hopeful, Kansas.* She can't wait to meet Hugh."

Oh, God. I put down Denise Swindell's essay, "How Needlepoint Helped Me Understand Calculus," and rub my brow.

"She swears the party will be an all-out, black-tie extravaganza. Caviar. Champagne. Salmon flown in from Norway and lobsters from Maine. A band at the club. Aren't you thrilled?"

"Maybe the pool boy could have twisted the screwdriver."

"Please, Genie. Stay on track. I'd have expected you to be squealing!"

"Oh, I'm squealing all right." In my head. Can't she hear?

Aaaaggghhhh!

An engagement party! For me *and* Hugh? Now how am I going to pull this off? I mean, people will expect him to show. It's not often that couples are thrown engagement parties and only the bride turns up. Unless . . . Hugh were in the military. Yes! That . . .

No. No one would ever buy Hugh as a soldier. He's too old. Too pasty white.

Then my mother says, "Of course, you're going to need to register soon because once word gets out about your wedding, people are going to start sending you gifts."

Gifts! Shoot. Lately, I've been worried about the legal issues that might arise in this gift-getting

141

activity. Isn't accepting Cuisinarts and Williams-Sonoma knives under false pretenses some sort of criminal offense? Theft of quality kitchenware by unlawful betrothal, or something? I'd be just like those people who shake down customers at the grocery store by claiming their dear Aunt Helga is dying of restless leg syndrome when really they're pooling spare change for a bottle of Mad Dog.

"Mom, I can't have an engagement party . . ."

There is an ominous pause.

"No one turns down Tula Abernathy. Honestly, Genie, I'm disappointed. You're supposed to be excited about planning this wedding. Instead, I feel like I'm weeding dandelions, tugging each stubborn detail from you until I'm exhausted. Good-bye!"

Her silence is short-lived and, as if I have just passed through the eye of a storm, my phone blares a brief twenty minutes later. "Now what about a date, sweetie," Mom asks, all syrupy as if we haven't so much as raised our voices. "We can't plan anything without a date. Have you and Hugh picked a date?"

"A date?"

"Yes, a date."

"Oh. A *date*." This is a very clever tactic on my part, I think, stalling by repeating everything she says.

"As in August blank . . ." she reiterates.

Crap. She really is going balls-out with this wedding planning business, isn't she? Demanding dates and all that. I flip through my desk calendar and notice that I have conveniently scheduled the week of August 20 for vacation with Patty down at the Cape. "How about August twentieth?"

"Are you sure? Is that okay with Hugh? Won't classes be starting around then?" She spits out her questions faster than a Thompson machine gun. "Because once you pick the date, you can't change—not at this late date, you can't change a date."

"The date's fine." I underline a sentence on Andy Pringle's essay about the "Value of Euthanasia": *I don't know why it's wrong to let the sick just die. Isn't the world overcrowded as it is?* and jot a memo to his high school counselor: *Psychiatric evaluation?*

"But you haven't talked to Hugh about the twentieth, have you? Now, listen to me, Genie. Men can get *verrry* prickly if you don't ask them or, rather, go through the pretense of asking them. The sooner you learn how to give Hugh the impression he's making all the decisions, the sooner you'll have the upper hand in your marriage."

Ah, yes. Welcome to the Nancy Michaels course on Marriage by Manipulation.

"I'll tell you what," I say, folding up Andy's application to send it back to Spartan High School FedEx Overnight. "I'll pretend to have asked him and we can pretend he said yes."

"Perfect." The *scratch* is audible from my end. Another item off her to do list.

She hangs up and I have barely a chance to stretch and pour myself another cup of tea when my line

143

buzzes again. Only this time it's not Mom, it is her evil henchwoman, Lucy.

"Are you sitting down?" She doesn't wait for my answer. "Because I have terrific news. Guess who's throwing you your bridal shower?"

"Tula Abernathy?"

"No . . . me!"

This has got to stop. Engagement parties. Showers. "You can't throw me a shower. You're my sister." I'm no Martha Stewart, but even I know it's a breach of etiquette for a family member to host a shower.

"So what? These days sisters can throw showers. Really. Check out Emily Post. Page one-seventy-seven of *Wedding Etiquette.* She says it depends on individual circumstances, and you've got one doozy of an individual circumstance."

"What doozy is that?"

"Patty Pugliese. She's the most logical choice to be a hostess and Mom wants me to preempt her. Something about not wanting to be exposed to male strippers and battery-operated dildos."

"Patty wouldn't do that."

"Really? Think long. Think hard."

I think hard and long and have to agree that battery-operated dildos are not out of the realm of possibility in a Patty Pugliese-hosted bridal shower.

"Okay. How about I tell Patty I don't want a shower?" I suggest. "How about no one throws me a shower and I just get married under the willow tree in Mom and Dad's backyard? No engagement party. No church. No fancy reception. No gift registering. No guests. We just keep it simple. Five minutes and we're done."

Lucy lets out a long, pained sigh. "Lookit. From here on out you don't get to make any decisions. I'm taking over because you're suffering from some sort of pre-wedding stress disorder."

PWSD.

"Just do what I say," Lucy instructs, "and it'll all turn out fine. Now, first step. Register. You can do it online at Neiman Marcus or Bloomingdale's or Saks or Harrods, even. For the British friends of Hugh."

"Who?"

"Hugh. Remember? The dude you're marrying?"

Oh, right. *That* Hugh. "Well, maybe Hugh and I don't want gifts," I say, appealing to Lucy's do-gooder side. "Maybe we have enough stuff already. Wouldn't it be better for people to send the money to charity instead?"

"Like it's a funeral? Boy. You are a lot of fun, Genie. I can't wait to shop for bridesmaids' dresses with you. What are you gonna dress us in, hair shirts?"

Bridesmaids! Bridesmaids' dresses? I haven't thought of those, either. I feel something wet and note with dismay that sweat from my palms has smudged Benjamin Cadburry's ink signature on his pledge to maintain his grades through senior year if accepted.

"At least register so people know what to buy you. It's more work for them otherwise, trying to figure out what you want and need, if you've already got a fish poacher or not. That way after the wedding, if you're still playing the family role as Sister Eugenia, you can return the gifts for cash and write a big fat check to Save the Children."

That's a possibility, though I'm almost positive brides these days register with charities alone. I read it in *Cosmo*. Not that I read *Cosmo* religiously. Well, aside from the sex parts.

"Just make sure there's a lot of kitchen stuff in your registry because I'm throwing you a kitchen shower next month. Personally, I recommend asking for a garlic press. I don't know how you live without one, all that cutting with no press."

She's right. How *have* I survived?

"By the way, have you given thought to what you're going to do about your triceps?"

When she says this, I'm confused. I'm thinking dinosaurs like T rex, raptors, and triceps. I can't for the life of me figure out what dinosaurs would have to do with wedding planning. "Pardon?"

"Your upper arm muscles? You know, that little piece of flab that hangs down."

"I have a little piece of flab that hangs down?"

"Check."

I tap the bottom of my left arm, where supposedly my lazy triceps have been loitering about. My good-ness, she's right. It does hang down there.

"I didn't want to bring it up," she says, bringing it up. "I'm sure you're self-conscious about it. Don't worry. We *all* are."

We are?

"And because of that, Jason and I have purchased your first shower gift."

Oh, no. It'll be some sort of upper-arm caliper.

"A three-month membership to Joe's Gym right around the corner from your apartment. I made a Saturday morning appointment for you to meet with a trainer who's a specialist in upper body and abs. He'll do the best he can to get you buff by August twentieth. And maybe, if you work hard, your triceps will be tolerable for a strapless wedding gown."

"Why, Lucy!" It's so like her to zero in on my physical flaws. "How thoughtful of you to think of my arm fat."

"Yes, well, somebody has to."

Chapter Ten

"I can't believe Lucy called first dibs on hosting your shower. I should be the host. I'm your best friend, right?"

"Of course." No point bringing up the battery-operated dildos now that the shower's a done deal. "But have you forgotten I'm not really getting married?"

Patty stops stirring her Starbucks Caramel Macchiato, which is so sweet the sheer smell of it threatens to send me into diabetic shock. "You have got to drop that attitude, Genie. You are getting married even if you're not."

"That makes no sense."

"It does. Come here." Patty draws me away from the Starbucks fixings bar and drops her voice so low I can barely hear her above the soporific drawling of Norah Jones, who, I swear, plays in every Starbucks I've ever been in. "Look. You've almost got Hugh where you want him. Any day now, people are going to track him down in England and demand to know what's going on. His name is going to be mud."

"I've been thinking of that," I say, taking a careful sip of my triple venti latte that I ordered for the pure caffeine. I did not get any work done today, which means I'll be up all night reading essays at home. "Where does that leave me when everyone finds out the truth?"

"The object of pity, admiration, and empathy. The ultimate trifecta. You'll be a hero to every woman who's ever been screwed over by a long-term boyfriend, plus you'll have a newly outfitted kitchen."

I'm nipping this in the bud. "No. I am not registering for Lucy's kitchen shower."

"Are you shitting me?" Patty, as always, says this too loudly so that a mother in one of the leather chairs actually slaps her hands over her daughter's ears. "I hate to break it to you, but your kitchen is the pits. The only pots you have are missing huge chunks of Teflon, a proven cancer hazard, and your measuring cups are all cracked. Don't even talk to me about that coffeemaker you bought at Rite Aid. I've had airplane coffee that's better."

"So you've told me." Over and over and over.

Patty delicately wipes whipped cream from her immaculately polished lips. "Remember, Genie, this is not only to shame Hugh into submission, but mainly to kick-start your adult life. Give me one good reason why a twentysomething woman should have a kitchen shower simply because she's getting married whereas a woman in her mid-thirties who happens to cook doesn't qualify."

I open my mouth to answer something about tradition, but Patty beats me to the punch. "Exactly. You can't. This is why when my nieces graduate from college and start heading out on their own, I'm going to throw them Welcome-to-Real-Life showers so they can get decent towels and tool sets and matching cutlery. Life begins when you get your own job and apartment, not when some bozo signs a contract claiming exclusive rights to your vagina."

This declaration of vagina rights is too much for the mother who's been unsuccessfully trying to shield her child from Patty's vulgarity. As if she can't take one minute more, the beleaguered woman busily gathers her cups and napkins, tosses them in the trash, and with a look of utter disgust, escorts her daughter outside.

Patty, naturally, is clueless, so immersed is she in the audacity of wedding showers for women who have the audacity to get married in the audacity of their twenties. "I'll admit it, I'm envious. Ever since you told me about Lucy's kitchen shower, I've been thinking how I can get someone to throw *me* one of those."

"Why don't you get engaged?"

She blinks. "That's a brilliant idea. A fucking brilliant idea."

Oh, no. What have I done? I really have to make an effort to think before I speak.

"I *should* get engaged, like you. I mean, look at your upcoming haul. Parties. Showers. A gym membership and a trainer. Every woman should get this kind of royal treatment. You're even getting a free house."

"My parents bought Lucy a house. They haven't bought me one."

"Not yet. But you know they will. They *have* to. Unspoken parental law dictates that they have to treat each daughter equally. That is, if they ever want to see the grandkids."

Grandkids?

And with that, Patty takes off, exiting Starbucks and marching a mile a minute, her little legs carrying her little body across Copley Square. I have to run to catch up. "Where are you going?"

"Bickman's Jewelers to get a ring. I saw one there the other day that was perfect."

"I thought you were joining a client for drinks?"

"I'll call him and ask him to meet me here instead," she says, reaching for her cell phone, not slowing her pace one bit.

Patty is stunningly in shape for a woman who lives on caramel lattes and doughnuts and who never exercises. She manages to call her client and have a normal conversation while I'm quickstepping and almost out of breath.

When she hangs up, I say, "You can't buy yourself an engagement ring. You don't even have a boyfriend. I dated Hugh for four years. My family and friends expected we'd get married. He proposed on national TV. But you . . . you haven't dated anyone."

She stops dead in her tracks. "I have too been dating."

"Casual sex with men you meet at the deli counter is not dating, Patty."

"The gourmet condiments aisle of Whole Foods, for your information."

"It's organic food, Patty. Not *orgasmic*."

We have arrived at the front of Bickman's Jewelers, with its tantalizing glass cases dripping with brilliantly lit tennis bracelets and diamond pendants. My heart takes a tiny leap. Jewelry stores always do it for me. They're the mineralogical equivalent of champagne.

"This is the one that caught my eye." She is pressed against the glass window, pointing to her object of desire—a garish fake cocktail ring.

It is the kind of ring my great aunt Rosalie from Tampa, Florida, would have worn had cubic zirconia been invented back in her day. Three oval-shaped stones, a large one in the center and two smaller ones on the sides, on white gold. The sheer weight of it would make typing impossible.

"It's . . ." I hesitate, careful not to hurt her feelings. ". . . huge."

"And people will notice it, right? That's what I want, an immediate recognizable symbol that I am engaged to a man with beaucoup bucks. I want their jaws to flap."

"Their jaws will flap, all right."

"Now, how about you?" Inside she directs me to a case featuring the far less expensive cubic zirconias. "You need something classic like a basic solitaire. Something that is without doubt an engagement ring."

I dillydally by the diamonds, stunned by the price tags. Five thousand dollars?

"Here it is." She stabs at a rather large solitaire in a genuine platinum setting. "That's exactly what people expect in an engagement ring. No sapphires or rubies to confuse the mix. Just a nice, simple solitaire."

"I don't know. I always imagined my ring, when I got engaged, would be more antique. Maybe something my fiancé's grandmother would have worn. Filigree and emeralds. Or old-fashioned, like pearls."

Patty is regarding me with incomprehension. "This isn't your *real* ring, numbnut. This is the fake ring. This is *the* ring for you or my name isn't Patricia Ann Minelli McGowan Pugliese."

"Minelli?"

"No relation. Trust me. My people do not do show tunes."

"Looking for something special?" A stylish young blond clerk in a black pantsuit with flawless skin approaches. How do they get that skin, this new generation of women? Is it just youth? Tons of bottled water? Bronzer? Tanning bed? Because, I swear, we did not have skin like that when we were in our twenties.

"We're looking for an engagement ring," Patty announces. "The both of us."

The clerk takes stock of Patty and me. "You mean you're looking for a *commitment* ring. For your right hand."

"No. Engagement. I like this one here, don't you, Genie?" She is still stuck on that Aunt Rosalie cocktail special.

"That's nice," says the clerk, who must sense an imminent sale because she informs us her name is Keira and insists on shaking our hands. "But, considering your unique situation, perhaps you'd be more interested in our Love and Honor collection or maybe Love and Power. They're very popular among couples like . . . you."

"Us?" Patty turns back to her obsession, as if being drawn by an invisible tractor beam.

"Celtic rings are also popular, or matching three-stone rings symbolizing yesterday, today, and tomorrow." Keira pulls out two bands, each with three glittering stones. "Of course, if these were diamonds it'd be prohibitively expensive. But these are made of a material with more refractive qualities than cubic zirconia called Moissanite."

"Sounds like something Curly of the Three Stooges

153

would buy, right, Genie?" Patty nudges me. "Hey, Moe! How about some Moissanite."

She snorts at her own joke while I'm thinking, why matching rings?

Keira smiles indulgently. "How long have you two been together?"

"Omigod." Patty waves this off. "You don't want to know. We go back forever. We were roomies all through college."

"Aww. That's sweet. It's nice that couples like you can finally make it legal."

Which is when I get where Keira's coming from. "Patty, Keira thinks we're a couple. A *romantic* couple."

"Huh?" Patty does a double take of the rings. "Oh, no. I'm not . . . we're not . . ."

"Not that there's anything wrong with that," I add, in case our clerk happens to be a lesbian.

"Of course not." She smiles nervously. "So your fiancé . . ."

"Oh, there is no fiancé. For either of us." Patty is back to her Aunt Rosalie ring. "Do you know how much this is? I love it."

Now, thoroughly confused, Keira reaches in the case and turns over the tiny white tag. "In white gold that's 997 dollars. However, we also have it in platinum at 1,994 dollars."

That's outrageous.

"Two thousand dollars?" Patty yells. "For glass?"

"Manufactured diamond," Keira corrects. "There's a

154

lot of work and design that goes into creating a quality CZ engagement ring. It's guaranteed to last five years. A lot longer than many marriages."

Boy, am I bummed. Not about the five-year-marriage statistic, though I can't say I'm surprised. It's just that I had no idea I'd be putting up thousands of dollars to get a half-decent ring.

Seeing our disappointment, she says, "If there's no fiancé, then, can I ask, what do you need this ring for?"

Patty checks with me to make sure she has the green light to explain. "It's a long story, but the bottom line is that it has come to our attention that there are many distinct advantages to being engaged women. Therefore, we'd like to partake of these opportunities."

"You mean, being engaged right now solves a lot of problems," she clarifies.

"Kind of," I say, before Patty starts boasting about her plans to haul in free kitchen appliances and gratis gym memberships.

"I totally understand. You wouldn't believe how many women come in looking for cubic zirconia engagement rings just for themselves." Now, finally understanding what Patty and I are about, Keira sighs and unlocks the window. "Especially women who have to deal with the public and are fed up with men trying to take advantage of them because they're single."

She gently removes Patty's garish ring from its velvet display and holds it up to the light so that the stone sends out shimmers of rainbow colors. It's even bigger than when it was in the case. Patty is practically swooning.

"The entire customer service department at Sears in Woburn is filled with unmarried women who swear by their CZ rings. Let's face it, people are so much nicer to you when you're married. Want to try it on?"

Patty doesn't have to be asked twice. She slips on the ring and splays her hand. Her French manicure does it justice and I cringe knowing that when it's my turn I'll have to curl the tips of my fingers to hide my ugly nails.

Meanwhile, Keira hands me a very tasteful solitaire. "Traditional. Simple. Affordable. People will recognize it right away as an engagement ring."

Like Patty's, it, too, catches the light. Yet, I can't help yearning for something different, even if it is fake.

"You know what?" she says, sensing my dissatisfaction. "Antique settings always add a little flair. I find that a stone in filigree gets a lot of comments and seems more sentimental. People will think your so-called fiancé really loved you enough to pass on an heirloom."

She wiggles onto my finger a ring with a huge stone that, while not heirloom quality, is a damned good imitation. Lots of filigree and an antique touch—kind of. "Is that platinum?" I ask.

"It's brass. With rhodium electroplating to make it

look like platinum. It's really quite spectacular, considering."

"Brass," snorts Patty. "Oh, boy. That *is* cheap. Say, how much are real diamonds?"

Keira reappraises my rich lawyer friend in her Escada suit with her black Lanvin bag and doesn't waste a second. "Actually, many are very reasonable and it goes without saying that they're also a sound investment. Want to see?"

Within seconds I and my tacky cubic zirconia are all but forgotten.

The ring's a bit loose, so an elderly clerk named Robert silently measures my finger as he takes over Keira's sale. He promises that the resizing will be "but a moment" and returns ten minutes later with my tighter "engagement ring."

As he walks off with my credit card, I wonder if I'm paying for something I could just as easily have found in a Cracker Jack box.

"What do you think?" Patty is back from the high-rent district and showing off a hulking marquise diamond. "It's estate jewelry. Weighs a ton. But it's real."

I cannot discern this diamond from the Moissanites, but I don't tell her that. I'm just relieved she has been steered away from the Aunt Rosalie cocktail number.

"Do I dare ask how much?"

"Not that much." She tilts her hand so it catches the light. "Under ten thousand dollars."

"Ten thousand dollars!" Now I'm the one who's

loud. "You're nuts, do you know that? That's not even a real engagement ring."

"Close enough. Hey, there's my client," she exclaims, waving maniacally. "Let's see if he thinks your ring is the real deal or not."

When I look to the door for Patty's client, I don't see anyone but a dark man in a navy blazer and white button-down shirt slightly open at the neck. Immediately, I feel the familiar rush of heat up my neck.

"What's Nick doing here?" As my voice has inexplicably turned hoarse, this question is more like a croak.

"I'm taking him out for drinks this evening and trying to get his business. Nick's interested in investing in some real estate and he might benefit from my, uh, assistance."

Which is Patty's fancy legal way of saying she hopes to take him home and rip off his clothes.

Nick scans the store until his gaze falls on Patty and her flapping hand. He starts to smile and then, seeing me, breaks into that knowing grin.

"Maybe I should go," I offer. "Leave you two alone to work."

"Nonsense. Besides, you've got to keep him company while I get sized."

As he passes the emeralds, a woman who must be at least in her sixties peers over her Valentino sunglasses to check him out. She might be worth a few million, but she's no more immune to Nick's magnetism than the college girls standing outside Club Mercury.

"Hello, Patty." He kisses her first on the right, then the left cheek.

To me, he says, "Nice to see you again, Genie. Hope you're feeling better."

"I'm fine, thanks." Modestly, I lower my eyes. There's something about his gaze. It's so penetrating, almost . . . rude.

"She was feeling bad?" Patty barks. "You didn't tell me that, Genie. Were you sick?"

"It was nothing," I say, tucking a strand of hair behind my ear. "Nick was there the other night at Club Mercury when I had that fight with Todd."

"Ohhh." Patty nods, remembering what I told her about the virginity conversation and Steve outing me. Judiciously, she changes the subject by shoving the ring in his face. "How do you like it? Isn't it gorgeous?"

Nick takes Patty's hand. "You have good taste. It's an estate piece, isn't it?"

"How'd you know?"

"I can tell by the quality craftsmanship. There's a distinct difference between hand-tooled jewelry and inferior pieces stamped from a machine. My uncle was a jeweler to King Constantine and he taught me everything I know about Hellenic metalworking based on a Greek tradition dating thousands of years."

Carefully, I slip my hand behind my back. Perhaps now is not the best time to be flashing my cubic zirconia, not with a Hellenic jeweler apprentice on the premises.

159

Keira motions that she's ready for her and Patty excuses herself to get sized. Before she leaves, however, my bestest friend in the whole wide world is thoughtful enough to ask Nick the Expert Hellenic Metalworker to check out my engagement ring.

Thanks, Patty.

"Well?" Nick holds out his hand, ready for inspection. "Let me have a look at what you and your famous fiancé have chosen."

Reluctantly, I put my hand in his large warm one. His fingers are surprisingly long and artistic, more like a musician's than a carpenter's.

In contrast, the skin around my knuckles is red and my nails are short and ragged. I wish I were like Patty, perfectly manicured and ready for spot inspection.

"You have lovely hands, do you know that?" Nick says, apparently unconcerned about my lack of pink gloss.

I want to gush *Really? I was thinking the same thing about you.* "That's nice of you to say."

"Do you play the piano?"

Funny he should mention that. Lately, I'd been debating whether to take lessons. Hugh always said it was pointless, that unless you started as a child it was impossible to master the instrument because the adult brain is so inflexible. He, of course, had been studying since age three and could play Beethoven's Piano Sonata no. 29 in B-flat Major perfectly. Not that I or anyone I knew had actually seen him do it.

160

"No. The flute was my deal."

"Ahh. That's too bad." He seems saddened by this. "My sister has hands like yours and she plays beautifully. Her teacher used to say she was born to it. Though it's never too late to start, you know. The human brain is an amazingly adaptive organ."

For a second, his dark eyes meet mine and, foolishly, it crosses my mind that he has ESP. That's so silly. I'm like a smitten teenager with a pop star. Nick's only being polite after what happened the other night with Todd. He probably feels sorry for me or something.

Turning his attention back to my hand, he peers at the ring and frowns. "The stone's big, that's for sure."

"Too big?"

"No, but it raises concerns."

Of course it raises concerns. It's glass.

"I hope you won't be offended by this, but are you completely sure this stone is . . . real?"

He knows. Why wouldn't he? He's a court-appointed Hellenic metallurgist. Snatching back my hand, I snap, "Are you saying my fiancé bought me a fake?"

"There's nothing wrong with a cubic zirconia," he replies patiently. "Diamonds are very expensive and some men don't see the point in wasting all that money on a tradition that essentially started as a De Beers marketing campaign."

I can't tell if he's slamming Hugh as cheap or suspicious.

161

"Believe me," I say. "Hugh buys only the best, the most authentic stuff." I try to think what authentic stuff Hugh would buy. "Like Irish wool. Single malt scotch. Hand-tooled Italian leather . . ."

"A six-day vacation in the woods watching another man build a post-and-beam house."

"Yes!" Wait a minute. Has he been talking to Todd? "I mean no. I mean . . ." I try to gather my wits. "What I'm saying is that Hugh comes from a very refined English background. He grew up on a six-hundred-acre estate in the Cotswolds and he went to St. Bart's in Scotland and his great-grandmother was a personal friend of King Edward. He would not, under any circumstances, even consider buying for me, his future wife, the mother of his future children, anything less than the most flawless, perfectly cut diamond."

"That'll be $24.95, Miss Michaels." Robert slides me my credit card slip. "Good news. Ten percent off all cubic zirconia solitaires. Only today."

I snatch the receipt and sign, not even daring to check Nick sidewise. "It's a duplicate," I say, scrawling my name with a flourish. "For insurance purposes."

"Perfectly understandable. For insurance purposes. Exactly what an Englishman who grew up on a six-hundred-acre estate in the Cotswolds would insist upon."

I turn to him, shocked. And with that, Nick winks and goes off to join Patty.

He knows I'm a fraud, but I'm no longer worried he's going to out me to Todd, oh no. He's going to hold this secret over my head, toying with me, teasing me, until I break down and confess it all.

Chapter Eleven

NEW YORK POST
PAGE SIX

July 10—Hot-stuff author **Hugh Spencer,** whose tearjerker *Hopeful, Kansas* continues to dominate major bestseller lists, isn't identifying the woman to whom he proposed recently during a **Barbara Walters** prime-time interview, though **PAGE SIX** sources have confirmed she is Spencer's longtime girlfriend, Genie Michaels, an admissions counselor at **Thoreau College,** where Spencer teaches English.

Michaels declined to comment publicly, noting in an official Thoreau College press release that their relationship was a private matter. However, she has been reported wearing a HUGE new diamond on her left hand and rumors are that an August 20 wedding is planned at her family's home in Belmont, Massachusetts.

When reached in London, where Spencer is promoting the British edition of his book, he said only, "What?"

TO: genie.michaels@thoreaucollege.edu
FROM: hugh@hughspencer.com
SUBJECT: What the ???

Genie:

Again, let me state how much I appreciate your discretion regarding my on-air betrothal. I am very impressed that you have not sought out the press as a sounding board for whatever bitterness you may be harboring. Truly, I had expected and was prepared for the worst. It was so refreshing to see you put my public image first. Thank you.

That said, I am a bit distressed that, in being wonderfully supportive, you have, inadvertently I'm sure, created the impression that we are truly engaged. In particular, as I stated in a recent telephone message, your parents' statements to Pippa were of concern. So much so, it briefly crossed my mind—though I know this can't possibly be the case—that you might be lying to them that we really are getting married. (Ha, ha!) I realized later this was nonsense; only a mentally disturbed person would promote such a fallacy and no matter what flaws you possess, Genie, mental illness is not one of them. (At least, I hope.)

Needless to say, your noble desire to remain mum on inquiries regarding our nonexistent marital status have, unfortunately, caused a bit of confusion/anxiety here, and though I have explained to my fiancée that you are just being supportive of my career, this explanation is fast becoming insufficient in light of the numerous e-mails/phone calls/telegrams and faxes congratulating me on my upcoming wedding to you.

I strongly suggest that, should anyone ask, you simply state that, no, I did not and never will ask you to be my wife.

Also, I am at a loss to understand this August 20 wedding rumor. Was this your idea? If so, I can't imagine what it was that possessed you to mention a date. You need to disabuse friends and colleagues of this notion forthwith.

Lastly, the ring. I find this thoroughly audacious. If your purchase of an engagement-type ring (I do not remember you owning one before) was meant to somehow mock me, then I suggest you remove it immediately. Weak attempts at sarcasm or, worse, desperate attempts to draw attention, do not, Genie, put you in the best of lights.

I trust you will proceed accordingly,

Hugh.

P.S. On a side note, the foreign rights to HOPEFUL have been sold to Thailand and the

Republic of Fiji Islands for a whopping total of 40 countries. I know you are as excited as I am.

TO: hugh@hughspencer.com
FROM: genie.michaels@thoreaucollege.edu
SUBJECT: RE: What the ???

I might be wearing an engagement ring. I might be getting married August 20.
    But who said anything about *me* marrying *you?* Life does go on, you know.

Genie

P.S. Congrats on the foreign rights. You have no idea how that thrills me to my very core.

Chapter Twelve

Let me just say this: I am *loving* the ring.

I've never felt so pretty and special, as if overnight I've become a princess. As if suddenly I'm a gorgeous, glamorous woman who deserves nothing but the best. I don't know why I didn't buy it years ago. Every woman should have at least one.

And the ring is so motivating. It even gets me to wake up early Saturday morning to meet the trainer Lucy arranged for me at Joe's Gym. Do I want to wake up and be abused? No. I want to sleep in and hang around in sweats all day.

But then I see my ring and remember how it is starting to change my life, and I get out of bed. Drink a cup of foul-tasting coffee from the Rite Aid coffeemaker (Patty's right, I really do need an upgrade), pack a bag, and head down to Joe's.

The joint is hopping at 5:45 when I stagger through the double glass doors. Clearly these people have never cottoned on to the concept of a nightlife. They are running. They are spinning. They are chatting as they run and cross-train. They are smiling, for God's sake. Don't they realize it's six A.M.?

"Hi there!"

Oh, Lord, save us. It's Kip Boynton in a Joe's Gym unitard. I met Kip the trainer during a six-week blizzard of fitness fanaticism when I let my former neighbor Robin talk me into taking a kickboxing class with her, an event that, apparently, they still discuss in the weight room. (Though I did not kick the bulletin board off the wall. That was a total exaggeration. It simply fell when I happened to come near it.)

"Ready to become a buff bride?" Kip slaps his hands. *Slap!* "Hold on. Let me see that gorgeous engagement ring."

Okay. This is when I discover if the ring can withstand the scrutiny of strangers, not just my friends or expert metallurgists like Nick. If it passes here, at Joe's Gym, I might very well summon the courage to wear it to work. That is, if I can fabricate a plausible backstory of its origins. (I'm thinking Hugh's great grandmother Serena from Cornwall who bequeathed it to Hugh's transsexual uncle Waldo, who never had much use for it, aside from the occasional Mardi Gras party.)

Also, along with a backstory, I'll be needing a manicure.

I've become very self-conscious about my ragged nails now that I understand that, according to Nick, I've got beautiful fingers. In the past, manicures always seemed so self-indulgent to my Yankee soul. I couldn't imagine paying a total stranger sixty bucks to push back my cuticles and polish my nails when I could do it at home for free. (Though I never do.) But now my perspective might be changing.

I find I'm holding my breath as Kip inspects the cubic zirconia in its antique rhodium-treated brass setting. Will he notice it's glass? Will he notice it cost less than his sneakers?

No. He doesn't!

"Donatella." He calls over to the peppy girl behind the counter. "Come look at Genie's engagement ring. It is Genie, right, from kickboxing?"

I refuse to answer that question on the grounds that I may incriminate myself.

"Holy . . . !" Donatella stops herself from a full swear. "That is beautiful. Did your fiancé design it?"

I smile like a dope. Less said the better is my philosophy.

"I bet it's a hand-me-down, say?"

This goes on for a few minutes, them speculating on the ring and where it came from and how much Hugh must love me to have given me such a *huge* diamond in such a gorgeous setting. I wish Nick were here so I could rub his face in it.

Another fit and peppy person comes to ooh and aah and then Kip notices it's 6:03. We are behind schedule.

I have no idea what my mother did in her day to get ready for her wedding. But I doubt she had a man in a unitard with his foot on her back as she executed knee push-ups in ten-rep intervals. Did she do forty chair dips, several sets of double crunches? Was she on the treadmill, ratcheting up the program to HIIT (High Intensity—don't ask me why there's an extra *I* or a *T?*)

Kip won't let me attempt the dumbbells, not until I've lost a few pounds. He recommends ten-pounders. "Nothing drastic," he says. (I have to inform him that—outside fitness fantasyland—ten pounds to the average woman in her midthirties is, indeed, drastic.) Then he provides me with your run-of-the-mill no-fun diet and an exercise program that, according to my cursory brief glance, requires me to visit the gym with disturbing frequency, like every day.

I'm not sure if I'm getting married or joining the marines. I'm reaching the conclusion there's not much of a difference.

"We don't have much time, but I promise you, Genie, that come August twentieth you will be fitter and sexier than you are today," he pledges.

Sexier. You know, I'm getting a bit tired of the message that as well as being smart and financially prudent and well-groomed and a good housekeeper, as a new bride I've got to be sexy, too. I mean, men don't get this kind of treatment. Men are praised for being hard workers, savvy negotiators, sage investors, or "real family men"—as if that's a rare, esteemed quality. (When was the last time someone observed that a mother was a "real family woman"?)

I haven't read anything in *Cosmo* about "Groom Boot Camp." Fathers don't take their affianced sons aside and privately advise them to drop a few pounds, maybe six-pack the old abs in order to keep the bride happy.

Still, hearing Kip say this, I feel that I am on the road to sexy. Granted, it's a very steep road and I've gotten a late start. For instance, there's my personal stash of big, cotton underwear at home. Comfortable, sure, but not exactly man bait.

The thing is, I buy bras for ease of wear, not for how they lift my breasts or squeeze my cleavage. And— yes, this might come as a shocker—I have never once bought a bra or panty with a man in mind. Here's why: Men don't have to wear the damned things for fourteen hours a day, whereas I do. Let them deal with scratchy lace against their crotch and see how they like it.

My lack of underwear finesse is further driven home when I arrive in the women's locker room to shower and change just as the Advanced Spinning class has let out. All around me are women with flat abs and high tushes prancing about in black or red thongs and—though I try not to look—an unnatural lack of hair. I mean, most of us have hair there, don't we? But not these women. They're practically bald.

How do they get so bald? This might be the Brazilian thing I've been reading about. Connie goes Brazilian. I am privy to this information because she and I have the same hairdresser (Melody at Stairway to Style, fantastic!) and I've heard stories. Wild stories, like the fact that Connie gets a design. Sometimes it's a heart or a simple triangle. One Christmas it was a merry bell. In the summer, Melody (who actually has to perform these Brazilian waxes on all shapes and sizes and ages of people) says most women go floral, their preference being a daisy.

A daisy.

As I try to make myself and all my au naturel hairiness inconspicuous in the corner by the inconvenient lockers, I decide Connie's daisy is just a symptom of a larger disease. The Aggressive Sexual Woman's Disease. It's not only the daisy, it's also that Connie keeps her body fat to less than twenty percent, that she has maxed out her Victoria's Secret credit card and owns a library full of books and DVDs on how to please a man, how to bring him to the point of arousal and back so that he's on his knees, begging and crying for relief.

In fact, I would accuse Connie of being Hugh's mystery woman if she hadn't admitted to me once that while she envied my relationship with a stable, successful, mature man, she, personally, could never date a "thin, pasty white, slightly effeminate" Brit. Apparently, Connie is so much of a woman that she requires someone with vast stores of testosterone—big, strong men with muscles who engage in daily physical labor. "Real men," as she put it, "built for insemination."

Like Nick, I think, my neck instantly going hot again. Why in the world would I have thought of him?

"Genie?"

I stop musing about Nick and look up to find Tracy Gridell naked along with two perfectly formed globes that, in some plastic surgery circles, must pass for mammary glands. These have to be upgrades because Tracy and I went through junior and high school gym class together and though my memory is not the best, I am positive she never sported basketballs instead of breasts.

"Genie Michaels? I haven't seen you since forever. How *are* you?"

I would like to say that I pride myself on being beyond the realm of pettiness, but those breasts are my tipping point. In a moment of impulse I know I will regret later, I hold up my hand and say, "How am I? I'm *engaged,* that's how I am!"

Squeeeal!

That is so satisfying, that squeal. I hate to admit it.

Tracy practically tears off my hand, inspecting the ring. This is even more nerve-wracking than Kip's review downstairs because with her new plastic anatomy, I bet Tracy is an expert in all things false.

"Oh, my God. It's gorgeous. Who?"

See, now, this is where maybe I should shut up. Though, of course, I don't.

"Hugh. Hugh Spencer. You know"—I actually flutter my eyelids—"the author of *Hopeful, Kansas*? We've been going out for four years so, whew, finally, right? August twentieth. That's the big day."

Tracy has no idea who a Hugh Spencer is or what or where is *Hopeful, Kansas*. Nor does she care because I've just said something that could affect her life and, as we all recognize, a conversation improves dramatically when it's about ourselves rather than the other person.

"You're getting married in August? Do you have a house yet?"

Just when I'm about to get a handle on this engagement thing, she throws me a curveball. A house. Everyone wants me to buy a house.

"Because I'm a real estate agent now with Hennicker Realty, so if you're looking, give me a call. I can get you a terrific deal even in this seller's market." Tracy reaches in her gym bag and produces a business card. Sure enough, it says Tracy Williamson, Hennicker Realty. She can now write off this month's gym membership.

"Williamson? Did you get married?"

"Already divorced. What a cliché, huh? Get divorced, become a Realtor. Anyway, that's the way the cookie crumbles. Hey, how's Todd?"

Todd. I'd forgotten Tracy had a huge crush on him in high school. "He's okay."

"Still single?" Tracy drops her towel and slips into a hot pink silk thong. She, too, is bald. In fact, she's smooth and curvy and white all over. I feel like some lice-ridden cavewoman in comparison.

"Uh-huh." I wrap my own towel more securely as I step into my flowered Fruit of the Loom cotton briefs. Tracy shoots a glance at them, a glance that says volumes.

"He's in home remodeling now," I say, pretending that I've come to terms with my Fruit of the Looms. "He's been working on a great house by the golf course, on Peabody."

Slathering on moisturizer, Tracy says, "Not the Victorian two-family with the stained-glass windows."

"That's it." Surreptitiously, I bring out my white cotton bra (a meager 36C) and try snapping it in the back.

"But that went on the market yesterday."

My bra snaps off. "What?"

"If it's the one I'm thinking about. The one with the poplars in the back. The one abutting the golf course, right?"

"That's it." Could it be for sale so soon? Todd didn't say anything.

"Yup. I swear it popped up on the MLS listed for about five hundred thousand dollars. And, you know, there was a note on it about needing some work. Guess that's the renovation Todd's been doing, huh?"

The notion of yet another dream house once again slipping through my fingers to someone who doesn't appreciate it is maddening. My life is one long stretch on the bench watching other lives go by. Just when will the coach pick me to play?

Hold on. Isn't this the whole point of what I'm doing—to get my butt off the bench and play? Why, yes it is!

"I want to buy it." I can't believe I just said that.

Tracy slaps her hands on her narrow hips, her uncovered pink nipples pointing at me accusatorily. "Are you serious?"

"I am. Only . . ." Oh, man. I wish I knew if my parents were going to give me the money or not. "I'm not sure I can rake up the deposit."

"A hundred grand is what you'll need. That is, if you're not going balloon—and I definitely recommend in this economy that you not go balloon."

It's hard to face those breasts and not go balloon.

Retrieving my bra, I say, "It was just a thought. I really love the place, is all."

"Then you should get your money together and buy it. I can't tell you what a steal it is at this price." She comes closer, bringing with her clouds of lavender and rose. "I shouldn't be telling you this since Todd's involved, but the rumor is that the woman who owns the house has a boy toy out in California. She hates Boston and wants to be rid of all memories of it and her ex as quick as possible. Which is code for you know what."

I know what. This means Cecily Blake wants cash and that she might be willing to drop the price if she gets it. Todd said she was running out of money, but a boy toy is better. Much more motivational.

"So, think about it and if you do decide to act, call me. But act fast because this will be gone by Sunday. You can take that to the bank."

Chapter Thirteen

It is pathetic that this is my first visit, ever, to Victoria's Secret.

Thirtysomething years old, almost forty, and I've never been. Why? Because every time I scrounge up the courage to walk in, there is some guy in a raincoat by the door looking both awkward and kind of, well, *turned on,* as he ogles women picking through the central display of lace-etched thongs. And no, he is not a bouncer. (Although, it's an idea worth considering.)

I keep thinking of all those male fantasies (delusions) or that movie, *St. Elmo's Fire*, where Judd Nelson goes to buy Ally Sheedy some fancy lingerie and he ends up getting *extremely* personal attention from a clerk who has just added a whole new dimension to customer care. I just love male screenwriters and their *absurd* imaginations.

Okay, so the creep by the door is probably a boyfriend or a husband, but how can I be sure? What if he's your garden-variety perv who gets his thrills looking at women picking through underwear? This is why I don't go to Victoria's Secret.

But that was before. Now, with my ring, I visibly belong to some other man and I am not to be messed with. (Hands off, pervert by the door.) As I walk past him, I make a big display of my left hand so that the glints from my fake diamond practically blind him with their supermarital powers. Take that! And that! And that!

After I successfully *kapow* him with cubic zirconia, he doesn't dare stare at me. He has to look away until a dumpy woman approaches, displaying for his approval a long, high-necked nightgown from what must be the "Victorian" end of Victoria's Secret. So ends the male fantasy.

Let's see. Where to start? First I have to figure out what I'm doing here with all these sexually adventurous twentysomethings who think nothing of picking up $60 leopard-print, gel-filled Very Sexy push-up bras. I'm not sure they're getting adequate support with those. They'll live to regret it when they hit middle age and find they've become dependent on the gel.

But I am getting distracted. I must concentrate on the business at hand. My goal is to achieve a complete underwear overhaul, to execute the kind of purge a real bride would undertake in preparation for a sex-filled honeymoon. It's a daunting task, eschewing my high-waisted cottons, and I'm not entirely positive that my body, which is beginning to mount a full-scale protest of this morning's physical activity, can pull off something called a "flutter thong" or a "satin lace-up tanga."

Oh, what the hell. Why am I sweating this? This is not brain surgery. Soon I am randomly gathering anything in a size 5—thongs, which I will have to resist constantly yanking downward; plunge bras; "keyhole panties" (whatever they are); and a couple of baby-dolls.

Surveying my basket filled with feather-light pink, purple, black, and emerald green lingerie, I swell in new sensuality. Yes, this has been my destiny, a secret life as a sexual ingénue, one denied me by Nancy Michaels's upbringing. From this day forward, I will be Genie with the hard body and purple lace-up, keyhole panties. (Doesn't sound like much coverage, does it?) I may even shave places heretofore declared unshavable.

Though no daisies. Or holiday bells, either.

As I saunter to the counter, I try to keep in mind that, naturally, this transformation will not take place overnight. But if I work out every day and smooth my skin with baby oil, perhaps darken it with some spray-on tan, by August 20 I bet I'll look like . . . no. Not her.

Karolina Kurkova is pouting at me from a display above the register, her thighs so hard you could bend steel on them.

Okay, so maybe it might take a bit longer than a couple of months. Still, I'll get there, I really will.

And won't that be rich when Hugh returns from England to start the new semester with his new fiancée and he bumps into me on campus, barely rec-

178

ognizing my highlighted hair, my taut triceps, and my sculpted figure.

He'll have to ask himself who is this beautiful, sexy woman with the keyhole panty? Could this be the warm-hearted Genie Michaels whom I *sponged off* for four years while I wrote my bestselling sap fest? No, this couldn't be the woman who never turned me on, because this vision of sexuality could turn granite on.

"My God, what a mistake I've made!" he'll cry, as he runs at breakneck speed to break up with said fiancée, who will plead and beg but who, upon seeing the New Me, will have to admit I am too fabulous for any mortal man to resist.

Eventually, he'll win me back with a real diamond and a fervent pledge to spend every day of his life making up for the hurt he inflicted. And we really will be married. In a church, not the backyard. Maybe even in England like my mother wants. There will be six bridesmaids and shower gifts I won't have to return or donate to charity. And best of all, Hugh will be so madly in love with me he'll never think of looking at another woman and will spend all his free time berating himself for having strayed in the first place.

"That'll be 165 dollars," the girl at the register says.

One hundred and sixty-five dollars. Yes. There'd better be an English countryside wedding for that kind of money. I pull out my Visa and, with a slightly tremulous hand, submit it.

In a weak attempt to distract me from this astronomical bill, she observes, "That's a beautiful ring. Engagement?"

"It is!" With each lie, I grow more comfortable exclaiming this. "Getting married August twentieth."

"No way! Me, too." She thrusts out her hand, on which sits a smaller diamond, though one that probably cost more than $24.95. "I can't believe it's the same day. What a coincidence."

Patty claims there's no such thing as coincidence, everything is destined by God, I think.

"Where's your ceremony going to be?" Hoping, praying, that it will be at All Saints Episcopal Church and I'm off the hook as far as a church wedding is concerned.

"St. Nicholas Greek Orthodox Church. My boyfriend's from Cyprus."

Patty would call this a sign from God. But do I see it?

No.

My divine insight has been obscured by the dazzling temptations of the Great Whore of Babylon. Also known as the Victoria's Secret 30 Percent Off Table.

Next stop after Victoria's Secret is the porn section of Barnes & Noble.

Yes, yes, I know there's not really a porn section since very few books on erotica have actual pictures. Those you're supposed to invent in your mind. That's what makes them literature.

Actually, erotica is not where I want to be. That's not going to help me become a more sexually skilled woman. What I need is a manual of some sort, a book that tells me what to do and how to do it with easy-to-follow instructions. Otherwise, I'm afraid I'm doomed to a life of sexual sluggery.

Look. I have all the underwear. Not much point in spending one hundred and sixty-five dollars on flutter thongs if I'm just going to lie there on the bed, arms frozen to my sides in sexual paralysis. No! I need to take action. Practice with bananas and all that.

Normally, I'm a bit shy about lingering in the Sexuality section. You never know whom you're going to meet and then, of course, there's the issue of appearing to be a failure. *What's so wrong with her that she has to consult a book?* is what I fear people are asking themselves as they walk by to Gardening or Home Improvement or other perfectly normal sections.

My answer to that is *Hello, have you met my parents, Don and Nancy Michaels?* Todd once told me that in his estimation our parents have had sex exactly four times: on their wedding night; on the night they conceived him; and then, a prudent fifteen months later so Todd and I would be born exactly two years apart, on the night they conceived me; and lastly, after the Schiffmans' Halloween party where they got drunk (no surprise there!) and conceived Lucy. Lucy "our spooky accident," my father calls her. Also, "our freaky mistake."

The point is that I did not grow up in a family where physical affection was often displayed. There was my father's good-bye kiss to my mother each morning and their Christmas smooches under the mistletoe (my father wearing the most gawdawful bright green plaid pants). But that was pretty much it as far as displays of hot, unbridled passion were concerned.

Nor did we ever discuss sex in the Michaels house. Never. While my friends' mothers were taking their teenage daughters to the OB/GYN to get outfitted with all sorts of protection, the only prophylactic my parents made available to me was the threat of a one-way ticket to St. Mary's Episcopal School for Girls.

Which all adds up to me, Genie Michaels, repressed woman in the high-waisted floral underwear. A woman so unsexy that the man she was dating for four years couldn't bring himself to bear spending a lifetime of unsexy nights with her. Well, I'm here to say that the old unsexy Genie Michaels is officially dead.

Because here in the Sexuality section, I have just found the book that's going to change my sex life: *The Good Girl's Guide to Naughty Sex: A Step-by-Step Manual on How to Ride Him Hard and Get Put Away Wet.*

Yes!

Quickly, I open the book to hide the cover. Oh, my. This *does* have illustrations. Wait. What is that? That can't be . . . no.

I scan the contents:

How Many Licks Does It Take to Get to the Heart of a Man?

The Pen(is) Mightier Than the Word, Not: The Art of Talking Dirty
Lock Me Up, Tie Me Down: Sex Tricks That Are Illegal in at Least Three Southern States

Oooh. That sounds interesting. (And it's an excellent civics primer.) I flip to this chapter and am told, right off, that *extreme cleanliness* is very important if I wish to undertake any of these activities. Perhaps this book is slightly over-the-top for me.

Even so, I'll buy it. I have no choice. I need to know about those Southern states. At least, that's going to be my explanation at checkout.

Then again, I don't have to worry about what they're thinking at checkout, do I? I'm engaged. I'm about to be married. I *should* be purchasing sexual technique books since, as my religious radio station reminds me often, a "healthy sex life is at the heart of a solid marriage relationship."

Also, I will get *Sensual Bathing and Orgasmic Massage: What You Don't Know Could Be Ruining Your Love Life.*

That covers all the bases, doesn't it? Kind of a one-stop-shopping deal. Yup. And, of course, *The Cosmo Kama Sutra* because, after all, it's *Cosmo*. And *How to Blow Everything . . . Including His Mind.* These books should set me up perfectly. But, hold on. I throw in *Fouralarmsex*, which until this moment I was not aware was one word.

Great. I can't wait to get home and start reading, just

as soon as I squeeze past this rather large man in black with the funny white collar and . . . "Reverend Whitmore?"

"Genie?" Reverend Whitmore turns, his thumb keeping the page he was reading in place. "Funny running into you here."

Okay, who was the wise guy who positioned Spirituality across the aisle from Sexuality?

"Um . . ." I discreetly hide the books in my Victoria's Secret bag and take a chance the passing clerk doesn't think I'm shoplifting. "Actually, doing some research. You know, for work."

He puzzles his brows. "But don't you work in Thoreau College Admissions?"

"Kids." I give a what-can-you-do-with-them shrug. "Gotta know what they're up to." To prove my point I point to *Fouralarmsex* on the shelf. "This is what they're into. Isn't that sad? That and hooking up. I swear, no one builds real lasting monogamous relationships anymore. It's all sex on the fly."

But despite the tantalizing topic of *Fouralarmsex* and my moral consternation, Reverend Whitmore is not staring at the naked bodies on the cover. He has zoomed in on my ring.

"Is that what I think it is?"

Oh, no. Here goes. I'm about to lie to my minister, to the man who baptized me and led me through eight weeks of confirmation classes. "That depends on what you think *it* is."

"My word, little Genie Michaels is finally getting

married. Seems like just yesterday you were a babe in my arms." He pouts in sentiment. "You've grown up so fast."

Why do people keep saying that? I'm thirty-six. I've been living on my own for fifteen years. I have an automatic bill-pay on my checking account. I have spider veins in my calves.

"Yes, well. We children will do that, grow up, you know."

"Have you set a date? Because I have to tell you, the church's Saturday calendar fills up very fast."

"Er . . ."

"And don't forget it will be necessary for you to take my six-week pre-marriage counseling course, that is if you plan on an Episcopal ceremony. Then again, I'm sure you know all that from Lucy's experience."

Which Lucy described as "six hours of excruciatingly boring Q and A that would make even the sanest person in the world ponder the virtues of self-immolation."

"I'm afraid we can't. You see, my fiancé, Hugh"—I nearly choke on the words—"is British and he's in England for an extension of his book tour."

"*Hopeful, Kansas.* I read it. Such a powerful message of hope and redemption. He must be a wonderful, sensitive man. I do look forward to meeting him."

"Oh, and I'm sure he looks forward to meeting you, too. Just that we don't have much time. We plan on getting married August twentieth and he won't be back until August fifteenth. I can't imagine how we'll fit in your classes."

His forehead wrinkles even more. "Are you telling me someone else is performing the ceremony? I hate to think the church is losing a Michaels."

"No, no. It's just that I haven't gotten around to asking. It's all happened so fast."

"I see." He shoots a glance downward, what everyone does when I tell them our wedding borders on shotgun.

"That's not it," I say. "It's . . . complicated."

"Yes." His old fat fingers tap the binding of *Biblical Families: Raising Honest Children in a Dishonest World.*

I cannot stop staring at that word, *dishonest.*

"I have no idea what my calendar is for August twentieth, but for you, Genie, I'll make room. For heaven's sakes, it seems like I've been waiting a lifetime for this day. For a while, there, I figured I wouldn't live to see it. But God is merciful and patient. What for us seems a lifetime, for Him is but a blink of the eye, and He seems to have blessed you with a wonderful life partner."

We chuckle weakly. I think, if I don't get out of here this conversation is going to last a lifetime.

"And don't worry about the counseling sessions . . ."

Thank God! I'm off the hook for that one.

"I have worksheets you can send to Hugh. Even e-mail."

"Worksheets?"

"It's not ideal, but we'll muddle through. Some of the questions are tricky. Brain benders, I like to call them. You know, what happens if one of you becomes paralyzed. What if one of your children is born severely retarded or dies. What if one of you falls in love with another person. How would you cope should one of your parents move in and need round-the-clock care. What if one of you loses his or her job and can't find work."

Boy, marriage is depressing.

He squeezes my shoulder and whispers, "You know, the kinds of issues married couples face after the honeymoon." He taps the Sexuality bookshelf. "Ah, yes. Those were the glory days. I remember them vaguely," he says, before waddling off.

I am so stunned by this statement that it takes a few seconds for me to realize that not only does he engage in sex but that he has also walked off with my Victoria's Secret bag—thongs, orgasmic massage book, and all.

Chapter Fourteen

Reverend Whitmore cannot take my bag of thongs and sex manuals, especially since I haven't even paid for them. If he leaves the store with them, he'll be busted for misdemeanor theft and thrown in jail!

I can see it now: him waddling through the shoplifting sensor oblivious to the sixty dollars' worth of stolen sex manuals in his possession.

Alarms ringing. Security personnel closing in from every side. And there will be the good minister, flush-faced and baffled to find he is holding my hot pink bag of naughty undies along with *How to Blow Everything . . . Including His Mind.*

"No!" I scream, dashing from the aisle, turning the corner, and running—*smack!*—into, of all people, Nick.

"Hey, hey, hey." He grips my shoulder, laughing as if we're playing a game of tag. "You all right?"

Actually, I'm not since, aside from being filled with heart-pounding anxiety, I have had the wind knocked out of me after impaling my solar plexus on his elbow.

"Did I hurt you? I didn't mean to. You sort of side-swiped me."

Never mind my agony or the fact that, in his dark navy carpenters' union T-shirt, Nick is spellbinding. I have no time to talk—even if I could.

"Sorry," I gasp, when I get my breath back. "Gotta run." Wiggling from his grasp, I make it as far as the railing when I spy Reverend Whitmore on the floor below, pushing open the double front doors. Miraculously, he has passed the sensors without so much as a beep, despite my pink bag securely in his grasp.

Too late, I realize, letting out a long sigh. I am just not meant to enjoy good sex, that's all. I should be a Puritan like my alleged ancestor, the famous John Howland. Except for the all-day praying on hard benches. That's a bit much.

"Lose something?" Nick asks, joining me at the railing.

"A friend of mine walked off with all my stuff."

"Can't you catch up to her?"

"Him," I say. "And, no, it'd be too embarrassing."

"Right. Of course. Horribly embarrassing."

We are silent, watching the customers perusing tables below. Nick is no doubt at a loss to understand what the crazy woman next to him is up to now and, frankly, I don't have the energy to explain.

"What are you doing here, anyway? Not that I think carpenters don't read," I hasten to add, lest Nick peg me for a snob.

"Killing time." He holds up a slim copy of *Fear and Trembling*, which I haven't read since a college philosophy class and I'm not sure I really read it then. "I've just gotten to the good part where the spy is being double-crossed by his Russian lover who's selling nuclear secrets to the Chinese. Typical Kierkegaard, violence on every page."

"Gee. I'll have to give him another try, now that I know there's that much action. How's the sex?"

"Not bad, though he's kind of conflicted. I think Søren's about to break off his engagement to the love of his life, Regine."

Is Nick hinting he knows my secret? Or is this true? Damn. Where's my reserve of Kierkegaard trivia when I need it? "Well, it's hard to keep a good Danish existentialist down. At least, that's the way the song goes."

He laughs. "You're great, Genie. Very funny. I wish

189

I were going for coffee with you instead of the person I'm supposed to meet. Anyway, I'm beginning to think she's stood me up."

She? What *she* would stand up Nick?

"I wouldn't mind a cup of coffee," I offer cheerily. "Besides, I'm a good placeholder if she shows. First rule of being stood up—never be alone. Always pretend to be having the time of your life in case she arrives late."

"Really?"

"Oh, absolutely. The last thing you want is for her to find you looking forlorn and worried, milling around the remainders table and checking your watch. That'll be a total turn-off. She needs to see you already in the company of another woman."

He's smiling now. "Meaning, you."

"If you're game. My recommendation is to grab a table by the window. That way, when she walks by, she'll catch us in deep conversation and will curse herself for being tardy. You know what they say, 'Those who dither, suffer.'"

"I thought it was 'Those who procrastinate, mas—'"

"Shhh! Please. I'm a respectable woman. We'll have none of that talk."

"Sorry," he says, feigning seriousness. "I forgot about your prior history as a virgin."

"You can erase the memory of that conversation from your databanks, thank you very much," I snap, narrowing my eyes at him. "Now, do you want me to help or not?"

"How could I refuse?" And with that, he slides his arm around my waist and gives me a slight squeeze. "Is this too much?"

Not enough, I want to say, drinking in the smell of his clean shirt, the faint hint of soap. "Perfect. She'll be seething with jealousy." We head toward the escalators, scanning for his date. "What's she look like, anyway? I need to know so I can make a pass at you when she walks in."

"Tall. Rail thin. White, white skin. Kind of scary, actually."

"Sounds delightful. Do you always go out with skeletons?"

"Beggars can't be choosers, not with all the best women spoken for." He lets go so I can step in front of him on the escalator. What am I doing with this make-a-pass business? I am playing with fire, is what I'm doing. And I better take care that I don't get burnt.

Luckily, we do find a table by the window, where I wait while Nick orders us two coffees. I decide it's not just his Mediterranean magnetism, as Todd calls it, that attracts people to Nick. It's his overall demeanor. He is one of those naturally friendly people who talk to total strangers as if they've known them for years.

Like the girl behind the counter, for instance. Something he's said has her giggling, and it appears as if she's throwing in a chocolate croissant for free. (Oh, goody.) Sure, his good looks help. The longish wavy dark hair. The masculine jawline and trim physique. The shoulders out to there.

Nor does it hurt that he just stuffed a wad of cash in the tip jar. Hugh never would have done that.

Hugh boycotts tip jars. In his opinion, tip jars put the *slack* in *slacker.* "Mere mendicants," he used to say. "That's what we're becoming. A society of lazy mendicants."

"Can I tempt you?" Nick slips the croissant onto a napkin and slides it to me. It is bursting with dark chocolate. My very favorite, next to almond.

"I couldn't. Too fattening." Such a hypocrite. The cream and sugar in my coffee is worth at least two *pains au chocolat.*

"Come on. You know you want it." He breaks off a corner and pops it into his mouth. "Man, is that good. Dark chocolate. Pastry. How can you say no?"

Trans fats, Hugh would point out.

"A real date wouldn't eat a chocolate croissant," I observe. "She'd demur. Until . . . later."

He raises an eyebrow. "Later?"

"Until after we got to know each other better. You don't want to pig out in front of a guy before he sees you naked for the first time. A girl's got to create the image that she's almost, well, divine, a goddess who has no need of mortal food."

"I see." He sips his coffee, mulling this over. "I've never thought of that but, looking back on my previous dates, I guess you're right."

How long have Nick's women had to wait before they could eat, is what I want to know. My guess is not more than a night.

"So," he says, "I've bought you a coffee. We have the table. The next step is for me to take your hand, don't you think?"

A flutter ripples through me as I extend my hand with its newly done nails. "You learn fast."

"I have a good teacher."

Instead of chastely touching hands, we link fingers. Oh, God. We have just linked fingers and Nick is grinning that grin of his. I know it's an act. We're putting on a show for his date.

Still.

"Now," he says, "what should we talk about? Our hopes? Our dreams?. . . Hugh?"

Quick. Think of something, Genie. Anything but Hugh. "I know. How about the house?"

"The house?" He squints. "What house?"

"The house you and Todd are working on. I was at the gym this morning and ran into a woman I knew from high school. She's a real estate agent now and she said Cecily is finally putting the house on the market. She wants to sell it fast so she can go to California and be with her boy toy."

Nick doesn't let go of my hand. In fact, he absently strokes it with his other, his fingertips gently caressing my wrist. Clearly, he is an innately sensual man.

"Boy toy, huh? I knew she was eager to go to California, but Cecily never mentioned a boy toy."

"But you did know about her selling the house." I am trying very hard not to seem as if I'm at all excited by what he's doing with his hand.

"Of course. We've been in deep negotiations about me buying it for weeks now."

"Buying it?" He can't, I think, yanking my hand back and mulling over what he means by *deep* negotiations. "How come?"

"Excellent investment. Plus, I can finish the downstairs bathroom and kitchen while I continue to live upstairs."

"I didn't know that's where you lived."

"Yeah. I moved in when we started the project, part of a deal I cut with Cecily to keep her costs down. What's wrong?"

"I don't know if Todd mentioned this," I start, worried that I might sound like my brother's spoiled baby sister, "but I want to buy it, too. It's my dream house. I love its location, the fireplace, that it has a backyard big enough for a garden. I have visions of planting roses all along the front. Big red roses. Mr. Lincolns."

"Roses," he repeats, smiling. "You really must love it then."

"I do. You could even say I feel sort of desperate."

"Then how come Todd said Hugh wouldn't go for it?"

"Todd doesn't know squat. If I want the house"— here comes another whopper of a lie—"Hugh will agree. Sight unseen. He totally trusts my judgment."

Nick brushes a few crumbs off the table. "Well, then why haven't you two made Cecily an offer?"

Good question. So good that I don't have a decent

answer to it. "To tell you the truth, not enough money."

"Got that right. Cecily's looking for cash. A half a million at that. She's out of her mind."

"Who's she going to sell to? Drug dealers?"

"Fine by her. As long as the house is off her hands and she can go to California without waiting a month to close."

Cecily the real estate flipper. Poor Todd, having to work with her all these months. What a nightmare.

"We have to think of something," he says. "We can't let that house fall into the hands of some wise guy or a gun runner."

"Okay. Let's think. Let's resolve not to leave this place until we have a solution."

Nick and I drink our coffee in mutual silence and wrack our brains. A half a million is a lot. No matter how happy Mom and Dad are to have me married, they'll never go for it. For one thing, Lucy would have a fit.

Finally, he says, "How much cash can you scrape up? If you don't mind me asking."

"Right now, about twenty grand if I close out a couple of CDs. However, I might be able to get as much as three hundred thousand dollars. That's what my parents gave Lucy and Jason when they got married—not that I'm assured of the same." Not that I'm really getting married.

A glimmer of shock passes across his face as Nick lets out a low whistle. "How do I know *you're* not a crack dealer?"

"You don't. How about you? How much can you scrape up?"

He twirls the napkin on the table, hesitating. "About a hundred grand less."

"So, we're both drug dealers, since I don't know too many carpenters who've been able to sock away two hundred thousand dollars."

"I keep my expenses down."

"No kidding."

"Genie," he says, looking up. "What would you say if I suggested we split it?"

"The house?"

"Hugh would probably hate the arrangement. But from what I hear, Hugh wouldn't live in a two-family on Peabody anyway. So it could be strictly an investment while you two live somewhere else. If you put in three and I put in two, Cecily gets her cash. We could turn it into two condos. I'd finish the downstairs, no charge, and I'd take out a loan to make up the difference. It'd be doable."

Yes, I want to say, but there's no way I could plunk down that much money and still live in my apartment. My parents would never understand that. What am I saying? My parents won't understand when I tell them Hugh broke up with me weeks ago.

"The thing is," I venture, "I'd have to live there. I can't afford to live somewhere else and also own a home."

"You?" Nick asks. "Or you *two?*"

"Do you care?"

He's about to answer when something over my shoulder suddenly grabs his attention. "She's here."

"Who's here?"

"Cecily Blake."

"*The* Cecily Blake?"

"On the up escalator."

I turn around and sure enough there's a woman who meets Todd's every description. Impossibly tall, rather thin, with a pout that seems permanent. Cecily Blake in a crisp black shirt and white pants accessorized by clunky jewelry is going up while staring down at us like a buzzard on roadkill. There's no doubt about it— she's pissed Nick is with another woman.

"Shouldn't I kiss you now?" Nick asks.

Spinning around, I say, "Kiss me?"

"So she'll seethe with jealousy." He starts to lean in my direction and stops. "Wait. What's your preference? Do you like the first kiss to be one of those prim pecks or should I go for more? I know, you don't have to tell me. No tongue."

A surge of emotion wells inside me, though I can't tell if it's because Nick is talking about kissing or that I've just realized he has a bigger advantage than I do in getting the house.

"Cecily Blake is your date? Why didn't you tell me that?"

"I'll explain later." In one fluid move, he plants his lips on mine. It is neither a pristine peck nor a sloppy fumble. It is an absolutely perfect kiss. Soft. Full. Entrancing. The contrast between this kiss and Steve's pass is stunning. Steve's kiss I barely tolerated; this kiss I don't ever want to end.

Nick seems to be enjoying it, too, since he gently cups the back of my head, bringing me closer to him.

Which is when I see Reverend Whitmore at the window holding up my pink bag and gaping in horror.

"Crap!" I gasp, pulling away and getting up to go. "Crap. Crap. Crap."

"Was it that bad?" Nick looks hurt.

"No. Not at all."

For a moment, our eyes meet and something so powerful comes over me that I have to turn to the window, even though that's where Reverend Whitmore is standing.

"It's my friend. He's got my bag." I give a finger wave to my "friend," who is still frowning. "If I don't run now, it'll be too late."

"Sure," says Nick, rapidly writing something on a napkin. "Here's my home phone number. Call me if you have any more ideas about the house." He hands it to me. "Or if you just want to pick up where we left off."

Tucking the number into my purse as if it's a treasure, I say, "I don't know about that. I'm engaged, remember?"

"I remember. My question is for how long? If that kiss is any indication, I'd say not very."

Wow, he's bold. "You might be surprised."

"I might be," he says, sitting back and folding his arms confidently. "Fortunately, I'm a very patient man."

That's good because, unfortunately, I'm a very impatient woman.

Chapter Fifteen

The good news is that Reverend Whitmore is discreet enough not to mention me kissing a man who is not my fiancé. The bad news is that when I turn to look back at the window and our table, I find that Nick is still there, though all his attention is focused on Cecily.

Oh, well. C'est la vie!

I have no right to be jealous. After all, it wasn't a real date we were on. We were just pretending, that line about him being a patient man probably nothing more than his usual flirtation modus operandi.

Besides, even if Nick is developing feelings for me—and I'm not claiming he is—it would be a stupid move, strategically, for him to blow off Cecily now. He wants the house and what better way to get it than through seduction.

Which is excellent motivation for me to take action, too, by driving over to my parents right now before I chicken out. Granted, it won't be easy sitting them down and asking them for—*gulp*—three hundred thousand dollars. A handout this huge completely grates against my nature as an independent woman.

I've always prided myself on being able to get by on my own without Mommy and Daddy there to catch me when I fall.

Then again, it is three hundred thousand dollars we're talking about, a windfall that could tilt the scales in favor of my future happiness. In which case, my independence can sit down and shut up for a Saturday afternoon.

Mom is in the kitchen repotting a plant in the sink when I come in, soaked and determined.

"What a rainy day surprise!" she exclaims, rinsing off her hands. "I'm so glad you stopped by, Genie. I drew up a rough invitation list. Take a look."

There are far more people here than we planned. "I thought we were keeping it to under a hundred guests."

"I tried and just can't. Once you invite the relatives from my side and the relatives from your father's side, we're already up to seventy. And that's not including Hugh's people. Do you have that list yet?"

"Not yet," I say, flipping through the names. Why is Mom inviting my former high school principal?

"Well, you'll have to get that to me soon. Also, Hugh's parents. Honestly, I can't believe we've gotten this far into the wedding planning and we haven't even contacted them. It's incredibly rude. It's practically scandalous."

This I've got covered, thanks to Patty. From my purse, I pull out an address for Susanna and Trevor Spencer c/o Giorgio Hermani, Paloma, Italia. Never mind that Giorgio Hermani is Patty's uncle George, who, being a former con artist and internationally acclaimed circus star, has agreed to answer all correspondence sent to him as though he really were an uptight British couple.

"No phone?" Mom says.

"Guess they're really roughing it." I point to Patty's name on the invitation list. "Why is she crossed out?"

"Oh, dear. You don't really want to invite *that woman*, do you? She's so loud."

"I have to. She's my only bridesmaid."

"No!" Mom grips the kitchen counter as if she's suffering a mild myocardial infarction. "Why?"

We have been over this every day, that Patty is going to be my maid of honor, that Lucy will be my matron of honor, and that that will be it as far as attendants are concerned. And yet, every day my mother acts equally shocked and put out, as if we need to get a pass from the warden to spring Patty from the penitentiary along with a pardon from the president to spare her the electric chair.

"Would it make you feel better if I tell you she's engaged?" I say.

"Some man is actually marrying her?"

Well, no, *not a real man,* I want to say. "She's got a huge diamond to prove it."

"Does Todd know?"

"I don't know. Why?" What would Todd care if Patty got married?

The wrinkles from my mother's forehead have

instantly disappeared. The heart attack is gone. She is back to being in the bloom of health. "Yes, that *does* make me feel better, as a matter of fact." And with that she takes out a pencil and erases the line over my best friend's name. "She's not so bad, really."

"Really?"

"She's very bright and hardworking, objectively. Almost principled, in a kind of honorable Don Corleone kind of way, wouldn't you say?"

To my mother, all Italians must subscribe to the code of the underworld as outlined in *The Godfather* parts I through III. "Your words. Not mine. Where's Dad?"

"In the den. Wimbledon is on."

Forget it. The timing is too lousy. Wimbledon is once a year and Dad does not want to be disturbed for one minute of it. I'll come back later.

You can't think like that, Genie. You're always finding excuses not to live out your dreams. Act now.

My inner voice is right. It is now or never. "Mom," I say, marching to the den. "I need to ask you and Dad a big favor. I hope it won't be too much of a burden."

She trots after me asking all sorts of questions, most of which have to do with the wedding. "Do you need to change the date? Expand the guest list? If you don't want to invite Aunt Elda, I completely understand. That woman is so unpredictable."

Dad is half asleep, his mouth open as women's tennis plays on the screen in front of him. "Oh, good," Mom says. "It's the Russian. He can't stand her."

I turn off the TV and Dad jolts to attention. "Hey. I was watching that!"

"Sorry, Dad, but this is important." Pulling up the leather hassock, I sit at his feet—the significance of my supplication not lost on either of us. "Look. I don't know where to begin, so I'll come right out and say it. I want to buy a house and the twenty thousand dollars I have saved is not enough. Could you please help me?"

Mom sucks in a sharp breath. Dad sits up and rubs his face to rouse himself awake. Then he grips and ungrips the armrests before asking me where I suddenly got this urge to buy a house.

"It's the house Todd's been working on in Watertown, the two-family by the golf course. It's a fantastic investment, ask him. The neighborhood is stable. It's on a dead-end street in a pretty good school district. Practicalities aside, I absolutely love it and if I don't make an offer by tomorrow it'll be gone."

Dad glances up at Mom, who is biting her tongue, I can tell.

"You've talked this over with Hugh, I suppose," he says.

Okay. This is the hard part. I don't mind lying about being engaged to prove a point, but I'm pretty sure lying to get three hundred thousand dollars is a felony.

"No. Hugh has no idea."

Mom exhales the breath she'd been holding. "Then why are you asking us? You're jumping the gun here, Genie. You're almost a married couple. You can't go

203

around making unilateral decisions as if you were still a single woman."

There's something about the word *unilateral* that sets me off. Maybe it's from all those stupid diplomacy courses I took in college when I thought, wrongly, that I wanted to major in international relations and work in the State Department. *Unilateral* sounds so one-sided. So selfish.

"My decision's not unilateral, Mom. It's smart."

"Say, Nance," Dad says. "Would you mind getting me a Coke with ice? I'm dying of thirst."

This, of course, is code for *Scram, Nancy.* Mom presses her lips together, shakes her head in disapproval, and stomps off to the kitchen.

When she's safely out of earshot, he says, "Why haven't you talked to Hugh about this?"

"I haven't been able to reach him. He's all over Europe."

"Even in this day and age of communication?"

I pat his knee. "It's Hugh we're talking about, Dad. He can't even work a landline. Besides, what does it matter? You helped Lucy buy a house. I know that doesn't automatically mean I deserve the same, but . . ."

"You deserve the same. Better, in my opinion. My only concern is what happens if you buy the place without consulting Hugh and he hits the roof?"

"Hits the roof" is one of my father's favorite expressions.

"Let me ask you something," I posit, curious. "What if I were single again and I wanted to buy a house.

204

Would you give me the same amount of money you gave Lucy? I mean, not adjusting for inflation."

Dad grins at my inflation line. He knows I'm clueless when it comes to economics. "And you weren't getting married?"

"Hence my use of the word *single.*"

"Then . . . no."

"Why not?" Though I expected this answer, a part of me secretly wished my father had enough respect for me not to say it to my face.

"Because what's the point? A single girl doesn't need a house. Houses are for families. They're places to raise kids. All a single girl needs is an apartment, a reliable car, and a closet full of new clothes."

My left hand balls into a fist. I must keep my cool if I want to win this battle. I cannot bicker about his erroneous use of *girl* for *woman* or his thoroughly insulting statement that houses are for families only.

I need to remember that he's not cruel, he's not intentionally sexist. He's my father who loves me and he is simply ignorant.

"But, if I were getting married—as I am—you would have no problem giving me how much?"

"Well," he says, pondering his slippered feet. "We gave Jason and Lucy three hundred thousand dollars so they could keep the monthly payments low. What's Todd's house going for?"

"A half a million and Cecily, the owner, wants cash."

Dad emits a knowing banker snort. "Good luck.

Real estate is an industry that thrives on debt, a system the IRS very much encourages."

Oh, no. Here it comes. The banker lecture number 47.

"It's the biggest federal subsidy, you know. Mortgages."

"Yes, Dad, I know. You've told me this a gazillion times."

"So you should know your Cecily is blowing smoke. No way someone's going to show up with a pocket of cash to buy that place."

Actually, he's made me feel much better. It's a relief to realize I won't be bidding against doctors and lawyers and drug dealers with Franklins falling out of their pockets.

Mom is back with the Coke. I'm amazed she went through the trouble of pouring it since Dad immediately puts it on the side table without so much as a sip.

"Well?" she asks. "Have you reached a decision?"

Dad gives her a newsy update. "Genie can't reach Hugh because he's in Europe and she's worried the house Todd's been working on will get snapped up over the weekend if she doesn't act fast. I think we should give her and Hugh the up-front money, at least."

Up-front money? What's that?

"I can't hide my disappointment, Eugenia," Mom says. "Your father and I planned on doing for you and Hugh what we did for Lucy and Jason. Only, we were waiting until Hugh returned. We were going to have a little party and surprise the two of you with our offer to help you buy a house and now it's all been ruined."

"No it hasn't, Mom," I say, getting up and hugging her, barely able to hide the happiness that's mixed with my frustration. "It's better this way."

"You mean without the party?"

"Actually," I say, "without Hugh."

Mom says, "You mean without Hugh here."

"Right."

It turns out that the "up-front money" my father has in mind is enough to put the house under contract, not enough to satisfy Cecily's whims. Though I'm grateful for his extremely generous offer—no matter how ticked I am that I had to pretend to be engaged to get it—I must recognize defeat.

There is no way I'll get the house. In this market, there'll be enough eager buyers who can gather the necessary cash so Cecily doesn't have to wait a month.

It's over.

This is the message I leave on Nick's machine, being mindful that Cecily might be in the room when he plays it. Then I hang up and survey my tiny apartment with its one-windowed kitchen, its makeshift living room barely big enough for a couch, and sit down to cry, Jorge staring up at me, bored. I don't even bother to answer the phone when it rings. I'm simply too depressed.

"Pick up!" Patty screams from the answering machine. "I know you're there, Sister Eugenia."

I pick up the phone and carry it to the kitchen, cupping it on my shoulder as I search the freezer for something inspiring. "Where are you?"

"At McGillicuddy's. Your buddy Steve's playing and Todd's here doing his award-winning rendition of 'Subterranean Homesick Blues.' "

"Don't let him get away with that," I say, choosing a Lean Cuisine orange chicken. "He didn't take home first place. He got honorable mention for artistic cue cards."

"He's still got 'em! They're awesome. Why don't you join us?"

I peel back a corner of the plastic. "I can't. I'm too blue. I just found out tonight that Cecily's put the house on the market and she wants cash. A Realtor I ran into figures it'll be gone by Sunday night."

There's murmuring in the background, Todd asking whether I'm coming and Patty explaining my house-induced depression.

"So forget the house," Patty says, getting back on. "All the more reason you should come out with us. It's Saturday night. It's summer. Everyone is roaming the streets. Even White Bob."

White Bob is the nickname we've given to a student street musician who, aside from being white and probably from Kingston, Ohio, instead of Kingston, Jamaica, operates under the painful delusion that he's the reincarnation of Bob Marley.

208

"No, really. I think I'll just take a shower, turn on the air-conditioning, and go to bed."

"We'll get you drunk on Cap'n and Cokes!" As if that is somehow enticing.

"I don't want to get drunk on Cap'n and Cokes. I want to buy the adorable Victorian on Peabody."

"I give up. Talk to Todd."

Todd gets on. "Let the house go, Genie. I've been in real estate long enough to know if it's meant to be, you'll get it. Otherwise, forget it."

My microwave beeps and I give the still-cold chicken a turn. "Todd, that's how I've been living my life, going with the flow. I'm tired of it. I need to act. I need to do something. Take risks, like you said."

"Yeah, yeah, yeah. Listen, I gotta quickly ask you something while Pugliese's out of earshot. Is she really marrying this guy?"

"I don't know. I guess." Patty has not brought me up to speed on how far she's gone with this engagement story of hers.

"What bothers me is his name. It sounds so bogus. Moe Howard."

I stop stirring the chicken. Oh, Lord. Don't tell me she went with that one. That was her old standby when we were in college, the imaginary boyfriend for when she didn't want to get picked up. "Is this Captain Moe Howard of the U.S. navy we're talking about?"

"Have you met him? Because this is the first I've heard of the guy and suddenly she's engaged."

"Oh, yeah. Those two have been dating for years. His brother Curly's a laugh riot. Put Patty on."

Patty gets on. "Back from the bar, me and my Cap'n."

"That's not the only captain in your life, I gather. Honestly, Patty. What were you thinking?"

"It slipped out. Force of habit or whatever. Anyway, can I help it if I'm a sucker for men in uniforms?"

"Claiming Captain Moe Howard as your boyfriend may have been moderately amusing when you wanted to put down obnoxious fraternity brothers in college. But it's not going to fly at your firm. Pretty soon someone's going to remember the Three Stooges."

There's a slurp and a crunch of ice. "First of all, you don't have to use *obnoxious* as the modifier of *fraternity brothers*. It's redundant. Second, I seem to have convinced Todd and he's not dumb."

"Yes, he is."

"No, he's not. He's smart. Really smart. And I'm not just saying that 'cause he's buying. I think he finally appreciates me, now that I'm the object of another man's infection, as they say."

Albeit an imaginary man. "What about Nick?" I ask, testing the waters.

"What about Nick? He's a client, nothing more. You know I never step over the line of attorney-client relationships. Geesh, Genie. I may be a slut, but not in the workplace. Only at Whole Foods."

Actually, if memory serves, there's no place, work or otherwise, Patty *hasn't* been a slut. But I'm not going to debate the point. I'm just tremendously relieved that she and my brother seem to have finally found common ground. It's a miracle.

A miracle that gives me hope. If Patty and Todd can get along, then maybe it's not so impossible to think that I might be able to buy the Peabody Road house after all.

Hey. You never know.

Chapter Sixteen

My miracle doesn't take long.

The next morning, as I'm leaving to go to the gym, I find Patty's yellow Porsche parked in front of my house, Patty asleep at the wheel. She is in her clothes from the night before. A white halter dress with a big Coke stain right on the front.

Classy.

"Are you okay?" I shout.

Patty shakes herself and groggily rolls down the window. "Freaking tired. I stayed up all night and then, just to cover all my bases, went to the sunrise Mass. I've been waiting for you."

There is the niggling question as to whether she stayed up all night with Todd, but I don't dare ask.

"Get in." She leans over and opens the door.

I get in, leaving my gym bag on the sidewalk. Jorge, having made it as far as my front step, eyes us with suspicion. Once again I'm going someplace and not taking him.

Patty's car smells of fine leather, coffee, and mint gum—Patty smells.

"I wanted to make sure I caught you, but I didn't want to call and wake you up. So I parked here." She covers a big yawn. "I think I know how you can buy the house today."

This is my friend Patty. She never stops scheming. "Are you serious?"

"It might work. It might not. Todd's not so sure."

"Todd?"

"Yeah, he hammered out the details with me until the wee hours."

Therefore, she did spend the night with him.

"He loves you very much, Genie. He wants you to be happy and he's willing to do whatever it takes. Also, he feels guilty for blabbing to Nick about how Steve popped your cherry."

"Thanks." I love my brother, too.

Taking a healthy sip from her white Starbucks cup, she says, "All you have to do is stop by the house around eleven forty-five when Cecily's Realtor's showing it to a couple of doctors. Dress nice and keep your mouth shut. Todd and I will do the rest."

"What's your plan?"

"I'd rather not say. It might be"—she pauses—"somewhat illegal."

"Oh, brilliant." Great. First I fake an engagement and now I'm scamming property. How the mighty have fallen. "If it's too much of a risk, we can forget it, Patty. I don't have to own this house."

She plunks down the coffee. "Yes, you do. It's your destiny."

"It is not my destiny."

"Of course it is. Yesterday you ran into two people—Tracy, the real estate agent, and Nick—both with crucial information about the house. That's the Holy Spirit, baby."

"No it's not. It's coincidence."

Patty slaps her hand on my knee. "Oh, honey. There is no such thing as coincidence. I keep trying to tell you that. Everything, and I mean every little thing, happens for a reason."

"It's nice to believe, Patty, but it's not true."

"Yes, it is. The Holy Spirit is the most powerful force in the universe. Praise God. God is great!"

Okay, I'm not going to get in a religious debate with her on a Sunday morning in her Porsche. I will smile politely and wait until she's done giving testimony and then be on my merry way.

"Do you know," she says, shifting in her seat to look at me, "that when I wake up in the morning, I say three things? I thank God for giving me another day to live on this planet, basking in his love and asking for his help in returning the favor. Then I say Jabez's Prayer."

"I dread to ask."

" 'Oh, that you would bless me and enlarge my territory! Let your hand be with me, and keep me from harm so that I will be free from pain. Amen.' " She crosses herself. "It's from the Old Testament, First

Chronicles 4:10. I say it because it reaffirms for me that all I need is to do my best and trust in God and all will be well. He never lets us out of His sight, Genie. Never."

"All right," I counter. "If God never lets us out of His sight and wants us all to prosper, then how do you explain starvation and murder? How do you explain wars and AIDS and children in Third World countries who are slaughtered in front of their mothers?"

Patty slaps her steering wheel. "It's that damned free will. Why do you think I pray? So that He'll intervene once in a while. Frankly, I just don't know why He doesn't take free will back. The world would be so much better off."

"Also, more boring."

"True."

Patty and I sit there, staring at nothing, thinking about free will and destiny.

"What's the third thing?" I ask.

"Pardon?"

"The third thing you say every morning before you get out of bed."

"Oh, that. Yeah. Filing deadline. I pray that I haven't missed a filing deadline 'cause that could lose me a case. Man, the law can be one nitpicky bitch."

I have known Patty for almost twenty years and still I haven't figured out how a ruthless lawyer who swears and drinks and sleeps around and breaks the speed limit whenever possible can also be such a devout Catholic.

When she's not praying or going to confession or attending Mass or donating wads of her personal income to charities, she's cursing the male-run, hierarchical nature of the Church to which she is devoted, body and soul. It's a contradiction I don't understand.

I don't ask; I just accept.

Chapter Seventeen

I arrive at the Peabody Road house at 11:45 on the dot.

Already, there are a bunch of cars parked at the dead end—Patty's Porsche, Todd's pickup truck, a Lexus (which must belong to the Realtor since it's a statute Realtors in this area must drive Lexuses), and a late-model Volvo. Probably the doctors'.

Everyone's inside and I have absolutely no idea why I'm here or what Patty and Todd want me to do. Take a risk, I think. That's what.

The Realtor is already showing off the house's features when I walk in. With great arm flourishes, she gestures to the marble fireplace and then to the high ceilings, emphasizing the space and gushing about the southern exposure and hardwood floors, the excellent schools and unique privacy.

There is no sign of Nick. Then again, why would there be? He knows every inch of this house, including the upstairs, his home.

Meanwhile, a couple I'm assuming are the doctors are behaving as if they, too, know everything. He is snapping gum and nodding rapidly, motioning with his hand for the Realtor to get on with it. The woman isn't even paying attention. She's punching numbers on her cell. Might be checking a page. Or maybe that morning's crossword puzzle.

While . . . Patty. Wait! What's she doing?

Patty is in a very suburban Dolce & Gabbana miniskirt and pink, sleeveless cotton top, the exact outfit someone like Lucy would wear to an open house. Her hair is in a bouncy flip and held back with a black headband and she is dripping with diamonds. A diamond tennis bracelet. Diamond studs. Her to-die-for Tiffany watch with its diamond face and, of course, her new diamond ring.

The Realtor clears her throat expectantly. "If you're here to bid on the house, please get a form. Right now, we're entertaining only preapproved applicants."

Geesh. I'm not preapproved for anything except the five thousand credit card offers I get each week in my spam folder. The male doctor regards me over his half-glasses as if he, too, is well aware that I'm an imposter.

"She's with me," Patty says, grabbing my hand. "We're together."

Between the jewelry store and this showing, we're going to get a rep. We're going to have to start buying purple cars and rainbow license plates.

"Excuse me, Sheila," the male doctor says. "But can we cut to the chase? My wife and I are on a very tight schedule and I think all of us here are up to speed on the house's features."

"Are we?" asks Patty. "I'm not so sure. There are a few questions I'd like answered before we move forward." And from her tote, the one that carried the infamous bottle of tequila on that infamous night we forged the Sleeping Beauty Proposal, she produces a long white legal tablet jam-packed with a question on each line.

The doctor groans and I'm tempted to object as well. I've seen Patty in this mode. She can drag out a cross-examination so long even the most ardent plaintiff is moved to settle—or commit suicide, whichever comes first.

"My first question concerns the percentage of lead in the window paint." She clicks her pen. "Now my preliminary research shows that most houses in this neighborhood were built at the turn of the century, which means that all of them likely were painted with a lead-based primer.

"As you may know, by law a house cannot be sold unless the paint is no more than six hundred parts per million lead. This raises the issue of—"

"I don't care if it's solid lead. I'm going to take down all the walls anyway," the doctor barks. "I'll offer ten grand above the asking price."

He's going to gut the place. He's going to rip out everything and start over. Now, I absolutely cannot let him get it, even if he is offering more money than Nick and I could amass together.

Sheila says, "You realize you're going above your original bid, Dr. Norman."

"So I can seal the deal. What time is it, Sandy?" Dr. Norman nudges his wife, who looks up from her cell, startled. Tetris. Definitely Tetris.

"I dunno. Twelve fifteen?" Sandy doesn't seem too concerned.

More important, she doesn't seem to care.

Patty and I quickly exchange looks. One of the benefits of having a long-term friend like Patty is that our communication often doesn't require words. She's thinking what I'm thinking, that Sandy's not gaga about the house. I'm as sure of this as I'm sure Patty's going commando.

"Put this house under contract by twelve thirty and I'll personally chip in an extra one percent to your commission," Dr. Norman declares.

Sheila laughs slightly and says, "Dr. Norman. That's not necessary."

Though we all know damn well it is.

"Is this water damage?" Patty rocks back and forth, causing a tiny, almost imperceptible squeak in the flooring.

"I don't think that's water damage," Sheila snaps. "That's just what you get with an older house. Now, about that offer—"

"Really? It certainly smells like there might be water damage."

We all sniff. It could be my imagination, but there really is a vague scent of rotting wood.

"It does seem a bit . . . damp," Dr. Norman observes.

Patty says, "You know, you're right. Almost like mold. Does this house have a mold problem, Sheila?"

That captures the attention of Sandy, who pauses from aligning her digital bricks to comment that mold makes her cough and that she's highly allergic to all sorts of spores as well as bees and certain varieties of berries.

"Could be black mold." Patty opens her eyes wide in alarm. "That shit will kill you dead."

It's appalling, Patty's hyperbolic redundancy.

As if on cue, the back door to the kitchen opens and Todd tromps in carrying a huge tool chest and wearing a leather tool belt, work boots, even a yellow hard hat. The works.

"Howdy!" he hollers. "Don't mind me. Just finishing a patch job."

Todd never says *howdy* and he never wears a hard hat if he can help it—certainly not for a patch job.

Clearly annoyed, Sheila excuses herself to have a private chat with my brother in the kitchen. I'm sure Todd's not supposed to be here, though he's doing a superb job of acting confused, taking off his hat and scratching his head. I actually hear him say, "I got my orders."

Sandy tugs at her husband's sleeve. "Do you think there's mold?"

"No." He sneers at Patty. "This woman's just trying to queer the deal." Then, realizing his politically incorrect faux pas, says, "No offense."

"None taken," Patty replies politely. *Cough.*

Oh, she's good.

Cough. It's a tiny feminine cough. "Excuse me." Patty points to her throat. "Just a slight tickle." *Cough.*

Patting her on the back, I inquire, "Is it the dust?"

"I don't think so." *Cough.* "It's the kind of cough I got that summer in P-town. That summer of the Red Tide."

"Brevetoxins," Sandy gasps, herself releasing a contagious cough. "Similar reaction to the molds. Remember that vacation we took to the Outer Banks?" She coughs again. "It's deadly."

"You're imagining things," her husband says. "Coughs are psychologically contagious. Everyone knows that."

Patty, still coughing, gestures to Todd. "I bet he can tell us if there's mold."

"Good idea." Sandy deposits her cell in her purse and, moving like a warship, glides toward the kitchen.

Dr. Norman gives us a dirty look and follows.

"I have a question," Sandy says to Sheila and Todd, who are in the middle of a confrontation.

Sheila holds up a finger. "In a moment. We're finishing up and then we'll go over the terms of the contract. It's right here on the kitchen table."

"Is there mold?" Sandy addresses Todd. "I'm asking you because you've been doing work here."

Todd shuffles his feet. "No, ma'am. There's no mold. Not in this house."

"There. Does that satisfy you, Sandy?" Dr. Norman asks. "Now, let's go back—"

"Not on this floor, but in the basement, absolutely," Todd interjects. "Tons of it. Black stuff in all the corners. Hard to see with a naked eye, but you can't miss it once you get your nose in the cracks."

The three of them stop. I don't dare make eye contact with Patty. Nose in the cracks. Where does he come up with these lines?

"In the basement?" Dr. Norman is incredulous. "Why? This house is at the top of a hill. It's not even near any water."

"It's one of them stone basements. You know, dug out. All these houses on the streets, the ones what haven't been refinished, are crawling with mold. Course it's a bitch to remove, even if you do finish them off. You could tear it down to the foundation and never be rid of it. No, sir."

Sixteen credits short of a Harvard degree, my brother is playing the dim-witted yokel.

On cue, Patty erupts into a full-blown coughing fit. "I knew it. I just knew it. You can have this house. You couldn't get me to buy it for free."

"Me neither," agrees Sandy. "I knew there was something fishy about this place, the way the owner was selling it before the renovations were complete. Everyone said the owner just wanted out so she could move to L.A. But that's not it. There's mold here. *Black* mold."

Dr. Norman is not as sure as his wife, but since he's

already behind in his busy, busy schedule he doesn't stick around to argue. As he follows Sandy out the door, he leans toward me and growls, "You tricked your way into getting the house, missy. I just hope it's got dry rot."

I truly despise that word, *missy.*

We stand in the kitchen dully, listening to the Normans arguing outside, listening to the doors of the Volvo slam and then it backing off. When the Normans are gone, Sheila says, "I could report you."

"To what?" Patty screeches. "The Board of Sneaky Home Buyers? Give me a break. You were about to accept an illegal offer for a one percent bump on the commission. Mess with me and you'll never buy or sell real estate in this state again, toots."

Sheila is shocked, never having suspected that the tiny woman in the Dippity-Do flip and pink top is a legal whip.

Composing herself, Patty says calmly, "Now let's discuss a reasonable purchase price."

"These people were willing to pay 525,000 dollars cash." Sheila fiddles with the contract nervously. "Are you willing to pay that?"

Patty says, "Four seventy-five, not cash. It has no downstairs kitchen, no downstairs bath, and might even have mold. Take it or leave it."

The front door slams. Shoot. The Normans are back and immediately we all shut up.

"Stop everything, Sheila," an imperious voice

declares. "I've already accepted an offer. The house is sold."

"Uh-oh," says Todd. "Godzilla."

Cecily Blake in a head-to-toe snow white pantsuit has suddenly appeared in the living room holding a set of papers. It might be my imagination, but I swear she is saving her dirtiest of dirty looks for me.

Her heels pound across the hardwood floor as she marches straight past Patty and me and thrusts the papers into Sheila's hand. "Five hundred thousand, cash, just as I requested. No thanks to you."

Once again, Sheila's speechless.

"Let me see those." Patty snatches the contracts and starts reading, her face falling lower and lower the farther she gets into the paperwork. "Holy hell. He really did pay cash."

"Who?" I'm dying to know who stole my dream house. Who could have been so cruel, so devious as to go straight to Cecily? Who could have come up with that much money?

"You'll never believe it. Nick."

Chapter Eighteen

TO: genie.michaels@thoreaucollege.edu
FROM: steven.taylor@point107.com
SUBJECT: When are you going to forgive me?

Okay, to count I have left fifteen messages on your home phone/seven at work. Alice says you're in the office so don't tell me you're too swamped.

I can't believe you're still avoiding me.

To repeat my many messages, I sincerely apologize for stepping over the line and telling your brother and that other guy that you and Hugh were having sexual problems. I don't know what else to say. I fucked up.

BTW, how are things with you and Hugh? Better?

E-mail me back or I will get a total complex.

Steve

TO: steven.taylor@point107.com
FROM: genie.michaels@thoreaucollege.edu
SUBJECT: RE: When are you going to forgive me?

I forgive you. Of course, I forgive you. I'm not some psycho.

And I really am swamped. (That's my official line and I'm sticking to it.)

BTW—what's wrong with you that you can't haul your butt over here to take me out for a make-up lunch?

P.S. Todd says you're in love with some young thing named Alexi. Tell me, are her parents letting her stay out past midnight?

P.P.S. I am no longer discussing my sex life (or lack thereof) with you, fink.

TO: genie.michaels@thoreaucollege.edu
FROM: steven.taylor@point107.com
SUBJECT: FWD: Request for tact

Genie? What gives? Is this a joke? Inquiring minds want to know. (P.S. I never asked him about his goddamn potboiler.)

Steve

TO: steven.taylor@point107.com
FROM: hugh@hughspencer.com
SUBJECT: Request for tact

Steve, ole fellow. How delightful to hear from Genie's best (male) friend. Thanks so much for the toasts and all that. Yes, yes, I've gone and done it. Well, sort of.

Listen, as I did this with both guns blazing, I am now trying to regain my privacy regarding my personal life, so I'd appreciate any effort you can make to nix the gossip. If her other friends ask about Genie and me, my suggestion is to feign ignorance. Thank you in advance.

I can't tell you what it's like to be hounded by the press. It's as if, overnight, I've become Mick

Jagger of the literary world. If you haven't heard, my blockbuster HOPEFUL, KANSAS has reached a printing that portends to pass THE DAVINCI CODE or, dare I say it, HARRY POTTER. Naturally, I'm as thrilled as you are.

How did I manage to write such a huge hit? I get asked that question constantly and, though I don't mind if you inquire, really it's becoming a bit of a bore. Anyway, I suppose the crux of the answer is that I've just developed a certain skill, an ability to tap into the collective yearnings of the female species, if you will. The jealousy of my fellow writers is darn near palpable. Soon, I fear I will need around-the-clock security.

So there you have it. Don't worry. I won't let my fantastic success go to my head, even if I've just found out that Miramax is in negotiations with Colin Firth to play Dick Credo. I promise that I'll stop by and say hello when I return to Boston next week.

Cheers,

Hugh.

P.S. Alexi sounds splendid, you lucky dog.

P.P.S. Please don't circulate this e-mail address among the hoi polloi. Fans are ruthless!

Gotcha!

It is killing Hugh that I might be engaged to someone else. Though, I'm a tad bummed to hear that he might be cutting his book tour short and returning from England next week.

Picking up the receiver, I'm about to dial Steve and make amends when another call comes in. It's Todd, who is irrationally worried about me lately.

"How about you knock off early and come down to Hingham with me," he says. "You've got to see this house I'm working on. Eight fireplaces and I swear there's a ghost. Afterward I'll take you to dinner at Harry's Clams."

Ever since that night of the Bob Dylan look-alike contest, Todd's been going out of his way to be nice. "Thanks. But I have too much work. Besides, I'm not ready to look at yet another house I can't buy. It'd just bum me out."

"You have got to get over this, Genie. Remember what I've been saying, that when Hugh gets back from England you two can go house hunting together. Probably, with Hugh's royalties, you'll end up with that huge colonial on Concord, something much better than a crappy two-family in Watertown."

"You don't get it, Todd. It's not only losing the house. It's the fact that Nick went behind everyone's back, straight to Cecily, and stole it from me."

"Stole it from you? You didn't have that kind of cash in the first place. Get real."

Yes, but that's not the point. "We talked about splitting it. I figured that at least he'd call me to ask if I was still interested in doing that. But I haven't heard anything. I'm telling you, he's stolen the whole thing."

"Stop using that word, *stolen*. He saw a good investment opportunity and took it. He'd been looking to invest in real estate for some time. End of story."

"Investment, ha!" That makes it worse. "I wanted to live there. I wanted to pass it on to my grandchildren. He just wants a source of rental income."

"Or not. Patty says he's got a girlfriend back in Greece he plans on bringing over here to marry. For all you know, that house will be brimming with little curly-haired, olive-eating Greek kids in a few years. Now wouldn't that make you happy?"

Nick has a girlfriend in Greece? That completely knocks me for a loop as I recall our kiss over coffee. Though, I don't know why I should care. I mean, good riddance is all I have to say. A woman would have to be a fool to assume a man like Nick Spanadopolous would be loyal for a week, much less a lifetime. Look at the way he treated me, pretending to be smitten one minute, and then not even calling to explain about the house the next.

Yes, good riddance indeed.

Still, as soon as Todd gets off, I call Patty on her cell.

"What's this about Nick having a girlfriend in Greece?"

Patty must be multitasking because she answers in a monotone. "Girlfriend? I think her name's Elena. He mentioned her the other day when we were drawing up papers for the house. Rumor is she's gorgeous."

Gorgeous Elena. Figures. I picture a fecund woman bursting out of a white peasant's smock, lots of wavy black hair cascading over her porcelain white shoulders. "Did she help him come up with cash for the house?"

"I can't answer that."

"Why not?"

"Lawyer-client confidentiality."

"Oh, please. We're talking about Nick here, the megalomaniac who stole my dream home."

"He didn't steal it, Genie. His reasoning was very sound and his approach was completely aboveboard. Todd and I were the ones who were cheating, not Nick."

I hold the phone away at arm's length, as if this will allow me to verify whether I'm really talking to my best friend—or a robot who's answered her cell. "You can't be serious."

"I also can't get into it. You might think I don't take this lawyer-client shit seriously, but I do. And this is a lousy time, anyway. I'm drowning in paperwork. Talk to you later."

How about maybe never. I can't believe my best friend has turned on me. That is so unlike Patty.

There's a lot of stuff you can say about her, but one thing you cannot say is that she's disloyal. Patty defends me first, shoots questions later.

Okay. I have got to get back to work. Our new student review meeting is in a few minutes, and I still haven't drafted a plausible explanation at to why we should not retract our acceptance of Hob Cooper as an incoming freshman. Hob was a stellar student until he contracted what appears to be an almost fatal case of senioritis, garnering a bunch of Bs and even a few Cs in his high school back in Salt Lake City.

Now Bill wants me to give him the boot, according to revised school policy.

Recently, there's been a lot of pressure on us to rescind our offers of admission if students don't maintain their grade point averages. Personally, I think this is just plain mean. The spring of senior year is the last opportunity some of these overachievers get to goof off. And, as we all know, goofing off is a vital part of a well-rounded life. It's essential to our health.

Thanks to my own proclivity to goof off, I am able to jot down no more than one measly note about Hob when the door opens and Alice barges in holding a huge basket of roses.

"Two dozen." She rearranges my photos and puts the basket next to the one of Hugh and me at Thanksgiving. "Guess who they're from."

I eye the card and see the envelope flap askew. Good thing peeking in flower mail isn't a federal offense or

Alice's photo would be gracing every U.S. Post Office.

"Tell me."

She acts shocked. "How would I know? I don't go sticking my nose into other people's business. Though I bet I have an inkling." She drops her gaze to my ring. It is driving her nuts that I refuse to officially, finally confirm that Hugh and I are engaged.

So far, my policy at work has been to provide only vague, suggestive answers when my coworkers ask, "Did Hugh give that to you? I heard you two were engaged."

I've found a blush on the cheeks and a slight shrug of the shoulders do the trick. Also, when forced, a very blasé "We're very excited. Yes. August twentieth. Right around the corner."

Skirting all questions is the safest route, the one that will steer me clear of hot water should Hugh demand to know why I've been telling people we're getting married. This way I can honestly state that I have, in fact, told no one (on campus) that he is my future husband.

Can I help it if people jump to conclusions? It's only rational since he was my boyfriend for *four years!*

Alice is determined to stay until I read the card, though I make no move to. While I review Hob's essay and transcript, she lollygags around my desk, pretending to straighten my framed painting of Thoreau, dusting a plant with the cuff of her blouse, and chatting as though we're hanging out in the Laundromat waiting for the spin cycle to finish instead of preparing for another high-tension meeting with Bill.

"It must be pretty awesome having a boyfriend—I mean, fiancé—who sends you flowers. Trey sent me flowers once, you know, after he smashed in the front end of my car."

I look up. I love Trey stories. I simply cannot get enough of the Mullet Man and his beer-fueled, car-maiming antics. "Trey smashed the front end of your new Saturn?"

"Last year. Why don't you read the card?"

I ignore this. "Hope he repaired your bodywork, too."

"What happened was that Trey's brother Ray and their cousin J. C. stopped by unannounced one after-noon to watch the Patriots. Course J. C. and Ray showed up with a case of Bud paying no attention whatsoever to the fact Trey had just quit drinking."

Trey has always just quit drinking.

"And then they ran out of Bud and started talking about going for more. They wanted me to drive over to the packy and get two six-packs, but I said no sir. So Trey got his keys and headed for his truck. That's when I ran around the back and blocked him in with my Saturn. I didn't want him out there driving over mailboxes . . ."

Or people.

". . . blowing a point oh eight."

Point eight oh.

"He got mad, of course."

"Of course."

"And bashed in my front end with a tire iron. Next day, he told me it was the best thing I'd ever done. I'd saved his life and kept him out of jail and it was proof I loved him."

"That is so touching," I lie, wishing Alice would find a better man. She's too smart for Trey, too good a person. I keep thinking that if she made more money at work, were made an admissions counselor instead of staying as a secretary, for example, she might feel financially secure enough to dump him.

"Later, after he stopped puking in the toilet, he sent me roses. I saved one of the buds and squished it in my *Joy of Cooking* for preservation. It's still there next to 'Cuts of Pork.'" She collapses in my black-painted Thoreau chair and shoots another glance at the flowers. "Aren't you kind of curious? It'd kill me. I'd have to open it up right away."

I divert her with the eternal question. "When are you and Trey going to get married?"

She tips back her head and studies the ceiling. "Soon, I hope. You know how Trey has been wanting to marry me for years. He swears he will just as soon as he gets his Mustang out of his ex-wife's driveway."

This will end up making sense. I have faith.

"It's not any old Mustang. It's a 1968 Shelby with a 428 Cobra Jet engine. The original muscle car. But if we get married, she'll never give it up. He can't take the chance. It's worth, like, two hundred thousand dollars."

"Whoa." I had no idea American cars could be so valuable. "Why doesn't Trey just go get it when she's at work?"

"Jeanine doesn't work. She's on welfare. Though that doesn't keep her from spending her child support when she goes out every night."

"In the Mustang?"

"Oh, God, no. She doesn't have the key. Only Trey has a key, but he's afraid she'll sabotage the car if he so much as lays a finger on its bumper. Jeanine's very attached to it. She calls it her lifeline since that car's the only thing she has over him, to make sure he keeps up on the support payments."

Right. Why hadn't I thought of that? Then a superb idea pops into my head. "You could steal it."

Alice stops staring at the ceiling. "Trey would kill me. So would his ex."

"Not if you hot-wired it, maybe took it to a friend's garage or hid it in one of those storage places. Then you could show Trey what you'd done and he'd have no excuse not to marry you."

"It's not an excuse. It's a legitimate reason."

"Sorry." Shoot. Alice is so sensitive about Trey. "I didn't mean to call it an excuse."

Though I did. It amazes me, the "reasons" men come up with to stay single, from Hugh's amorphous marriage-is-an-archaic-construct to Trey's ultimately practical I-need-my-wheels-from-my-old-old-lady line. And yet they lack the guts—or ethics—to tell a woman she'd be better off with some other man. Why should they, when they're getting free HBO, free shelter, free food, and free sex?

Then again, I might have to rethink that. Sex was one reason why Hugh wouldn't stay. Too bad for him. There ain't nothing I don't know about how to give an orgasmic massage, now that I've been reading up.

Alice notes it's past ten and that the meeting has already started so we better get moving. My stomach clenches. I am not at all ready to argue in Hob's defense.

Alice says, "Just read the card before we go."

"Why?"

"Because." She picks it off its plastic devil's fork. "It's from the florist the college uses."

How extremely unsettling.

It could be from Publicity. They're promoting the heck out of *Hopeful, Kansas* and they've been begging me to provide more details about our engagement to include in the latest press release about Hugh.

"After the meeting," I say, heading for the door.

Alice trots behind. "Okay, but you swear to tell me who it is."

"Sure." Though that's ridiculous as Alice already knows who sent the card. Which is why her insistence that I read it is all the more unnerving.

Chapter Nineteen

I cannot remember Connie Robeson ever missing a new student review meeting before. Now I understand why Alice is making such a big deal about her unexpectedly going out of the country and being gone for such a long time. Something is definitely afoot, as they say. Connie never bypasses an opportunity to suck up to Bill.

We all take our seats, the clerks, the IT people, the other admissions counselors, Alice, Kevin the wunderkind assistant director of admissions, and me. I arrange my transcript file, yellow tablet, and pen neatly, preparing myself for a barrage of questions about Hob, when a sparkle of pink catches my eye.

My ring. Spectacularly colorful under the conference room's fluorescent lights. The wise move would be for me to quickly slip my left hand under my tablet before anyone else sees, but I can't resist making it glint and sparkle, twirling the ring from side to side playfully until Bridget, one of our traveling admissions counselors, says, "So there's the famous diamond. Wow. That *is* huge."

Kevin, who's been chatting with David Smythe, our summer intern, whips around. "Hey. I heard you got engaged. Let me see."

And before I know it, I'm being peppered with questions about Hugh's television appearance and how come he's not here to celebrate, about when we're getting married, *where* we're getting married, if I'd expected him to propose, how long we had been going out anyway, what finally changed his mind, if we're going to have kids right away, if we're going to buy a house, if Hugh's going to stay here at Thoreau or quit and write and, if so, what I'm going to do, if it's going to be sit-down or buffet reception and where we're going on our honeymoon—the one question, supposedly, that pushes politeness.

It's exhausting. I don't know how real brides-to-be do it.

Felicity Trinkle, a computer clerk, wants to try on the ring, but I won't let her, ostensibly because "I won't part with it for a minute," but really because I'm afraid she'll see that the inside of the rhodium-coated brass band is engraved with "Bickman's Jewelers" instead of the initials of its designer.

That's when Felicity says, "You should make sure that ring is covered by Hugh's insurance policy. My sister left her ring on the bathroom sink and forgot about it. Came back five minutes later and it was gone. Their insurance hadn't covered it since she'd been negligent. Now if someone had mugged her . . ."

This opens up a torrent of advice from women in the office who have never before given me the time of day because I was single. It was as if in being single there was no way I could possibly understand the trials and tribulations they endured as put-upon matrons. Now that I'm engaged, however, I have been silently initiated into their secret club.

The matrons urge me to insure not only my ring, but also my entire wedding should "a sudden cancellation arise." (Considering my circumstances, this is not a bad idea.) Also, speaking of wedding costs, Kevin (who isn't married, mind you) suggests I draw up a wedding budget and not overspend. (He's such a perfect nerd.)

Margery Rothman, one of Admissions' dinosaurs, cautions me against serving white wine at the reception. "People guzzle it like water. It'll bankrupt you."

Karen Caruso adds that I shouldn't make the mistake she made of stamping NO CHILDREN on the outside of the reply envelopes for her wedding invitations. Her cousin—and mother of five—hasn't spoken to her since.

Nor, apparently, should I have a "standby" guest list to cover the ten to twenty percent (on average) of people who "decline." I find this horrifying. Do some couples actually do this? And, if so, do they also have a "frequent" guest list and a "first class"?

We are all so abuzz, hashing over weddings do's and don'ts, that we barely notice Bill. He walks in, throws his own files on the desk, and pushes back his coat—Bill language for "enough." Everyone takes his or her seat as his arresting gaze sweeps the room.

Now is when I hide my hand under the tablet.

"Where's Connie?" He nods to the empty seat at the end of the table.

Yes. Where *is* Connie?

Alice raises her hand slightly. She is petrified of

Bill. He's so mean and such a backroom player with his cigars and campus politics, I don't blame her for being scared. He scares me, too.

"England," she says.

England? Alice never mentioned Connie went to England. She just said out of the country. What the heck is she doing in England?

Bill cocks an eyebrow, looking for more information.

"She's meeting the parents of her"—Alice shoots me a furtive glance—"boyfriend."

A boyfriend? In England? Connie? She never mentioned a boyfriend in England. She doesn't even like British men. They're too pasty and white and effeminate. She'd go on and on. . . .

The lady doth protest too much, methinks.

Like magic, the reason for Connie's frequent trashing of Englishmen becomes crystal clear. She doesn't hate British men. She loves them. Oh . . . my . . . God.

Hugh.

Suddenly, my chest freezes, unable to expand or contract. I feel as if maybe I'm having a heart attack and I grip the table, trying to remember the symptoms. Pulse racing. Chest pain. Arm pain. Heart pain.

"Are you all right?" Kevin whispers in my ear.

Across from me, Alice has the oddest expression. Her eyes have narrowed and she clearly is trying to communicate to me that she knows something I don't. I can't tell if she's laughing or accusing or . . . busting me.

That's it. That's all the confirmation I need.

Connie is in England with Hugh.

My archnemesis across the hall is my ex-boyfriend's mystery fiancée.

"Well, that's too bad," Bill is saying. His voice seems very, very far away. "Because we have a lot of ground to cover today. Okay, let's start with the incoming student update."

Margery jumps in with a glowing report about how all her choices managed to maintain their grade point averages since she did such an excellent job of weeding out the fly-by-nights and fakes. Someone's talking about cutoff GPAs and another's bringing up high school rankings, maybe Karen, I don't know. I don't care because I can't focus for the life of me.

I can't think of anything else besides Hugh and Connie, the woman he claimed on national television to love, desire, and worship. And the more I think of them together, the more I think of him longing for *her soft, warm lips,* the more I realize how much sense it makes.

Of course. Connie's been after him for months!

There was that period last year when she started escorting applicants over to the English Department to sit in on Hugh's classes. Then she lost all that weight and got breast implants over Christmas vacation. She really did look like one of those Victoria's Secret models, especially after she let her hair grow and got the highlights.

And let's not forget that warm evening this spring

when I was working late and came outside to find Hugh and Connie sitting on the picnic bench waiting for me, her long, bare legs crossed and silky smooth (I remember that).

Well, Connie wasn't waiting for me. She was waiting for Bill, who was taking her to the wine-and-cheese reception over at the dean's house. It doesn't matter. What matters is that she and Hugh were sitting close, very close, and Connie was giggling and tossing her long blond hair and Hugh was leaning back, laughing with her.

Oh! What about that week last April when Connie and I were supposed to hit the road for a Midwest high school evaluation with Bridget? But Connie came down with the flu and stayed home and Hugh told me he'd checked in on her once or twice to make sure she was okay so when Alice asked why Hugh's Saab was parked in Connie's driveway that weekend and . . .

God! I am *such an idiot!* Why didn't I see it before? Connie and Hugh have been carrying on for . . . forever! I'm a walking cliché, the girlfriend who is the last to know. Probably the whole campus has been aware of Hugh's catting around. I bet the entire office has been sniggering behind my back, Margery Rothman and her ilk gossiping about how sad it is that Hugh's such a Lothario while I'm so . . . clueless.

Or was I blindly in love? (It's so easy to confuse the two, cluelessness and blind love.)

That explains why Alice kept making such a big deal of Connie being out of the country and how I, of all people, wasn't supposed to know where she was. I am so dense. I kept writing Connie off as a desperate spinster with a library full of books about how to get married after thirty-five when really I should have been on high alert. Those books work.

I'm not with Hugh. *She* is!

Which means—oh, triple crap—that Alice knew all along that Hugh hadn't proposed to me. So Alice also knows the ring is bogus. And the flowers! What does she know about those? I should have read that damn card.

"Genie?"

I look at Alice, who is busy taking notes.

"Genie?"

Bill is waving to me. "Daydreaming?"

"About *Huuughhh*." Felicity singsongs and everyone chuckles.

"What?" asks Bill.

Margery's about to fill him in when I summon my faculties and launch into Hob Cooper's dismal final grade point average. I can't believe my mouth is working so well and that I'm able to pull this off. Look, I have a memo. Here I am handing it to him. I have copies. There I am distributing them around the table. People are reading and nodding.

I am engaging in an intelligent discussion about the pressures on a devout Mormon leaving a Mormon community to attend a heathen East Coast college like Thoreau. My coworkers are smiling and nodding. I'm actually putting forward a cogent argument on why we should excuse Hob's C+ in chemistry and his F in badminton and no one knows that inside me, I have absolutely zero idea of what I'm saying.

I'm hurt. I'm mad. I'm on a roll.

"In sum," I say, having never said "in sum" in my life, "Hob is a dedicated student who clearly is capable of performing quality work at Thoreau. Frankly, I'd be worried if he hadn't slacked off a bit after getting our acceptance. I mean, he's been pulling down a straight three point eight and racking up fifty points per game as center of the Park City Panthers. Who cares if he can't keep his eye on the birdie when he's the next Larry Bird?"

Everyone laughs satisfactorily at the Boston basketball reference. I sit down and see that Bill is grinning at me with unabashed approval. What have I just done? I can't think of a thing I've said.

"All who vote to keep Hob Cooper?" Bill raises his hand.

So does everyone else.

"Excellent." Bill makes a note. "I hope the Coopers know just how lucky they were their son got you as an admissions counselor, Genie, and not some tough nut like Kevin."

Kevin guffaws. He loves being called a tough nut, seeing as his nickname around the office is quite the opposite.

"Now that Genie's done with her report, we can get to the big news everyone's been talking about."

Oh, please, no. Not after I've just found out Connie is Hugh's future wife. Margery and Karen both giggle. Kevin gives me a nudge and I want to slap my hand over Bill's mouth. Anything to shut him up from announcing what will surely haunt me for decades to come.

Remember when Genie Michaels told everyone Hugh Spencer asked her to marry him when he really didn't? Bill Gladstone even made an announcement. It was so mortifying.

Again Bill grins at me. I can feel it coming, the weight of my world crashing around me.

"Don't go sliding under the table, Genie. I don't want you, in particular, to miss a word."

Darn. He caught me. Kevin hoists me up and gives me a pat. "It'll be okay," he whispers.

Bill clears his throat importantly. "This weekend I learned a member of our admissions family . . ."

I have to cover my face. He's calling us his "admissions family."

". . . is moving on. And while that makes me sad, I've been in this game long enough to know that change, though hard initially, is necessary, and certainly Bowdoin's lucky to have Kevin join their team."

A round of applause breaks out. Slowly, I lower my hands and, feeling even more foolish, see Kevin is standing and shaking Bill's hand. No one is looking at me, not even Alice.

Why . . . this announcement has nothing to do with

my engagement. Kevin's leaving. He's going to Bowdoin!

"Yes!" I shout.

Bill and Kevin stop shaking hands. "You don't have to be *that* enthusiastic, Genie," Bill says to more chuckles all around. "Unless, of course, you want his job, which I certainly hope you do. I encourage Genie as well as everyone here to update your resumes, dress for success, and make a good impression. Because I plan to fill Kevin's spot from in house and, yes, I am open to bribes."

And with that, the meeting's over. When I get up, I find I've left two sweaty butt marks on my chair.

Kevin stops me at the door. He's so short, I can look down and see the prematurely gray hairs on the top of his head. "I'm going to miss you, Genie."

"Thanks, Kevin. I'll miss you, too." Though I won't, as Kevin treated me like a puppy that required training.

"I'll put in a good word for you to replace me. That'll count for a lot. Bill trusts my counsel."

Kevin relishes his role as Bill's right-hand man. I bet he'll miss that when he moves to Bowdoin and finds he's back to being part of the herd.

"Logically, Connie has to be Bill's first choice. She's been here longer than you and, hmmm, how to say this?" He furrows his brows. "She tends to be more professional. Admissions is more than a job for her. It's a career, a calling. You'd do well to remember that in future."

In future. How pretentious. Of course Connie will get Kevin's job. She was supposed to get it before *he* got it, but then Bill decided he needed a right-hand man, not right-hand woman, to attract the much-coveted male students and, so, she was passed over with the promise she'd be next.

Then she stole Hugh.

"Well?" says Alice, sidling up. "What do you think Connie's going to do now?"

"Get everything she ever wanted," I say sourly.

"What?" Alice rushes to catch up with me in the hall. "What was that?"

"Nothing. What do *you* think she's going to do?"

"Cut her trip short and rush home to claw and scratch her way into Kevin's office. Bad enough you got that rock on your finger. Wait until she finds out that Bill announced an opening for assistant director of admissions and she wasn't here. She's gonna go mental."

I stand by my door and watch as Alice takes out her master key, unlocks Connie's door, and deposits the memos from today's meeting on her desk. When she leaves, she doesn't bother to lock up, leaving Connie's office temptingly open. I enter for just a bit and consider peeking in her desk, searching for clues about Hugh. A picture of them on the beach. His phone number on her speed dial. Extra-large condoms. (Hugh insists he needs them.)

No. I have crossed many lines lately, but this one I definitely must not overstep.

Taking a deep breath, I return to my own office, locking the door securely behind me lest I am struck by a sudden urge to fling it open and run to Connie's.

There is a flash of red behind my desk. The roses. Might as well get to the next bit of bad news. I slide open the envelope and remove the card.

Genie:
   Meet me at Sussex Bank at 4:30 if you still want to split the house.
   What I did, I did for you.

Nick

Which is when I notice that the roses are not any old roses. They're Mr. Lincolns and they're in a root ball. They're not cut; they're supposed to be planted. Planted on Peabody Road.

Wow.

Chapter Twenty

As my father would say, "This is highly irregular."

That's all I can think as Tina, a mortgage processor who also happens to be Todd's ex-girlfriend, slides me a set of legal documents, all of which have been meticulously crafted by none other than my very own Patty Pugliese. No wonder she refused to get down on Nick—or break her lawyer-client confidentiality. At Nick's request, she was secretly drawing up papers so I could buy half of my dream house.

"It's a condo agreement," Tina explains, tapping the top sheet with her hard pink acrylic nail. "Nick Spanadopolous will own the upstairs apartment and the outside of the entire structure, including any outbuildings or a garage. You would purchase the ground-floor unit."

I know all this, but by some absurd bank stipulation, she has to go over the basics with me again.

"Per the agreement," Tina continues, "Nick has promised to finish the kitchen and the bathroom. In return, you pay the taxes on the entire property for two years. Do you agree?"

"I agree," I practically shout. "Oh, man, do I agree."

"Then sign at the Xs." She points out all the highlighted Xs and I sign merrily away, not reading one word of what I'm legally committing myself to.

This is all so stunning, I haven't even been able to absorb it. I'm finally buying my dream house. Well, not all of it, but that's okay because look! The purchase price is $250,000 and I don't even need my parents' money. Or, at least, much of it. Just enough to add to my savings for a down payment.

Somehow Nick got together the cash total, bought the property, and now we're refinancing. My monthly mortgage payment will be slightly more than my rent. And then there's the advantage of a tax break when I write off the interest every year.

Also, there's the advantage of Nick living on top of

me. Well, not on top of me. In the apartment above.

"What about the title search and all that?" I ask.

"Done. However, you'll need to put down forty thousand dollars, twenty percent, in order to get this low monthly fee." Tina shifts uncomfortably in her chair. "I guess your father's been involved because there's a note here that he's prepared to co-sign if necessary. You got the dough?"

"I do."

It's weird that Dad knows about Nick's house deal. Why didn't he say something? Though I'm not complaining. Compared to the huge sum Mom and Dad gave Lucy and Jason, my request for $20,000 is almost saintly.

Tina is stamping and initialing things, moving the paperwork right along with nifty efficiency. She's a woman who has done everything possible to make herself pretty despite her Clairol-colored eggplant hair. She also seems to have developed a personal relationship with Neutrogena spray-on tan. At least I hope it's spray-on tan because anyone this brown should have a dermatologist on retainer.

As she staples and clips papers together she says, "So, your dad tells me you're getting married. Is that the ring?"

"Sure is." Confidently, because I'm fairly certain Tina is not a certified gemologist or a Hellenic metallurgist, I thrust out my hand for her review.

She exhales a satisfying whistle. "That's gorgeous. Looks almost like one I bought down at Revere Beach for twelve bucks. Though that was cubic zirconia, of course." She laughs.

I laugh, too. Twelve bucks! I was ripped off.

"I was sure Todd would be the next Michaels to get hitched."

"Not Todd. He'll never marry. He's a confirmed bachelor."

"That's what all bachelors say. Next thing you know, you're bumping into them at Target, where they're buying a thousand dollars' worth of playground equipment." Putting the papers aside, she clasps her unnaturally dark hands and gets down to business. "Okay, so what's the deal with this Nick guy? Is he hot or what?"

"You met him already?"

"Sure. He's been in the bank all week and he's not exactly the kind of guy women ignore, if you know what I mean."

Irrationally, I take pride in Tina's compliment, as if Nick belongs to me. This is setting a dangerous precedent. I have to keep in mind that we're merely neighbors, nothing more. Business partners. Platonic acquaintances.

"He's also a very nice guy," I add prudishly. "Smart, too."

"Oh, I bet he is. Then again, you're one of those brainy women. You know, the kind who falls in love with a guy's mind instead of his ass."

"That's not true." As soon as I say this, I realize how wrong Tina is. Well, I'm not necessarily big on ass, per se, but I enjoy a well-built man as much as the next woman. (Though probably not as much as Patty, who enjoys well-built men a bit *too* much.) Anyway, who's to say just because a man has a great ass means he can't have a deep soul as well?

Tina says, "I don't know if you've noticed, but that Nick of yours has one fine caboose."

"Done signing papers?"

Nick is standing over us, smiling. I swear he knows exactly what we've been talking about.

"Done," Tina says, pushing back her chair. "I just have to run these upstairs and I'll be right back." As she passes by, she makes a big show of pretending to check the wall clock.

She is so transparent.

"Well," says Nick, sitting his coveted ass in the chair next to me. "I hope I wasn't too presumptuous circumventing the real estate agent and going straight to Cecily. It was the only way I could think of to ensure our house didn't fall into the hands of crack dealers."

He called it *our* house.

"You weren't presumptuous, you were brilliant." I just noticed he's model-grade handsome in that leather bomber jacket and now I've forgotten what I was trying to say. Oh, right. "It was so thoughtful and considerate of you to keep me in mind—right down to the roses."

"It was a pleasure."

"It was? Even putting up with Cecily?"

Nick gives me a puzzled look and it occurs to me

that maybe his tête-à-tête at the bookstore cafe with Cecily wasn't all business. Maybe they're seeing each other romantically.

"Unless you two really are an item," I add quickly. "In which case, I have to say she is a stunning woman with a splendid personality."

He grins slowly. "No, Genie. Cecily and I are not, as you say, an item."

"Then your meeting at the bookstore . . ."

"Strictly to discuss the house." Though, the way he says this leads me to believe that perhaps he is being a gentleman and not confiding that while all he wanted was the house, Cecily wanted more.

"Speaking of love interests," he says, casually grazing my knee with his hand. "How's Hugh taking the news that you bought a place he hasn't seen?"

His eyes aren't dark blue, they're brown. That is so weird. I've never seen eyes that change color before. Green to blue, sure. But not blue to brown. "Are you wearing contacts?"

"What?" He shakes his head. "No. Did you hear what I said?"

"Uh-huh. Maybe it's the leather jacket that turns the color of your eyes."

"Genie. You're avoiding my question. You did tell him, right? Hugh does know about the house?"

"Yup."

"You're one hundred percent positive Hugh's cool with this? Because I don't want to get in the middle of a lovers' quarrel. You guys have been going out for four years and I'd hate to think a stupid condo could screw things up."

"Won't screw." Wait. "I mean, it'll be fine. Hugh loves the house."

Tina's back and from the look on her face there's trouble. "Charles Denkins, the head of mortgages, would like to meet you, Mr. Spanadopolous."

Nick, who has gone from Nick to "Mr. Spanadopolous" in a matter of minutes, doesn't seem at all concerned he's being called in to the head of mortgages.

"Not me, too?" I ask, feeling left out.

"Maybe later, Genie," Tina says. "There's some, um, history in Mr. Spanadopolous's background that Mr. Denkins would like to discuss."

That sounds ominous. Drug charge? Bench warrant? Maybe a tryst with the former Mrs. Denkins, a woman my father described as Belmont's answer to Brigitte Bardot, only African American and not French.

"Don't worry," says Nick, getting up. "I'm used to it."

So he's *used* to being a felon and an adulterer. Super. I suppose I could call my father in, if it comes to that, but I really hate to pull strings. I'm a big girl now—as everyone keeps telling me these days.

With Nick off to explain his rap sheet, this is my opportunity to call Mom and squeal about the house. It's so exciting!

She answers right away. "Hi, honey." She must pull

up a chair by the phone and sit there until it rings. "We were just talking about you."

"We?"

"Your dad and I. We have big news."

"Let me guess. Tula Abernathy is adding crab to the dip."

"Funny you should mention Tula. Her name came up, too. She's set a date for your engagement party. August third."

"I don't know, Mom. Hugh might not be back by then."

"Not to worry. Hugh can make it. In fact, he's looking forward to it."

Hold on. I have to sit up and take a closer look. Nick and Clay McDonald, the bank president, are walking side by side down the marble hall together. They appear to be joking, shaking hands. Clay McDonald is practically salivating all over Nick. What gives?

Did she just say Hugh was looking forward to our engagement party?

"What was that about Hugh?" I ask.

"He's thrilled about the party. He's really very honored that Tula's putting on the dog for you two."

That pain shoots up my arm again. I feel faint and dizzy. "You called him?"

"No. You told me not to, remember?"

Thank God in heaven. If she had called him . . .

"Your father ran into him a few minutes ago."

Upon hearing these words, my heart literally leaps

out of my chest. I almost expect to see it beating at my feet. "Where?"

"On the doorstep of your apartment. Dad was driving by on his way home from work and there was Hugh ringing your doorbell. You should give the boy a key, Genie. He's your fiancé, for heaven's sake."

"HUGH!" I jump out of my seat, practically knocking over Tina's candy bowl. "HUGH SHOWED UP AT MY APARTMENT?"

Funny how easily sound bounces off granite walls. Tina is staring at me wide-eyed and Clay McDonald, too. Nick . . . I can't even make eye contact.

This cannot be happening. Hugh cannot be here in Boston. His e-mail to Steve said next week—not *this* week.

"Oh," Mom moans. "It was supposed to be a surprise and I ruined it, didn't I? Hugh told Dad it was a surprise and Dad, naturally, let it slip his mind. Men are so clueless about things like surprises. I was just so tickled because Dad did remember to make sure Hugh knew about the engagement party."

Okay. Hugh's in town and Dad invited him to the engagement party. Scratch that. *Our* engagement party. This after I've hinted in an e-mail to Hugh that while I might be engaged, I'm not necessarily engaged to *him.*

Which was probably why he was at my door, curious to know who, exactly, could replace him. Though there's no doubt now, is there? I mean, now that my father has told Hugh point-blank that not only

255

are we getting married but that Tula Abernathy, Belmont socialite, possible murderess, is throwing us a blowout bash.

"Everything okay?" Nick asks, hands in his pockets.

"Fine." My phone clicks shut.

"Sounds like Hugh's back in town."

Quickly, I search through the papers on Tina's desk for my copy. "Yes. It was supposed to be a surprise. When can I move into my new house?"

"Hugh eager to settle in, is he?"

"Not Hugh, me. So when?"

Nick frowns as he calculates the work to be done. "Let's see. The kitchen needs to be finished and there's no bathtub or shower." He shrugs. "I dunno. Three weeks maybe. Four weeks tops."

"In other words, tonight. Great. See you then," I shout, rushing out the door and heading home to make a fast escape.

Chapter Twenty-One

"I don't see why you have to pack up this apartment you've been living in for fifteen years and move out overnight," Patty asks.

"Because Hugh's back in town and he showed up on my doorstep."

"So?"

"So, if he showed up once, he'll do it again. And the next time he'll bring Connie, just to rub my face in it."

"You want I should take her out?" Patty looks up

from her box of plates. "No marks. My people don't leave evidence."

Someday I'd like to meet Patty's people. Or, on second thought, not.

I stuff one more sheet into the garbage bag. Filling garbage bags with linens is not the tidiest of methods of relocation. (Nancy Michaels would be shocked!) But I'm not going for tidy. I'm going for fast.

The good news is that my landlord, Mr. Collins, was initially going to give me a hard time about moving out since I recently renewed my lease. As ammunition, he brought out my contract and pointed to where I had agreed to find a sub-tenant should I have to leave before my term was up. (Who reads the fine print on those leases, anyway?)

So I pointed to where he was supposed to remove all vermin and hadn't. (Mice. They live in my stove and Jorge does nothing to stop them. Just sits and watches them like they're kitty TV.) Which was when Mr. Collins saw my ring.

After that, it was hunky-dory. He was overjoyed that I was getting married after living in his apartment for nearly two decades. Kept saying he thought it would never happen, that I would end up in a nunnery, et cetera, et cetera. As a wedding gift, he ripped up my lease and brought out a can of Tab to toast.

It's amazing, the awesomeness of that ring. Has the power to destroy leases and produce really bad diet soda.

Patty wraps a plate in newspaper and slides it into a

box. Then she takes another sip of wine. This has been her snail-like process. Pack. Sip. Pack. Sip. At her rate, I'm not only going to be hauling a bed, a bureau, a couch, several appliances (including my crappy Rite Aid coffeemaker), but also a midget drunk.

After she closes and tapes the box, she dumps it rather carelessly by the door. Then she spends a great deal of time looking out the window for Todd or Hugh, whomever should come first.

Todd has promised to help move my bed and couch into Peabody Road so I can sleep there tonight. If only the evening were ten degrees cooler. I have completely pitted out my sleeveless white shirt. Even my hair is sweating.

Taking a break, I pour myself a glass of wine and add an ice cube. Then, dumping some salsa into a bowl, I carry that and a pack of fat-free baked chips to the tiny front porch where Patty is sitting, her arms around her knees, on Hugh patrol.

"How's the engagement going?" I ask, setting down the bowl and the chips.

"Fantastic. I'm almost done registering. Just in time for the party."

Patty's firm is throwing a huge black-tie couple's shower at the Harbor Hotel for Patty and her fiancé, the illustrious Moe Howard. I'd give anything for a shower at the Harbor Hotel.

Forget that. I'd give anything for real fried tortilla chips. This baked stuff definitely does not cut it. "Yeah? What have you registered for?"

"More like what *haven't* I registered for." She goes inside and comes out with her purse, from which she pulls a file folder overflowing with white sheets. Her registry records.

"A tad greedy, wouldn't you say?"

"I like to think of it as giving my guests a wide range of options."

"You don't have any guests."

"Yes, I do. I've got one hundred and forty. All I'm missing is a living, breathing groom. Here's my favorite list."

She hands me a sheet from Hammacher Schlemmer. At the top is the Mechanical Core Muscle Trainer for a whopping $1,999.

"Do you really think people are going to buy this?"

Patty swills some more wine and says, "Can't hurt to ask. If you'll notice, I've also registered for a Professional Rotary Belgian Waffle Maker at a very modest seventy-nine ninety-nine. And then there's the cat hammock for forty dollars."

"Are you high? Because, last I checked, you don't have a cat."

"You never know. What if Jorge visits?"

Jorge's fat butt rounds the corner, searching for escape. Like all cats, he dreads being moved and has been inching away from us all evening. I am safely assured he won't get much farther than the back steps before, exhausted, he sets down his satchel and takes a snooze.

"Jorge doesn't visit."

"And whose fault is that? If you weren't so stingy with the car keys, the poor fellow could get around more." She huffs, scoops up some salsa, and hands me another sheet from her registry file. Tiffany & Co.

Oh, for heaven's sake. She really has gone over the edge. "What happened to good ole Macy's and Bloomingdale's?"

"They're there, too. You know what I've noticed? That men like me more now that I'm engaged."

Reluctantly, I draw myself away from the $775 Birds of the Nile mini vase, the kind of item that screams "extravagantly impractical." "Men always liked you. What's so strange about that?"

"Now they *really* like me. I mean, I've had two clients ask me out since I've gotten the ring and these are clients I've known for years. They asked all about who I was marrying and if I'd thought long and hard about the consequences of settling down. Then they insisted on wining and dining me, as if they're trying to change my mind."

"Don't complain. I'd love for some rich man to wine and dine me."

"I think it's a biological thing. Like, now that another male has marked me as his own they suddenly have to fight for me, the desirable female."

Could that be true? With me men haven't been . . . no. Hold on. What about Steve? He's been flooding me with mushy e-mails fretting over my upcoming nuptials. That's after decades of friendship.

And then there's Nick. Not that he's interested in

me. I mean, he *might* be interested in me, but only as a downstairs neighbor, a partner in our real estate venture, so to speak. Besides, there's Elena back home. I must be a poor excuse of a woman compared to her.

"This is what women who want to get married should do: Buy a ring. Tell people you're engaged and you're guaranteed to get propositioned," Patty says, as Todd pulls up in his truck. "Uh-oh. I've got to get myself together." Whereupon she flees to my bathroom.

What is going on with her and Todd?

Todd is beat, sweaty, and sagging. "Hard day at the office?" I ask.

"Just finished unloading twenty sheets of drywall." He wipes his forehead on his sleeve. "I hope you have beer."

Darn. I always forget. "I *will* get beer. I promise. In the meantime, how about a nice refreshing glass of white wine?"

"And after that should we go shoe shopping?"

"All right. All right. No need to be sexist." I try to get him to eat some salsa, but that's the last thing he wants. He wants to get the heavy lifting done with so he can go home, take a shower, and collapse.

"Where's Hugh?" he asks, lifting a chair. "Mom tells me he's in town. Shouldn't he be moving you?"

"Jet-lagged."

"That's no excuse. You're moving. You're going to be his wife. He shouldn't be leaving all this hard work to his future brother-in-law."

"You're right. It's a crime." I grab the bag of sheets. "Ready?"

Todd grunts, still not satisfied that Hugh's not helping. We carry our stuff to the curb, where Patty's Porsche is parked, locked, and loaded.

"She here alone?"

I have no idea what that's supposed to mean until I remember Captain Moe. "Yeah. She has the night off to help me pack. She's inside, um, packing, right now."

He lowers the box to the sidewalk. "You have to talk her out of this."

"What?"

"This stupid wedding. I mean, this guy's never around. Never. He could be leading a double life with another wife for all we know. Some scum after her hard-earned money. That's what I think he is."

"Captain Moe is not a scum after her hard-earned money," I say, defensively, having grown rather fond of Captain Moe. "He's a devoted family man, very close to his brothers."

"Captain Moe," Todd scoffs, setting the chair in the back of his truck. "It's gotta be bullshit. Sounds like one of the Stooges."

Close call.

Patty reemerges having done the magical makeup thing she does that makes her eyes sparkle and her lips shine. At the sight of her, Todd straightens up and starts hauling stuff he doesn't have to.

We drive up the street to Peabody, Patty following in

her Porsche with Jorge in his cat carrier meowing all the way. Though my condo is only about a quarter mile from my old apartment, I know he's going to have a hard time adjusting. Jorge fears change.

With Nick's help, we set up my antique sleigh bed in the spare, but large, master bedroom while Todd, Nick, and Patty bring in the couch.

Todd, Nick, and Patty bringing in the couch pretty much means Patty holds open the door while Todd and Nick heave and huff in. Now I'm certain my brother's trying to impress her, because he insists on single-handedly hauling more unwieldy furniture: my kitchen table and chairs, an upholstered chair for my living room, and the television and television cabinet. All the while bragging about how strong he is.

"Like to see Captain Moe try this," he says from underneath the loveseat on his back.

"Can Captain Moe lift a solid oak table with one arm? Well, can he?" he barks, carrying the table into the dining room.

If Todd only knew.

The midsummer sun is setting by the time we finish. Nick and Todd crack open beers and help themselves to a bucket of fried chicken from the KFC in Watertown. Using leftovers from my refrigerator back in the old place, Patty whips up a salad and somehow manages to find another bottle of white wine.

We end up heading to the golf course to catch the Boston skyline and, when it turns dark, for an invigorating, slightly risky game of nighttime golf using balls Todd painted with glow-in-the-dark paint. I keep sneaking glances back at my house—*our* house—its windows glowing warmly. I am going to be very happy here. Very happy.

Finally, Todd and Patty leave, Nick and I waving good-bye from the porch as if we're already a couple. It's not until their cars turn off Peabody that it dawns on me how very comfortable our coupledom is. And how, ironically, that makes me feel all the more awkward.

"Well," Nick says, folding his arms and leaning against the porch railing. "Here we are."

"Yes. Here we are. Home sweet home."

He looks rather sexy with the streetlight on his hair and I can't help thinking what it would be like if we were really a couple. We'd clean up the cups and bottles, chatting about the evening, and then he'd take my hand and say softly, "Ready for bed?"

Or maybe we'd blow off the dishes and instead we'd pour ourselves another cup of coffee and enjoy the summer evening, Nick casually placing his arm around my back while we rocked on the wooden porch swing (note to self: get one of those), occasionally leaning over to kiss my cheek or playfully unbutton my blouse as we discussed whether to spend our vacation at the Cape or save up for a trip to Italy next spring.

"Too bad Hugh couldn't make it," he says.

Crash! Back to reality. "It's jet lag. Takes him days

to recover," I say, gathering up the trash, hoping he'll leave it at that.

"Do you expect Hugh to be moving in right off or are you two going to do it the old-fashioned way and wait until after you're married?"

I cannot tell, because his face is shadowed, whether he's grinning. "The old-fashioned way. If you met my mother, you'd know why."

"I'd like to meet your mother if she's anything like you."

"She's nothing like me. At least, that's what I keep telling myself."

Nick takes the empty bottles as I carry the plates inside, our footsteps hollow in the bare rooms. The kitchen suddenly strikes me as depressing with its unfinished counters and cabinets, the bare light fixture hanging from the ceiling. I dump everything in a black garbage bag and want to cry—though I have no idea why.

That's when I feel Nick's arm around my shoulders, warm and consoling. "The kitchen won't always be like this, Genie, I promise. I'll have everything finished by your wedding. Cabinets. Counters. I'll bust a hump so Hugh won't hate it. That's what you're worried about, aren't you? That Hugh will hate it."

No, I want to say. I'm worried that you'll hate me when you find I've been lying all this time about my engagement, especially after you "busted a hump" to get the kitchen done.

"It's not that," I lie. "I'm just tired. And filthy." God.

I can smell my shirt from here. "I could really use a shower."

"You don't have one. You'll have to use mine."

I must seem shocked because he adds, laughingly, "It's fairly clean. I even have, believe it or not, soap. Come on. I'll show you."

To get to Nick's apartment, we go through my kitchen and up the back stairs. I'm expecting the standard bachelor pad—La-Z-Boy recliners, a big TV, a computer, beer cans scattered about—and am delightfully surprised to find that while it's no Taj Mahal, his apartment has a refreshing order and warmth to it.

There is a red leather couch and what appears to be a hand-carved coffee table. Two nice accent lamps and a high-backed chair with a reading lamp. Also, a stereo perched on a shelf and artwork scattered about on the walls.

Plus books. Tons and tons of books. Most of them in boxes.

"I haven't had a chance to do any work on this place." He's actually tidying up for me, snatching a newspaper and balling a pair of dirty socks on the floor. "Gives you an idea what the house was like before Todd and I started the renovations. A 1970s special."

A woodstove extends from his fireplace and whereas my living room is spacious and open, his has been divided into two. There's worn green wall-to-wall carpeting on the floor that, underneath, is probably oak, like mine, and all the woodwork is brown instead of white. The kitchen, painted a hideous yellow, features a vintage General Electric stove in the retro style of Harvest Gold.

"It's like night and day." My diplomatic way of calling his kitchen the pits.

"I call it Hell's Kitchen. Not very original and I'm sorry that the bathroom's not that much better."

The bathroom is above mine, just like his bedroom is above mine. I can't help myself from sneaking a quick peek. Rumpled navy duvet over a queen-size bed with a plain oak headboard. More books. What's with the books?

Nick catches me looking and smiles to himself while I feel my face flush red again. Busted.

"The shampoo's in the corner and the soap's in the bottle. There's a relatively clean towel on the door. Okay?"

"Okay. Thanks."

"Enjoy yourself. I can't wait to take one next."

He leaves me in the bathroom, which some unfortunate soul painted a nauseating pinky peach. Nick's toiletries are scattered about—shaver, shaving soap (interesting), deodorant. The basics. Not like Hugh's expensive supply of Kiehl's Eye Alert, N.V. Perricone M.D. Skin Fitness After Shave Prep, and Jack Black Face Buff. And that didn't include his premium stock inside the medicine cabinet.

I shower up, wash my hair, and feel a billion times better. I do not let my mind wander to how many women have been here, how many have studied his use of shaving soap as if it were a clue to the mystery that is Nick. No. I turn off the water, reach for the brown towel hanging on the hook, and find it can barely reach around my body. Great.

"Hey, Nick?" I call, discreetly opening the bathroom door a crack. "Your towel, um, is kind of small."

He comes down the hallway, his shirt unbuttoned, revealing a relatively smooth chest with almost no hair. "That's all I have. How about I get you something else?"

In a second, he's back with a white T-shirt that barely covers the tops of my thighs. It'll have to do as I inch out of the bathroom, keeping my back to the wall. "Thanks again."

Nick's sitting on his bed, his legs propped up, reading. "No problem. In the morning, just let yourself in. Todd and I are out by five to get to Hingham. You'll have the place to yourself."

"I'll remember to bring my own towel."

"Wise idea. Feel better?"

"I do."

I'm stalling. I don't want to leave. In fact, I want to sit myself at the end of his bed and pepper him with questions. Why do you read so much? Did you go to college? Why are you a carpenter? How come you're in your midthirties and still single? Who's this Elena person? Why don't you have much of a Greek accent? What do you think about me? *Do* you think about me? What do you want out of life? Because intuition tells me I want the same thing, too, and I think I'm falling in love.

But all I say is, "Good night."

Chapter Twenty-Two

Since my old address is defunct and I refuse to let my mother give out my new one (lest Hugh should find me), wedding gifts are piling up in my office.

White boxes with silver bows and billows of white tissue paper. Plate after plate of heartbreakingly beautiful Chauteaubriand fine china by Bernardaud, the edges etched in gold with cheerful sprigs of pink thistles. Coordinating Waterford stemware with tiny gold bands along the base. Teacups. Saucers. Even creamers and dessert bowls.

And the miracle of it is, I've registered for not one piece. Someone must be signing me up for Reed & Barton, Spode, Orrefors, and Bernardaud in my place. Naturally, my first suspect is Lucy. Only she would have taste this ornate. If it were my mother, it'd be her plain white Wedgwood all the way.

"Here's another one." Alice kicks open the door. "It's heavy."

Oh no.

"This is the life, eh?" she says, watching as I untie another silver bow. "Get engaged. Go online and sign up for gifts and bingo, the next you know you're pulling two-hundred-dollar platters off the UPS truck."

She is referring to a Roman antique gold salmon platter I received—correction, Hugh and I received— last week from Zoe Murray, my mother's college roommate. Alice found the idea of serving smelly fish on a glass platter etched in 14-karat gold to be terrifically ridiculous. Then again, the only fish Alice likes is followed by the word *stick*.

"Yowzee!" she exclaims, reading the card as I pull out a heavy cut-glass cake platter. "It's Baccarat. It's from the dean." Before I can stop her, she is at my computer indulging in her newest hobby: checking the prices of my gifts on the Bloomingdale's registry.

The dean! Oh, man. This is really getting out of hand. How does he know I'm getting married? Please tell me my mother did not send a wedding invitation to the dean, who hardly knows me. I keep reminding her to keep the list to close family and friends. And she keeps "forgetting."

We are now up to over one hundred and fifty guests. This is not what I had planned at all.

"That cake platter's over a thousand dollars!" Alice pushes back my swivel chair. "A thousand dollars for a cake platter. Can you imagine? What if you left it at the school bake sale?"

"Well, I wouldn't, would I?" I say this calmly though my shaking hand belies my utter horror. A one-thousand-dollar cake platter. Of course, this is to curry favor with Hugh, Thoreau's hottest celebrity.

The card from the dean reads:

For Hugh and Genie:
A treasure for Thoreau's finest treasures.

May you always have your cake and eat it too.
Best wishes on your fabulous adventure,

Bob and Paula Crichton

It's an adventure, all right. Now I've got the dean to add to my list of apologies. And thank-you notes. I've been writing thank-you notes every night after work while Nick paints trim in the kitchen.

Nick and I've been doing a lot of talking during our painting and note-writing sessions. Mostly he tells stories about his childhood on the island of Leros, which happens to be the home of the goddess Artemis, a fierce feminist, who once sicked dogs on a mortal man because he saw her naked. Somewhat over the top, if you ask me.

Perhaps not coincidentally, the tradition on Leros is for women to pass property down to their daughters instead of the more traditional patriarchal route. To Nick, it is perfectly natural for me, the future wife, to present my future husband with a marital home. I think I might like Leros.

Especially the way he describes it—Grecian blue skies and the turquoise Aegean lapping the white beaches framing the island's scrabbly hills. No wonder the Germans, the Italians, the Crusaders, the Turks, even Homer's Argonauts have all sought to conquer the place.

The good thing about Nick, aside from his being a halfway decent raconteur, is that he's encouraging me

271

to be a self-reliant home owner. For example, when the faucet in the bathroom started dripping, he didn't just change the washer, he showed me how. (It's really easy. Just replace a worn rubber ring with another. Men have gotten so much mileage out of this one stupid act.)

But no amount of self-reliance could help me a few weeks after I moved in and disaster hit.

It was a Saturday night and I was alone, naturally. Patty was off doing her thing and Steve was playing at a club that was way too loud and crowded with teenagers for me to consider visiting. I was in the dining room cutting out French toile curtains for the windows that face Mrs. Ipilito's house and trying not to think about where Nick went on his date.

At least I was pretty sure it was a date. Around six, I heard him leave, taking the steps two at a time. He was whistling and he looked good. Freshly showered with damp hair. Denim shirt over khakis. Definitely date wear. Not that I was spying out my front window or anything.

Six turned into nine and nine turned into midnight. I had cut out all my curtains, plus linings, and had finished off an entire pint of Ben & Jerry's Pistachio Pistachio on the theory that I hadn't had any dinner, really, and it was hot. I refused to acknowledge that I was heartsick over the fact that Nick hadn't returned, which meant he might be having fun with another woman.

I don't know why it bothered me so much that night.

Certainly, he'd gone out before. Yet *before* he had always returned around nine. If he saw my light on, he might stop by and help himself to whatever was in my fridge, make his usual perfunctory inquiries about Hugh (the going lie was that Hugh was rushing to finish the rough draft of his follow-up novel before our wedding and could not spare one minute of socializing). We'd chat about our days and then he'd look at his watch and leave.

I'd come to anticipate his visits, cherish them, even downing coffee so I could stay up way past my bedtime until I heard his knock. That night, though, I feared his knock might never come—ever.

Resigned, I slipped into a loose T-shirt, brushed my teeth, and went to bed only to be awakened by the creak of bedsprings above. Nick and whomever in the heat of passion, and quite a lot of passion at that. Throwing my pillow over my head, I tried to block out the sounds, tried not to imagine him with someone else, kissing her neck, moving his naked body against hers, wanting her, desiring her. . . .

It was no use. I had to get out of there. I'd simply make myself a cup of tea, read a magazine in the living room, and wait for them to go to sleep. But no sooner did I turn on the kitchen light than I heard it. More than a *drip, drip, drip.* More like a *gush, gush, gush.* There was a leak. A serious leak at that.

My first thought was the freezer. Once when I was a teenager, I'd forgotten to close a basement freezer and it defrosted all over my parents' basement floor. My freezer, however, was securely closed. Nor was it my sink or the bathroom. The leak was in the basement.

Sure enough, a pipe had burst. Already there was at least an inch of water on the floor. Water was creeping everywhere—around the washer and dryer, around the boiler. It had reached the bottom step and was climbing.

What to do? I couldn't knock on Nick's door and burst in on him with another woman. Not that I would have minded breaking them apart. But I had my dignity to consider and also Nick's. This was truly a dilemma and I didn't have the luxury of time to debate my options.

Finally, I had a stroke of brilliance. I could call him on the telephone. That way I wouldn't actually have to *see* them together. So, I ran upstairs and did just that, listening to his phone ringing in the kitchen above me. No answer. Only his machine. I hysterically babbled something about an emergency with the pipes, hung up, and waited.

Nothing. He did not call me back and ask what was wrong. I did not hear him open his door and go to the basement. He didn't even go to the kitchen to check the message. Now, I was no longer sad or embarrassed. I was infuriated. How could he ignore this crisis? How could he ignore *me?*

That was it. I had to go up there and get his help if I had to rip the door off the hinges myself. Loaded for bear, I dashed up to his apartment and banged like a fishwife.

"Open up, Nick. I know you're in there. We have an emergency in the basement!"

After a few minutes came the sound of delicate footsteps and the click of his kitchen light going on. The door opened and there stood one of the most beautiful women I'd ever seen. Taller than I would have expected, but otherwise exactly as I imagined. Creamy white skin. Big pools of soft brown eyes. Black curling hair cascading over the shoulder of Nick's T-shirt. I knew that T-shirt because it was the same one I borrowed the night I moved in. Only it was a bit larger on her.

"Elena," I said.

She nodded, clearly pleased to be recognized. "Genie?"

Good. Nice to know that I was important enough for him to have mentioned me to his fiancée.

Fighting back my own flood of emotions, I said as calmly as possible, "I need to speak to Nick. We have an emergency in the basement."

Elena blinked. "Genie?"

"Yes?"

"Genie. No Nick."

Got that. I understood he wasn't mine and never would be and that I felt as if my life, for now, had lost its spark. There was still the flooded basement to deal with. "I need Nick." Gathering her English was about as good as my Greek, I pointed to the bedroom and added for emphasis, "In there."

She shook her head. "No Nick."

A man in the bedroom hollered something in Greek. Elena hollered back and suddenly Nick appeared in only his jeans. I was so mortified to have caught him in this intimate moment that I kept my gaze squarely on Elena.

"Genie," he said. "Nick's not here. I'm Adrien."

Adrien? Taking a closer look, I realized the man in the jeans was not Nick, but a much younger version with a boyish lanky body and wild unkempt hair.

"Nick's brother," he said in flawless English. Like Nick, he spoke with hardly an accent. "What's wrong?"

What's wrong? I wanted to parrot back. You're boinking your brother's girlfriend, that's what's wrong.

Seeing my incomprehension, he said, "Nick let us use his place while Elena's in town. I kidnapped her from her aunt's." He put his arm around Elena in the same loving way Nick sometimes puts his arm around me. "We're not supposed to, uh, you know, until we get married next year. Elena comes from a very strict, very traditional Greek family. They'd disown her if they found out what we were doing here."

She held up her hand, displaying a lovely sapphire-and-diamond ring. "Engaged!"

Yes, the one English word she knew. The one English word every woman knows, I suspected.

"You mean Nick's not engaged to Elena?"

Adrien laughed. "Elena's fifteen years younger than he is." He translated this for her and she, too, laughed, shaking her head and saying, "Nick. Old."

He was so *not* old. Nick was perfect. Handsome. Mature. Funny. Well read. Extremely sexy. He was fantastic!

Best of all, he was not engaged to Elena.

Adrien tapped me on the shoulder. "The emergency?"

Right. The emergency. "There's a pipe in the basement that's burst. Water's rising."

It didn't matter anymore. The house could wash away for all I cared. Todd must have misunderstood. Nick was probably going to lease the apartment to Adrien after he fixed it up. And Patty was so busy with work, she didn't pay attention to what I was saying when I asked about Nick's fiancée.

The important thing was, Nick was free. Free!

Unless—awful thought—he was engaged to a different Elena.

No way to find out because Adrien was already talking to Nick on his cell. I could hear Nick spouting instructions as Adrien ran downstairs, leaving me alone with Elena in the kitchen.

"Does Nick have an Elena?" I asked.

She puzzled her brows, trying to comprehend.

"Nick," I said. "Engaged?"

"No!" She shook her head vigorously. "No." Then, tilting her head coyly, she asked, "You like Nick?"

What the heck. She didn't understand English. "I do."

She broke into a huge smile. "That's good. Very good for Nick. I'll tell him."

Chapter Twenty-Three

The day after receiving the dean's cake platter, I am at my desk when Alice barges in with another gift—this one in the form of a bombshell.

"You have to call me when Connie gets back to her office today. I wanna be here for that Kodak moment when she walks in and sees all these presents."

"Connie's coming back today?" I ask, trying to sound neither alarmed nor homicidal.

"Didn't you know? She's been home for weeks."

"Let me guess. She flew in from London a month ago."

Alice counts on her fingers. "Yeah. That would be right. Around the time when you moved to your new house. She hasn't been to the office because of . . . Well, you know. It's sort of embarrassing."

"Right." Alice and I have been operating on a nudge, nudge system. She pretends I know she knows I know and she pretends she knows I know she knows. It's slightly confusing, but it's best for avoidance of an all-out cat fight.

Well, I would cross the Connie bridge when I came to it. No point in working up a lather before then.

"By the way, your noon appointment called. She's running on a tight schedule. A Kara Wesko from Bridgewater, New Jersey."

Kara, the debate club captain who plans to be on the U.S. Supreme Court before she's fifty. I've been looking forward to meeting her. No, really, I have.

The future Justice Wesko arrives at noon on the dot. Though a mere eighteen, she is in a full Prada suit, bag, and shoes, an outfit that by my estimation costs as much as my first car. Kara Wesko is going to be a laugh riot, I can tell.

"So nice to meet you." She sticks out her hand and as I pop up to shake it I temporarily forget who is being interviewed—her or me. "Please, have a seat," she says.

"Thank you," I find myself replying and sit down.

As Kara clicks open her briefcase I catch her perfume—Chanel No. 5 and Clearasil. "About your pre-law program. I have concerns regarding the statistics course. Is that taught by a TA? Because I've read some very unflattering reviews online. It's not easy learning statistics from someone whose native tongue is Polish."

"You don't have to take statistics if you don't want to. Only economics majors are required." Personally, you couldn't make me take that damned course if you pulled out my fingernails. Also it was at 8:30 in the morning. This is college, for heaven's sake. You're supposed to sleep in.

"Statistics is essential for the upper-tier law schools like Stanford and Chicago." She gives me a warning glare and makes a tick on her tablet. "You should have known that."

I am about to automatically spout "sorry," when I catch myself. I will not allow a kid who's not even old enough to buy beer to assess my professional criteria.

"I see." I counter with my own tick on a piece of scrap paper I was using to calculate the calorie content of the tuna salad I had for lunch.

Kara peers at my tick. "What are you doing?"

"This is a college interview, Kara. For some students it's not important. For others, like you, it's crucial." *Keep it snappy, the kid's onto you, Genie.* "Perhaps you can wow me with your renowned powers of persuasion, because, with only your application to go by, I have to say I'm not sure you're right for Thoreau."

"Not right for Thoreau?" She blows out her lips. "You've got to be kidding me. Thoreau's my safety."

We'll just see about that. I slide out her essay and look puzzled. "You write here that you plan to sit on the U.S. Supreme Court by age fifty. How do you think you'll be able to achieve that?"

"Quite easily. I have it completely planned out." And from her briefcase, Kara produces a paper that she unfolds. It is a tidy timeline, typeset and everything, in the design of a yellow-brick road. "This is my life plan. Our guidance counselor encouraged us to make one up so that we could set goals."

That Bridgewater, New Jersey, school system—literally laying out the path to success.

"See?" She is pointing to the drawing of an ivy-covered institution with the word *Harvard* written in crimson. "This is where I'll go to undergrad. That is, if I get into my top choice."

Yeah, yeah. You and every other senior in the top ten, I think, running my finger two steps down Kara's yellow-brick road. I pass the U.S. Supreme Court clerkship and her inevitable stint at the U.S. Attorney's Office to Darling, Smith & Kramer, a law firm that even I know is one of the top-grossing in Washington, D.C.

Patty, being Patty, had turned them down years before because of where they directed their political contributions. "What's the deal with Darling, Smith & Kramer?"

"The deal is Darling, Smith & Kramer is *the* place to be. I'll work my butt off there for fifteen years, make a name for myself and lots of money before I move on to circuit judge."

I do the math in my head. "Which means you'll work there from age twenty-five or so to age forty."

Kara checks her timeline. "Exactly."

"But it says here in your application that you plan on taking time off to have children—two, maybe three."

"Because I don't believe in day care. There's no logic to having kids if you plunk them in day care when they're three months old."

I'm looking for clues in her expression. Does the future Ms. Sandra Day O'Connor not get it? "You can't work for Darling, Smith & Kramer *and* take time off to raise kids."

"Why not?"

"Because you'll get fired, that's why. What law firm wants to keep around an attorney who's a no-show ten years running? Especially a firm that is regarded as a juggernaut."

Kara bites her lip, then gets out her pen and starts erasing *Circuit Judge, Third District* after Darling, Smith & Kramer. "No problem. I'll just have my kids after I'm forty."

"When it'll be harder to be pregnant."

"Marcia Cross did it."

I sigh. Marcia Cross. Sure. We all look up to Marcia Cross, married at forty-three, mother at forty-four. If she didn't exist, we'd have to invent her.

"All I'm trying to show, Kara, is that life isn't that easy to plan. Nothing is guaranteed—nothing. So why not allow yourself some flexibility for all sorts of hurdles, like failure? Or like love? Or like not finding love between the ages of twenty-five and thirty?"

Kara is clearly hurt. Her eyes are scrunched up and her lower lip is pouting. Apparently, no one has dared to criticize her timeline before.

"I'm not doubting your capabilities, Kara," I try to soothe. "I mean, we're all redrawing the rules, we women. What was true for our grandmothers did not work for our mothers and probably won't work for our daughters, either. There's a good chance you won't get married by age thirty. Actually, a big chance with the hours you'll be working at Darling, Smith & . . ."

"Okay. I get it. I get it." Kara holds up her hands. "Do you think I don't know this? I know. But . . . it's hard. What if I work too much and I never get married?"

Like the way you're working now and have never had a date, I think. "So what?"

Kara blinks as if I've just trash-talked the pope. "So what?"

"Maybe you will get married. Maybe you won't. That doesn't mean your life will be a failure. As long as you're doing what you love, as long as you don't hold yourself back because you're a single woman—and that's sometimes what single women do, hold themselves back—you'll have a fabulous, rich, fulfilling life ahead of you."

Kara is silent. This is not what she expected from a college interview. I may even be holding her up from her appointment down the road. (Standard operating procedure—Thoreau as warm-up for Harvard.)

"Are *you* married?" she asks, swallowing tears.

"No. And I'm very happy. I have friends and a great job where I get to meet bright students like you. I almost have it all." And I do, almost have it all that is. I have Nick and Patty and Todd and vacations on the Cape and nights out with Steve and my crazy family. "I even own a house. Part of a fabulous Victorian on a golf course with breathtaking views of the city."

"Cool."

"I bought it with a friend of mine. Actually, a guy who works with my brother."

She shoots a glance at the photos of Hugh and me on my bookshelf. "Not your boyfriend?"

"No. Never. Ha!" Teenage girls. Such silly romantics.

"But you own a house with him?"

"As a matter of fact, he lives right upstairs." I make another meaningless tick on my tablet.

"Is he cute?"

"Who, Nick? Oh my god, yes." Crap! I can't believe I just said that out loud. This is a student interview here. I have completely lost my senses. "I mean . . ."

"I know what you mean." Kara smiles and begins to fold up her timeline. "I may be only a senior in high school, but you don't have to tell me what's really going on. I'll remember that if I'm still unmarried and middle-aged like you, buy a house with a guy. Then get him hooked."

"No . . . it's not like that." Hey! Did she just call me middle-aged?

That's when I hear the high nasal giggle Connie emits only when she's flirting. Which means she hasn't come back to work all by herself.

I bet she's brought Hugh.

Chapter Twenty-Four

This is my resolution: I am not going to make a big deal about Connie and Hugh finally making their grand entrance as a couple. I mean, it had to happen eventually and now everyone will know at last that Hugh's not marrying me, that he's hooked up with Connie, who is no doubt flashing her ring, the huge Spencer diamond, and giggling about how Hugh swept her off her feet.

Yes. It'll be fine. How can it not be?

Too bad I just spent $15 to FedEx him all the mementos he'd left behind at my old apartment—razor, toothbrush, shaving cream, a pair of shorts, his extra pair of glasses, his complete set of Nicholas Sparks novels (which he used for "inspiration" for *Hopeful, Kansas*), his Krups coffee grinder, and his seasoned Calphalon omelet pan (or, at least, it *was* seasoned until I stuck it in the dishwasher).

It would have been lovely to carry them downstairs and, with much flourish, drop the entire box at his feet so everyone would get the point that he'd been practically married to me when he proposed to Connie.

This is the fantasy I'm entertaining when my phone rings, causing me to jump so hard I spill the entire contents of Kara Wesko's file. It's Alice and I bet she's buzzing to tell me how she knew all along my engagement was a fraud and how Margery Rothman and Karen Caruso have now officially kicked me out of the Married Ladies' Club.

"Prepare yourself," Alice says.

I swallow hard, preparing myself. "What's the word?"

"Bill's on the warpath. Whatever you said to that girl from Jersey must have been a whopper. She came down the stairs whining about you badgering her or whatever, so now Bill's trying to calm her down and also her father, who happens to be a potential bene."

Bene is admissions shorthand for *benefactor.* Terrific. As if I didn't have enough problems to worry about already.

Oh, well, at least Alice didn't bring up Hugh. Maybe he hasn't shown up after all. My imagination running wild and all that.

I ask, "Is Connie back?"

"Uh-huh. Have you seen her?"

"Not yet."

"Well, you're in for a shock. She's sporting a real shiner. The biggest one I've ever seen."

The Spencer family diamond. I knew it, just knew it. The bling of all blings. Hugh told me once it had been passed down from King Edward to his mistress, Hugh's great-grandmother Loria. He used to say it would be mine one day and that, together, we'd remove it from the Royal Vault in London and all the vault people would gather around smiling at us because only a Spencer truly in love would bestow the cherished Spencer diamond on a non-Spencer.

"You okay? 'Cause I know the suspense must be killing you," Alice says.

The truth is I am not okay. I am tied up in knots over whether to confront Connie immediately and get it over with or simmer on low until I explode. The Spencer diamond indeed.

"I'm fine."

Alice cracks her gum. "Keep telling yourself that. And remember my mantra: Fuck 'em if they can't take a joke."

"Didn't you have that made into a bumper sticker for Trey?"

"Yeah. When he was in the tank. Only it didn't go over with the cops that great."

Connie's door slams shut and I get off the phone with Alice. That's it. It's now or never. No point in prolonging the pain.

But first—makeup. Pulling a hand mirror from my top drawer, I brush out my hair and redo my ponytail, smack some Clinique Honey Blush on my lips, and refresh my charcoal eyeliner.

You've got to look good to bitch good.

Then I march across to Connie's office and rap my knuckles on the door.

"Come in," she calls out laconically.

Hugh's adoration fills the room. Flowers. Tons of them. White lilies. White roses. Freesias in pink, yellow, and orange. Plus lilies I've seen only in *National Geographic*. The perfume is so sickeningly sweet I nearly pass out, despite Connie's air-conditioner running full blast.

He really went overboard. Probably guessed I'd be in Connie's office first thing and wanted to be sure the message got across. *This is the woman I love now.* And to think I was beside myself the time he once sent me a half-dozen roses. Cheap date and cheap ditch. That's me.

"Hello, Connie."

Connie keeps her perfectly coiffed blond head bent over whatever essay she's reading as if I'm not even there. Probably she's just too ashamed to face me and, really, who can blame her.

"Please, go," she says.

All right. Apparently Connie is not familiar with the old expression "Pride goeth before a fall." "No, I won't go. You and I have to clear the air."

"I don't want to clear the air." Coolly, she flips a page and moves on to something else in her file. "I know why you're here. You know why you're here. Therefore, we have nothing more to talk about, Genie. Let's try to get through this period the best we can until it's over."

Amazing. Not even engaged two months and already their relationship is ending. Which proves a lingering suspicion I had that Connie, never enamored with British men, stole Hugh just to spite me. "And how soon, exactly, do you think it'll be over?"

"Any day now. The writing's on the wall."

And then will Hugh come back to me? Or did he use Connie as an excuse to end our relationship? Some men are like that—can't leave unless there's another woman in the wings. Especially Hugh, who has definite mommy issues.

"Maybe you don't understand what I've been through, Connie. This experience has been really painful."

"No more painful for you than for me."

I take a few steps closer, hoping she'll stop with the paperwork and pay attention to our conversation. "Really? No matter what you've been through, the

man you loved did not announce on national television that he was marrying someone else and then
admit that after four years in a relationship he was
never sexually attracted to you. Now *that's* pain. Not
yours, *mine.*"

Slowly, Connie raises her big blue eyes and I let out
a gasp before I can stop myself. Her eyes . . .

"Are you talking about Hugh Spencer, *the* Hugh
Spencer, your future husband?"

Her left hand, which, until now, has been hidden by
one leaf of the manila folder, is mostly bare. There is
no Spencer diamond. There is no diamond at all. Just
the dinky silver band she always wears.

Oh, shit. Shit. Shit. Shit. There's an excellent chance
I might have just made one terrible mistake.

"Or are you talking about what I'm talking about?"
she asks, tapping her pen.

"What *are* you talking about?"

"I'm talking about me taking over Kevin's position." Connie squints, an act that must be hard to do
with those swollen cheeks. "But it sounds to me as
if you're talking about something else. Are you
saying that when Hugh proposed . . . it wasn't to
you?"

"I . . . I . . ." I feel faint, queasy. Of all people to confess my secret to, Connie Robeson would be my very
last choice. But that's what I've done. I've told her the
truth and now it'll be a matter of days—hours?—
before the whole campus knows, too.

Panicked, I search for a topic change that will knock

her for a loop, and blurt out the first thing that comes to mind. "What happened to your face?"

Connie self-consciously touches her purple cheek. "It's a long story and no one's business."

All these flowers everywhere. On the bookshelves. The windowsill. Even on top of the window air-conditioner. Possibly from someone feeling very, very guilty. "Did some man . . . beat you?"

"You might say that. His name is Dr. Hakell."

"A *doctor* beat you?"

"More like cut me and mangled me. Of course, if I'd known he had an addiction to prescription painkillers, I might have gotten a second opinion before I let him near me with the knife."

The words don't add up until on further inspection I see her tiny pink scars.

"Plastic surgery?"

"Gone wrong. Very wrong. Even when he tried to correct it the surgery went wrong. There. Now you know. I'm suing him and he's trying to butter me up with flowers and various bribes, but nothing can change the fact that until I can rest up for more surgery I am stuck with this face."

"It's not so bad. Really."

"Please. My eyes may be black and blue, but I can still see my reflection."

So, that's why Connie was in England and why Alice didn't want anyone to know where she went. Also, why Alice shot me that look during the meeting when Bill inquired about Connie. Alice was

290

covering for her and the look was so that I'd shut up.

Poor, poor Connie. What an awful thing to have happened. And she was so beautiful, too. There was no need for plastic surgery. I should hug her, let her know we all love her just the way she is.

"Oh, Connie!" I cry, rushing over to her with open arms.

"Don't touch me." She pushes me away so hard I fly back into the filing cabinets. "Your sympathy is the last thing I want."

"But—"

"Your life is perfect. You're engaged to Hugh Spencer and you just bought a new house by the country club. And—shoot—you've gotten so fit and tan while I've been away it makes me sick. I've put on ten pounds, spending every day on my couch and hiding from the world."

I fight the temptation to say thank you, that, yes, I have been working out and doing my pre-wedding exercises and getting my nails done with Patty and using the spray-on tan Tina from the bank loaned me. And that, in fact, I happen to be wearing a pink lace-up tanga.

But that wouldn't be polite. Plus, there are more important issues to get straight.

"Listen, about Hugh. What I said . . . it kind of came out wrong."

Underneath the bruises, Connie's eyes flash. "Oh, no. It came out perfectly right. You said he didn't find you sexually attractive. Seems to me there's not much hope in *Hopeful, Kansas*."

"Actually—"

"You also said something about you not being the person he proposed to on television. Don't deny it. You *did*."

Damn. Connie never listens to me at meetings when I vote for Suzie Plain Cheese of Dayton, Ohio. But God forbid I let slip a teeny tiny personal fact I shouldn't and, *bam!* her brain's a sponge. And she's just the kind of manipulative, plotting coworker who wouldn't think twice about using someone's weakness to her own advantage.

"Gosh. I've got to be getting back to work," I mumble, backing to the door. "Sorry we had this little misunderstanding. Hope you feel better soon. Bummer of a nose job. I'm telling you it's not so bad. We should get together for a drink. . . ."

Knock. Knock. Knock.

Per usual, Alice doesn't wait to be invited. Throwing open the door, she bypasses Connie and targets me.

"Bill. He just finished with Kara Wesko's parents and he wants to see you, pronto."

My heart clenches. "How mad is he?"

"Babe, you don't know. I've never seen him this way before. It's scary."

I can practically hear Connie silently howl with vengeful joy.

Chapter Twenty-Five

Bill's humongous office is an impressive false front of leather couches and black wooden director's chairs imprinted with Thoreau's crest. Books abound, as do high mullioned windows facing the green quad where industrious and not-so-industrious summer students engage in the exchange of high ideas. (A euphemism for all sorts of activity.)

His mahogany desk looks to the fireplace that is always lit during the fall. It's what parents see when they enter the main hallway—Bill's fireplace with its antique gold mantel clock ticking steadily. The burnished autumn leaves fall from the oaks outside his window.

This is the New England collegiate atmosphere parents yearn for their children to experience. Many a tuition deposit has been written on his couch. Bill is a master in manufacturing image, which is why he always keeps his door open.

This afternoon, however, Bill's door is closed.

This is so not good.

Alice holds up a finger for me to wait as she buzzes him. Not for him is the knock-three-times-and-barge-in treatment.

"He's ready." Pressing her lips thinly together, she leads me to the door as if I am a dead admissions counselor walking.

I can honestly say that I have never so dreaded anything as much as I am dreading this meeting with Bill. I hate being in trouble. I go out of the way to avoid it at all costs. I pay my parking tickets as soon as I get them, my bills by the first of the month. I don't speed or drink and drive. Never cheat on my taxes. I've been pulled over once by the cops for a faulty taillight and I was so sick about it, I actually threw up on the officer's shoe.

And now, just because I gave Kara Wesko a bit of guidance, told her to ease up on the I've-got-to-be-married-by-thirty plan, I'm in boiling hot water. Because Kara Wesko (and her wealthy parents) are exactly the kind of people we in Thoreau admissions are supposed to be courting.

Not frightening.

"Remember," Alice says, "whatever happens is always for the best. Now breathe deep and good luck."

I breathe deeply.

Bill is standing at the window in a blue oxford-cloth shirt, his hands clenched behind his back. Oh, super. Hand clenching. That's it. I'm fired. Bill never clenches and unclenches his hands unless he's really, really pissed.

And I just bought a condo!

It's so bad, whatever humiliation I've inflicted on Kara Wesko, that he doesn't bother to turn around or tell me to sit. He just asks me how long I've been working at Thoreau.

I can barely do the calculations in my head, despite endless nights lying in bed asking myself why I still work in the same place after fifteen years.

"Fifteen years."

"Fifteen years." He shakes his head as if this is an amazing feat. "I hate to lose you after fifteen years."

Oh, please. Please no. I can't stand the prospect of being fired. The rejection. The explanations. Having to go down to the unemployment office and lie about searching for a job. Afternoons lying around the house watching *General Hospital*. Well, that's not so bad. . . .

"But that's what's going to happen if I don't do something right now. Lose you. It's happened in the past. Not that it was easy to let them go."

Think fast, Genie. This is your opportunity to save your job. Give him five good reasons why he shouldn't can your ass right now.

That's exactly what I'll do. I'll tell him that I meant well and that I was only trying to encourage Kara to enjoy life. Don't want superstressed kids throwing themselves off the top of libraries and all that.

"Then, years later"—Bill is rocking on his heels, staring out that stupid window—"you ask yourself, *'whatever happened to so and so.'* Wonder if they landed on their feet. If there could have been a way other than letting them go. . . ."

"There is a way!"

Bill turns to face me. "You're right. There is. Which is why I'm offering you Kevin's position. That is, if Hugh and you haven't already made plans to move on."

This is definitely a new low, even for Bill, who

often mistakes his cruelty for cleverness. You know, nothing awful. Just the personal jab about Alice's white pumps being the first sign of spring or Kevin striking out on a date with Lafonda James, the hottest fund-raiser at Alumni.

"I understand your hesitation. I'm sure a decision like this needs to be talked over with Hugh. Heck, that's what I would want my future wife to do."

Hold on. Is he serious?

"Bill?" My voice is suddenly so hoarse, it sounds like a scratched record.

"Yes?"

"May I sit down?"

"Oh, I'm so sorry. Please . . ." He gestures to the chair.

I sit and massage my temples, willing my brain to stop acting crazy. "This isn't one of your attempts at humor, is it?"

He leans over his desk and frowns to show this is not his attempt at humor. Though he's rumored to be sixty-seven, he's in very good shape. He could work as a model for Viagra ads. Lots of snowy white hair and a cleft chin. "You've known me for long enough now, Genie, to recognize when I'm being serious. I want you as my right-hand, um, woman."

He really is offering me Kevin's job. I can't believe it.

"You've paid your dues. You know the ins and outs of the admissions game. You're good at it. You select candidates who do well, who thrive, and you have helped to build a diverse student body. That said, I'll be honest and tell you that you were not my top pick."

Typical Bill to mix a bit of vinegar into the honey.

"There are other people here with more leadership potential. I'm sure you know who they are."

Connie.

"And, let's face it, you've never really set this office on fire. That is, until this summer." He walks around the desk and props himself on its corner, a position that is both casual and authoritarian. "I don't know if it's your engagement to Hugh Spencer—I mean, that's the only change in your life of which I'm aware—but you have suddenly blossomed into a bright, confident admissions officer, Genie, exactly the kind of person who should be the first contact for our higher caliber applicants—and their parents."

My throat is so dry now I can't speak. Seeing my distress, Bill gets up and personally gets me a cup of water from his water cooler. I have never known that to happen before. Bill never does anything for anyone else.

"Thanks," I say, downing it all.

"It was the end-of-month meeting that caused me to reevaluate your potential. Your speech defending Hob Cooper was articulate and insightful, containing just enough ardor supported by facts to win over even me. And, frankly, I was ready to can the kid, Mormon or no Mormon."

Bill is smiling and I smile back as I begin to develop a sense of pride in his words. He's right. I *was* really insightful. (Even though I was totally preoccupied with the erroneous revelation that Connie was Hugh's mystery fiancée.)

"And then there was your handling today of Kara Wesko. Her parents were just as impressed as I was by your directness. How did they put it?" He taps his chin, remembering. "Oh, yes. They wanted to thank you for doing what they and three psychologists had not been able to do—lift the lid on the pressure cooker. I guess Kara needed to hear it from another woman in your position that she didn't need to do it all."

I'm not so sure. Possibly, I dashed her dreams.

"I wouldn't be surprised if Kara takes a year off between high school and college. It'd probably be the best thing for her. And I also wouldn't be surprised if she ended up at Thoreau, a vibrant and happier student, thanks to you. Especially after the check her parents just wrote in gratitude."

Shoot. I'm near tears. These are the nicest things any boss has ever said to me.

"Now, I know that Hugh's career is taking off and that's great for you and, fingers crossed"—Bill crosses two fingers—"that'll be great for Thoreau, if we can talk him into staying here.

"But because of your special circumstances, the dean has authorized me to offer you a salary increase to one hundred thousand dollars, plus six weeks vacation and full health benefits. I hope that's enough to convince you to take the job and to persuade Hugh not to leave the area for Baja, or wherever it is successful writers go."

The numbers don't make sense. I've never made money like this. I've never even considered I'd make money like this. Six figures! And why? Not because I diligently punched the clock every day, but because, in a fit of pique, I mindlessly—yet, forcefully—delivered a powerful argument for some kid in Utah who flunked badminton.

"I'll take it. Thanks so very, very much."

Bill reels back, startled. "You don't need to talk to Hugh?"

Hugh. Right. Naturally, I'll be needing to talk to Hugh. That's what a really engaged woman would do. "Sure, I'll talk to Hugh. We'll discuss it tonight and then I'll give you an answer in the morning."

"Why wait that long?" Bill, jolly as all get-out, snaps up his phone and presses a button. "Alice, get me the dean."

The dean?

He covers the mouthpiece with his hand. "Hugh popped over for a visit to see Bob. You know how those two get. Talk, talk, talk." Then, getting back on, he says, "Hugh! Great to hear your voice. Say, I wonder when you're done over there if you wouldn't mind stopping by. There's a little lady you might know who has some very exciting news for you." He winks at me. "Five minutes? Super. I'll tell Genie to expect you then."

Oh, God. He's actually here.

I should be scared. I should be dreading his reaction when he finds out I've been spreading rumors that we really are engaged.

But that's how the old Genie would have reacted.

I'm the new Genie now. I'm in shape. I'm being promoted. I own my own home and, best of all, I am no longer dependent on Hugh for my future happiness. Moreover, I've been dreaming of this moment for weeks, planning and scheming exactly what to say.

Bring him on.

Chapter Twenty-Six

Because I am Nancy Michaels's daughter and have been raised to know that "sweat happens," I always keep a white button-down shirt in my office closet. I need this shirt. The one I wore to work this morning has been totally pitted out from my confrontation with Connie and my job offer from Bill. The only solution may be to burn it.

After changing my shirt, running some Ban under my arms, freshening my makeup, and downing a half a box of Altoids, I try the window in a last-minute urge to escape. It is nailed shut against the air-conditioner. I won't have this problem when I take over Kevin's job. There are three windows in that office. Also, because I won't be working here—not after Bill discovers I've been lying to his face.

There is a mild commotion downstairs heralding Hugh's arrival. Alice is shouting "Congratulations" at full volume and Brandon the handyman is saying something about "better you than me, buddy." Karen and Margery are screaming for him to sign copies of their books.

Guess I'm as ready as I'll ever be. I blow on my ring and give it a polish. Best $24.95 I ever spent.

Before I can figure out how to ideally position myself (on the desk with my legs crossed versus with my back to him, my legs propped on the bookshelf) the door opens and in walks Hugh.

For a moment my heart leaps as it used to, largely out of habit. Even after years together, his self-deprecating grin and sparkling eyes never failed to send a charge through my body. I used to sigh and marvel that a man so handsome, so witty, so debonair could find something of interest in little ole me.

Boy. Did I have that backward.

"Hey!" I sit up and give him a big smile, as if we are, and have always been, hunky-dory. "You're back!"

"I'm surprised this comes as a shock to you." With his trademark meticulousness, he carefully hangs his navy blazer on the back of my interview chair. (He'd actually had it slung over his shoulder.) Then, affecting a pose straight out of *GQ*, he shoves his hands in his khakis, his white shirtsleeves rolled neatly to his elbows, and studies me. "You look good, Genie. Very good."

If I were one of his students, this would be the moment I'd melt, because Hugh is giving me his I-know-what-your-heart's-desire-is stare, the one that's supposed to bore into my soul.

"And you've got mustard on your shirt."

Hugh falls for it, immediately inspecting his collar for the nonexistent stain. This is what happens when you go to an all-boys academy. He wouldn't have stood a chance at your average American elementary school.

"Gotcha." I shoot a finger at him.

He groans and rolls his eyes. "You may look different, but you haven't changed a bit."

That's what you think, pal. "Have a seat. Tell me what you've been up to." Poor choice of words. Next I know, he'll be rattling off his sales numbers and where *Hopeful, Kansas* is on the *USA Today* bestseller list and what miniscule European monarchy wants to buy the rights to Dick and Dora's sappy love story now.

He hesitates as if taking a seat might be a trap. "You know, I almost didn't come over when Bill called. I've been going out of my way to avoid you."

"Really?" I deadhead a rose hip from the plant Nick sent me. "Here we are engaged and you can't be bothered to pop in to say hello. How very rude."

"That's exactly what I'm talking about. You have got to put an end to these rumors." He's about to march toward my desk in some dramatic execution of urgency when he catches sight of the white boxes and stops dead. "Don't tell me . . ."

"See for yourself."

"Oh, darling. You have really gone too far," he says, clearly dismayed by the Benardaud teacup set.

"What? You think maybe I should have picked Wedgwood?"

"You know what I mean. Deferring answers when someone asks if we're truly getting married is bad enough. Planning a wedding. Registering for china and"—he gestures toward my hand—"buying a ring is downright psychotic. I'm wondering if you need psychiatric institutionalization."

"I knew you still cared," I say, flashing my imitation diamond.

"May I see that?"

"Maybe later. If you're good."

"It can't be real."

"Why can't it?"

"Because you'd never be able to afford a diamond that huge."

"I'll have you know that I had enough money saved to put a healthy deposit on my own condo. Besides," I add, "who says *I* bought the ring?"

He opens his mouth to reply and then stops. "Please. You really must stop this charade." Only he pronounces it *shar-rod*.

"It's no *shar-rod*. I've discovered there were things I didn't know about you, such as you sleeping around behind my back and cheating on me and pretending to love me when you didn't."

He casts his eyes downward, ashamed.

"Did you ever think there might be things you didn't

know about me?" I continue. "Maybe I've been conducting a clandestine affair, too. Some hot and heavy office romance."

"Don't be ridiculous." Pulling out a chair, he finally takes a seat. "You're an open book. Why, you couldn't even keep your Christmas gifts secret from me. Had to badger me with hints until I guessed long before December twenty-fifth."

This was true. Then again, I'd managed to keep a pretty big secret from my family and friends for weeks now. So maybe I was changing in that area, as well.

"Okay. Believe what you want to believe. Not like I owe you an explanation anymore." I go back to picking over the roses.

"Look. The only reason I'm here, besides pleading with you to cease and desist with this pernicious lie, is my curiosity. Bill Gladstone called me while I was at the dean's with the message that there was some big news that I'd be interested in that might, I gathered, involve you."

"It does."

"Does it concern *Hopeful, Kansas*? Because, if it does, I'll go downstairs and talk to Bill. Otherwise, I can't see the point of you and I continuing to play games."

"No problem. I'll call Bill up here right now. He's dying to meet you, anyway." I press the buzzer for Alice.

"Wait!"

It's too late. Alice is on and I am telling her that

when Bill has a chance, Hugh would love to see him.

"Wow. Must be nice to have such a cushy relationship that you can buzz in the boss," she snaps.

Hugh is resting his chin on his hand exactly like his author's photo. "Cushy relationship?"

"Back to that pernicious lie business. You must admit that I was roped into lying when you proposed to someone else on national television. What was I supposed to do? Tell everyone we know that you'd dumped me, big time?"

He drops his hand in disgust. "Genie. We have been over this I don't know how many times."

"Once, to be exact."

There is a rap on the door and Bill blows in, hale and hearty, blustering about it "being a great day for Thoreau" and how "super" it is to see Hugh and how impressed everyone is with the success of *Hopeful, Kansas.*

Bill truly is the master of the suck-up, injecting Hugh with his daily fix of compliments until Hugh is blushing and shaking his hand and doing an extremely poor job at being falsely modest.

"Couldn't have achieved this level of success without the support of this fantastic institution," Hugh gushes. "I suppose I'd be nothing but a starving writer if it hadn't been for my office here and the salary to keep me in pens for scribbling."

Blech. Hugh is never more saccharine than when he's channeling some eighteenth-century garret novelist.

"So you've heard the good news, I gather." Bill stops shaking Hugh's hand and slides an arm around my shoulders. "Hope you've given your blessing. I can't wait to have this lady by my side."

I know that Bill is talking about making me his right-hand woman, as Kevin was his right-hand man, but judging from Hugh's utter confusion, I'm not so sure that's getting across. Especially with Bill giving my shoulder an avuncular squeeze.

Bill says, "I didn't want to lose her, you know. Had to snatch her up before you dragged her off."

Hugh's jaw drops. He shifts his gaze from Bill to me and back to Bill again, horrified.

"Trust me. I completely understand if you object." Bill drops his arm and clears his throat, perceiving that Hugh perhaps is not pleased with my new promotion. "After all, I am known around these parts as a taskmaster, that's no secret. But let me assure you that I will personally see to it Genie gets plenty of time off for her new family. Because I'm betting there'll be lots of babies. Hazards of nonstop sex and all that."

The blood has drained from Hugh's complexion, indicating my hints at an office romance have wormed their way into his mind. And now, seeing Bill with me, seeing the ring on my finger, the wedding presents in my office, and how Bill is talking about me being by his side and asking Hugh for his blessing, Hugh has come to one horrified conclusion.

I really am engaged. To Bill.

My plan couldn't have worked better.

Chapter Twenty-Seven

"So what does Hugh think about your new job?" Nick asks from the other side of the bathroom door.

"He's all for it," I say, pressing my ear against the wall to hear what's going on. "Can't I take a look?"

"No. You cannot. I'm not ready yet."

Damn. Running my hand along the back of my sweaty neck, it's all I can do to keep myself from kicking the door down. Ninety-eight degrees and near one hundred percent humidity. I don't know how much longer I can tolerate this.

There is some Greek swearing and the sound of metal hitting the floor. Nick is taking forever. Forever!

Finally, the door opens and there he stands, shirt off, sweat beading his forehead. I can't help but notice the patch of dark hair in his armpits, his smooth, hairless dark chest and the *V* of slight hair below his navel leading to underneath his belt.

It's the *V* that makes my knees go weak.

"Now," he says. "I'm ready."

With that, he sweeps his arm to what I've been craving. My very own shower and bathtub.

Not any old bathtub, either. A high-backed, claw-foot porcelain tub that Nick found while working on the Hingham renovation. It had been left in the back-yard of an antique store for over a year and was covered with weeds and grasses when he spotted it while helping Todd search for a farmhouse kitchen sink.

It was a bear to carry in, weighing over 285 pounds. Todd threw his back out in the process and had to go home to a couch and Tylenol after helping Nick haul it into my bathroom. Plus, it had a funny drain that Nick's been wrestling with all day.

But now it's in. And I'm not going to wait until a curtain's up. I need that ice-cold water running over my body now.

Nick is smiling at my happiness. "I'm sorry it took so long."

"No. It was worth the wait. You want to do the honors?"

"Me?"

"Well, you're the one who did all the work."

"No, thanks. It's rewarding enough to see you so giddy about it."

I eagerly slip off my sandals. "You have to admit it's been a pain, me coming upstairs every morning to use yours." Without thinking, I rip off my T-shirt, remembering too late that Nick's in the doorway.

"Might need this." He hands me a towel and, being a gentleman, pretends to preoccupy himself with picking up his tools. "That desperate, huh?"

If he only knew my real source of desperation. There have been so many times—like now—when I've been tempted to gush *I'm not really marrying Hugh.* But then I think of the consequences and decide that Nick's reaction would be to write me off as a silly woman who invented her engagement to get attention. Not to mention the many long hours he's logged installing my kitchen cabinets, ripping up the floors—simply to make the deadline of my wedding.

No. There's no way to say what I want to say without him hating me. I've let it go too far.

"All right. Enjoy! I'll wait here in case you run into any problems." He closes the door and at last I'm alone, just me and my shower. Bliss.

I set out all the toiletries I've bought for the occasion—new shampoo and conditioner, lavender soap, a loofah, a washcloth, and the most vigorous exfoliant money can buy. Then, holding my breath, I turn on the water. It works!

"How's it doing?"

The floor is dry. "No leaks yet."

"Yet!" Nick plays at being incensed. "How dare you doubt me."

Leaving the rest of my clothes in a heap, I lift my leg over the high side and step in. The floor is way too smooth. A person could break her neck in here! I'll have to get a bath mat or those sand strips. Nevertheless, the water is divine.

Thoughtfully, Nick has installed an oversize showerhead so it's like I'm standing under a tropical waterfall as I close my eyes and let the cool water run over my head and face and down my back. I've always wanted to visit one of those waterfalls, the kind featured in the ads for Hawaii. Except I'd be worried about what sorts of creepy crawly things might be in the water.

Like snakes.

I sense it before I actually see it, the slithering green tail whipping back and forth in panic as its body makes it halfway up the tub's sides and then falls down in failure. The tiny head with its evil slanted eyes darting and retreating toward my feet, blindly searching for escape. Or something to bite.

"Snake," I whisper, too frightened to make my lungs work properly. "Snake."

Run, my brain tells me. *Just get out.*

But I can't. I'm frozen in place, the snake and I trapped in my high-backed tub. Forcing my legs to move is almost impossible. I hate snakes. Scratch that. I live in fear of snakes. Spiders, okay. Roaches, step on them. Bees, no big deal.

Not snakes. Snakes are my enemy. They are Satan and I am Eve.

Taking a different tack, I discard the snake approach altogether and keep it basic. "Help!" I cry, my voice louder. "Nick. Help!"

"Genie?" He pounds on the door. "Are you okay?"

"Snake!"

"Snake?" He sounds puzzled. "What snake?"

"In here. In the bathtub with me."

"You've got to be kidding."

"No joke!" I screech. "It's going for my feet."

"Throw it out."

Touch it? He must be nuts. "I can't do that."

"Okay, then you get out and I'll get rid of it."

"It's going to bite me. Help!"

"I'm coming in."

The knob turns and, quickly, I snatch the towel off the tub's edge. Nick bursts in expecting to find, I suppose, some sort of anaconda because he's completely unimpressed with my dire situation.

"Where is it?" he asks, searching the tub. "I don't see a snake."

"There." I point to the drain, where the awful creature has retreated, slithering and wiggling under the shower. "It's huge!"

Nick turns off the water and stares for a second before throwing back his head and howling with laughter. "That? It's a tiny garter snake. A baby."

"Kill it!" I inch back to the end of the tub, my towel protectively wrapped around me.

"I'm not going to kill it." In a move of daring, he gently scoops up the snake, opens the window, and deposits it outside. "Done."

"Omigod. I am never getting in this bath again," I say as I take Nick's hand and step out.

"Genie! You're shaking. Here." He grabs another towel, wraps it around my shoulders, and pulls me to him. I don't care that I'm naked and wet. I am never leaving his arms—though I'd prefer to have my feet off the floor in case more snakes abound.

"You're ophidiophobic," he says. "Afraid of snakes."

"That's an understatement. Todd used to torture me all through our childhood, chasing me with snakes, putting snakes in our canoe. Once, at camp, in my bed." That's when it hits me. "Todd did this, didn't he?"

Nick is holding me very tightly. "No. No. Todd wouldn't do that. Probably the snake was trapped under the rim of the tub. Yesterday he was in a patch of weeds in Hingham. Today he's in some crazy woman's bath and she's demanding his immediate execution."

I have to laugh, too. It is sort of funny. Now. It wasn't a few minutes ago when the snake was slithering around my toes.

"Are there others?" I ask, worried.

"Who knows? You want me to look?"

"Yes."

"Will do." He starts to move away and I grab him, one of my towels unceremoniously falling to the floor. "Don't go. Not just yet."

We stand there, me for the most part naked against Nick's own bare chest. His skin is against mine, my cold cheek against his warm, strong shoulders. I can smell him, his earthiness, the sweat, a faint trace of metallic grease. It's a heady perfume that has me intoxicated. We are both smart enough and mature enough to know that my refusal to let him go has absolutely nothing to do with reptiles.

"Genie," he says softly. "What is it that you want?"

"Do I have to say?" Hesitantly, I look up at him. I'm right. Words aren't necessary. It's all in his dark blue eyes. Passion. Love. Lust. Whatever. I'll take it.

"Is it okay . . . ," he asks, smoothing my wet hair off my forehead, "if I . . . ?"

Without wasting another second, I reach up and pull

him to me, eager for those lips that kissed me in the coffee shop what seems like ages ago.

His kiss starts off gentle, almost curious. Then, sensing that I have no hesitation, he brings me closer until my towel falls off my shoulders to the floor and he lets out a moan of pleasure, his thumbs grazing the sides of my exposed breasts.

I don't care what happens next. All I know is that I want him. I want to wrap my body around his body. Want to get those jeans of his off and see where that *V* goes. I want him inside me.

But most of all—I want the doorbell to stop ringing.

"Wait," he says, reluctantly pushing me away. "We can't do this."

"Why not?" At this moment I'm more of an animal than a human, incapable of intelligent speech. "They'll go away."

"It's not that, it's . . ." He looks down at my nakedness and closes his eyes as if he can't be tempted.

My addled brain is not comprehending. "If it's Hugh you're worried about, forget him. I don't care."

"You don't, but . . ."

"I don't love Hugh. I thought I loved Hugh, but I was wrong. Very wrong." Oh, God. Why won't he just kiss me again? Why won't those people go away?

"GENIE!" The shrill voice is harsh, unmistakable. It is the voice that haunts me in my dreams, that can trigger all my emotions.

It is the voice of my mother.

"Come on. We know you're in there."

313

"It's my mother," I gasp as all my sexual desire instantly vanishes. "What's she doing here?"

Nick is shaking his head. "I was trying to tell you this before you brought up Hugh. There's a surprise bridal shower waiting for you on the porch. That's why we couldn't do what . . . you know, I think we were about to do."

"Oh." Once again, I flush with embarrassment. "A shower?"

"Your sister and mother and Patty and some other women. Patty asked me to keep you away from the porch until they were ready."

I have never felt so much like a fool. Snapping up the towel from the floor, I wrap it tightly around my body even though it's too little, too late. "Well, you certainly managed a fine distraction. Ha-ha."

"Genie. Stop." He grips my bare shoulder. "I completely forgot about the shower just now. It never crossed my mind."

"Really? Or is that a line you give all your women?"

"Look. I understand you've been hurt by some man and because of that, bizarrely enough, you don't trust me. And maybe you shouldn't because you're weeks away from being another man's wife and it's taken every ounce of my willpower to respect and honor that and there have been moments, like now, when my willpower is no match for how much I want you." He says this in one breath so that he's almost panting by the time he finishes.

I'm speechless. He's been holding himself back

because he thinks I'm getting married when all along I wasn't sure he even cared.

"Nick," I whisper. "I had no idea."

"You don't love him, do you?"

"No." I shake my head slightly. "No, I don't."

"Then I can wait. Like I've said before, I'm a very patient man. When you're free, I'll still be here. Until then, it's up to you."

Footsteps come pounding down the hallway. An inner voice urges me to flee to my bedroom before my mother or Lucy catches me. But I don't want to. I want to tell Nick he doesn't have to wait, that I'm here for him now, that I've always been.

"Genie, where the hell . . ." Patty runs past the bathroom door and then, catching sight of us, slowly steps back. "Holy shit! What've you two been up to?"

"Hi, Patty," Nick says, sliding past her. "Genie's running a bit behind."

When he's gone, Patty stares at me and I stare at her. All I can say is, "There was a snake."

"Oh, I bet there was. And let me guess—it was huge."

Chapter Twenty-Eight

Patty has asked me not to tell Nick or anyone else the truth until her black-tie couple's shower is held in a week. After that, she says, we can both come clean together as the bogusly betrothed. Otherwise, she's afraid that if "certain people" (i.e., Todd) find out I'm not really engaged, then they will suspect *she's* not really engaged, either.

"One week. By then I'll have done the fancy party and gotten all the gifts and proved my point." Patty twirls in a lovely Carmen Marc Valvo embroidered white gown. "Besides, what's the rush? Nick said he can wait."

He might. I'm not sure I can.

We are in the bridal department of Neiman Marcus, where Patty is trying on wedding gowns and dresses for her engagement party. This is not mere frivolity. Several members of the extended Pugliese family have been feuding over who will get the various wedding contracts—the catering, linen, floral, et cetera. By buying her dress retail, and not through her cousin Carmen who has connections in New York's fashion district, she is aiming to save lives.

Meanwhile, as my wedding day approaches, Mom is near hysteria and has been leaving messages that are straight out of some 1950s book on bridal fashion.

"You should be radiant at each step, Genie," is the way her last message started. "At your engagement party. At your rehearsal. At your wedding, of course. At the reception and going away. You'll need at least two formal dresses, a wedding dress, a reception dress, and a going-away suit. It'll be a scandal otherwise."

A scandal otherwise. Patty and I love that expression. Or, at least, we're pretending to love that expression. Because now that we're getting closer to my wedding and Patty's black-tie couple's shower, Mom's not the only one who's getting hysterical.

I'm beginning to think that maybe we've gone too far.

Over a hundred ecru embossed wedding invitations have been sent hither and yon, overseas and across town, proclaiming that:

Mr. and Mrs. Donald Arthur Michaels
Request the pleasure of your company
At the marriage of their daughter
Eugenia Grace

To

Dr. Hugh Spencer
Saturday, the Twentieth of August
At Half Past Three O'clock
At Their Home On
234 Westwood Drive
Belmont, Massachusetts

"Patty Pugliese in a wedding dress," I say, fluffing out her skirt. "Like a hooker in a nun's habit. Never thought I'd see the day."

Patty turns for a side view, pushing in her stomach. "Me neither. On the flip side, don't be so smug. I never thought you'd be able to pull off a fake engagement this long."

"You thought I'd cave, huh?"

"I thought Hugh would come to his senses, dump his mystery ho, apologize profusely, and ask you to marry him. And then everything would be in place for the wedding you'd planned all along."

"You thought Hugh would really marry me? What about that feminist claptrap you were spouting about springing myself from the castle without the kiss and forgoing the prince and . . ."

"Admit it. There was a part of you that wanted that fairy-tale ending, too," Patty says, stepping out of her dress.

I open my mouth to object and find I can't. It's true. Yes, once upon a time, a teeny part of me privately hoped Hugh would return and see the error of his ways, that he would get down on bended knee and beg my forgiveness.

"That's not going to happen," I say, slipping the gown onto a hanger. "It's over between us."

"Let's hope so." Patty zips up an evening dress, a petite Eileen Fisher handkerchief linen tank in a flattering shade of blush pink. "The thing is, I have a problem, too. Roslyn, the new associate who is gunning for my job, has a brother who's a mucky-muck in the navy and he's been snooping around. Guess it doesn't take much to find out who's a captain and who's not."

Uh-oh. "You mean Roslyn has discovered . . ."

"There is no Captain Moe Howard in the U.S. navy." Patty smacks herself in the forehead. "Why couldn't I have chosen a name like Tom Smith or

Mike Jones? Why did I have to go with Captain Moe?"

"Maybe you've always had a crush on helmet heads."

"Maybe." She twirls around. "How does this look?"

"It looks great." And it does. Pink goes well with Patty's hair. "What are you going to do about Captain Moe?"

"I've got it all figured out. I just need to find a man who will step up to the plate and then I can go to the shower and introduce him as my real fiancé. I'll make up some story about needing to keep his true identity secret for national security purposes because he's with navy intelligence. And I'll tell them Captain Moe was his cover name. Something along those lines."

I think about this. "You spent a lot of time reading spy novels as a kid, didn't you?"

"I had eleven brothers and sisters and three bedrooms. What do you think?"

"Alternatively," I suggest, unzipping her, "you could tell everyone at your firm that you and your best friend from college pretended to be engaged so we could receive the same kudos married women get. Make 'em cry into their briefs at the unfairness of our sexist system."

"Yeah, right. My partners pull down seven figures a year filleting dedicated surgeons who happen to slip their scalpels a half a centimeter to the right. Somehow, I don't think they're going to—"

"Do you hear that?" I ask, trying to find the source

of a muffled buzz. Then I recognize it—my cell phone under the heaps of clothes. We actually have to dig it out.

"This is Christy Abramson of *The New York Times*," a droll voice informs me. "I'm trying to reach Eugenia Michaels."

"*THE NEW YORK TIMES*!" I mouth to Patty, who is standing in her bra and panties, a perfect matching set of beige lace.

"What for?" Patty mouths back.

Not for a subscription, I'm guessing. Please may this not have to do with Hugh and his stupid book. Lying to my family is one thing, but lying to *The New York Times* is really serious. You can get subpoenaed for that.

"We've received your engagement announcement," Christy continues, "and per standard procedure we need to fact-check it. Do you have a few minutes?"

"Engagement announcement!" Covering the phone, I inform Patty they're calling to fact-check my engagement announcement. The big question being . . .

What engagement announcement?

Patty slaps her cheek in horror. "They're ruthless fact-checkers at *The New York Times*. They check everything. They'll leave no stone unturned. How did they get an engagement announcement?"

Excellent point. I run this question by Christy.

"Well, you sent it to us, didn't you?"

Patty mouths, "Your mother."

My mother. Curse her. "Right. Mom did. Listen, you don't have to publish—"

"But we want to. Hugh Spencer is, well, *Hugh Spencer.* And while I don't watch TV personally, I understand it was on a national show with Barbara Walters where he first proposed."

"Oh, that . . . that you *definitely* don't have to print. An engagement announcement is so unnecessary. I really don't want—"

"Also, we're considering your wedding for our Sunday feature when you do get married next month. I know. It's very exciting."

It's not exciting. It's nauseating. Even the blasting cold air-conditioning of the Neiman Marcus dressing room is not enough to keep the blood circulating in my brain as I envision a front-page story in *The New York Times*, an exclusive investigated and reported by the paper's notoriously ruthless Weddings & Celebrations section fact-checkers:

LOSER BROAD SCAMS LIT HUNK
"I Did It to Get Stuff," She Claims.

And then, as if in a dream, I hear Christy Abramson utter the implausible. "Mr. Spencer said he would be quite amenable to that."

Patty, too, has heard this because she says, "Hugh?"

"Perhaps you two haven't had a chance to communicate since we spoke this morning. After verifying all the information, he was the one who suggested the feature. Our editor agrees that it might potentially qualify. Of course, I'm in no position to promise."

Could it be that Hugh is such a whore for publicity that he'd lie about an engagement announcement, just to be featured in *The New York Times*?

To prove she's really spoken to him, Christy rattles off his office number at Thoreau and his home number, his mother's maiden name, the age of their dog, Winston, when he died and sparked Hugh's literary career (don't ask). Even the name of his nanny, the one who took him to the train station when he was six to attend St. Bart's School for Neglected Boys.

Yup. That's Hugh all right.

"Christy," I ask, working hard to keep my voice level. "Do you happen to be familiar with the current circulation numbers of the Sunday *New York Times*?"

"It fluctuates, but the last reported figure I heard was one point six million."

Swooning with light-headedness, I lean against the dressing room wall for support. How can I lie to 1.6 million people that Hugh and I are getting married? How could Hugh lie, too, even if it would again boost book sales?

"I'll have to call you back, Christy. Something's come up."

Unfortunately for the new sundress I'm wearing, it happens to be my lunch.

Hugh is nowhere to be found. He has simply disappeared.

I try his apartment in Somerville, his office, Thoreau's library, and even Harvard's libraries (where he prefers to write on his laptop, the pretentious snot). Nothing.

This is not what I need right now, for Hugh to suddenly be telling the world that we're engaged when we're not.

I mean, it's hardly okay if *I* do it and I was the *dumpee,* whereas he was the *dumper.* Alms to the rejected and all that. I'm sure Emily Post would back me up on this.

Bogus engagement protocol aside, I can't for the life of me comprehend what he's up to. Then again, what am I thinking? It's *The New York Times.* Only an idiot author with no marketing savvy whatsoever would turn down an opportunity to appear in an exclusive *Times* feature about his wedding. Especially when this author is supposed to be melting the hearts of female readers everywhere.

I can't imagine that such a public announcement would sit well with Hugh's fiancée, whoever she is. I was too busy being pissed to ask him during our last confrontation, and Bill has allowed me no time to snoop during office hours.

Bill wasn't exaggerating when he told Hugh he was a taskmaster. My cluttered new office with its unpacked boxes of books and files are hallmarks of my current slavery. I haven't been able to so much as slap my name plaque on my desk or hang my Thoreau painting or even put up curtains so that every evening the campus can't see me working long after everyone else has left.

And tonight is no exception.

It is after seven and I'm still at my desk checking the incoming class spreadsheet while compiling a report for the dean, when I hear a strange sound and look up to find Connie looming over me like a vulture. It's true. She is the spitting image of a vulture. Thanks to her botched nose job, her one eye is slightly lower than the other and her ears aren't quite right. She's definitely scary.

"I need to speak with you," she says icily. "It's important."

Okay, this could be bad. Connie has never forgiven me for snaring Kevin's job even though I had nothing to do with the hiring decision. I've tried telling her that, but she won't listen. She won't even say hello or acknowledge me in the women's room.

"I'm all ears," I say, cheerily.

Slapping her professionally manicured hand on my desk, she declares, "You're not marrying Hugh Spencer. You never were marrying Hugh Spencer. You have been scamming everyone—including Bill—in a conniving move to get the job I deserve. And I'm going to see to it that you're fired."

Well, that was certainly succinct and to the point, I have to give her that. Tossing my pencil, I lean back in my fancy new all-leather swivel chair and call her bluff.

"Connie, I don't know what the hell you're talking about."

"Of course you do." She opens a manila file (Connie's mad for manila files) and pulls out a sheet of paper on which is stamped the familiar Thoreau seal. "I wouldn't have gone snooping around if you hadn't barged into my office ranting that Hugh had dumped you, that he wasn't sexually attracted to you."

"Did I say that?"

"Don't deny it," she says, waving the memo about. "You did. And even if you do deny it, I have evidence that you two never were engaged."

It is at this moment that my knees actually knock under the protective cover of my desk. Until now, I secretly doubted the knocking knee phenomenon. Not anymore. My knees really are knocking and for good reason. Connie does not issue idle threats. If she says she has proof, she does. And if she promises to go to Bill and out me, she will. Connie really, really wants this corner office.

Nor is she pleased that when Bill asked who I'd recommend to replace me upstairs, I heartily encouraged him to pick Alice. Alice is smart and intuitive. Plus, she's been working in admissions so long, she can sort the wheat from the chaff with one glance. Rumor has it that Connie threatened to quit if Bill promoted Alice to admissions officer, which, last week, he did.

Still clutching that Thoreau memo, she says, "At

first I passed off your ramblings as the typical Genie Michaels babble. But the more I thought about it, the more I began to wonder, especially after Alice told me Hugh never calls to talk to you. Never."

"That's because he has my cell."

"And he's only been by the office once."

True, true. She had me there.

"So I took Donna Mandretti out to lunch and we had a very interesting conversation."

Oh, no. Not Mandretti the Mouth, the blabbing secretary of the English Department with sodium pentothal running through her veins.

"It was Donna who told me you and Hugh broke up, and that the rumor was he'd been seeing another woman for months."

I sit up, now attentive. "No kidding. Who?" Wrong response. "I mean, *who* could believe a ridiculous rumor like that?"

Connie gives me a withering smile. "You are so pathetic, Genie. Here Hugh has already moved on to another woman while you cling to the desperate fantasy that he'll eventually marry you. God. You're so *Fatal Attraction.*"

Fatal Attraction. Man, I hate that stupid movie. Who lives in an all-white cinder-block apartment anyway? I swear. No other film has done more to slam single women in their thirties than that misogynistic hour and a half of Glenn Close with a bad perm. Married women=good. Single women=bad. Thanks, Hollywood, very insightful.

Connie's threats and memories of bunny boiling are quickly exhausting me.

"All right, Connie," I say, logging out of my computer. "What do you want?"

She squares her shoulders triumphantly. "Not much. Quit your job. Tell Bill that you want to go back to being an ordinary admissions counselor. Do that and our secret will remain our secret. Don't do it and I'll tell Bill everything."

I slap the spreadsheet closed. "You got yourself a deal there, honeybunch."

"You mean you'll quit?"

"No. I mean I'll take my chances with Bill." I reach down under my desk and fetch my purse. "In other words, you'll have to kill me to get this job."

Connie flutters her evidence hysterically. "But you haven't read what I've got here. This is indisputable proof that you've been lying and falsifying your personal information. Bill will fire you on the spot when he reads this. He might even blackball you so you'll never be able to work for another university again."

"And if so, you should know that the memo comparing incoming minority students to last year's total applicant pool plus an analysis of how we could improve acceptance rates for inner-city kids with SAT scores over two thousand was due on the dean's desk yesterday, so you might want to work on that now."

With that, I turn off the light and close the door, leaving Connie in the office she so desperately desires.

Chapter Twenty-Nine

I expected that after her dramatic presentation, Connie would have been perched outside Bill's office the next morning, her file folder in hand. But she wasn't. She spent the entire day holed up in her office and came downstairs only to go to lunch or fax something or pester Alice to make copies.

The next day it was the same routine. And the day after that. And the day after that.

It was really annoying. Let's get on with it, already.

All week, I checked my mailbox for an official notification from the dean that I was both *terminated* and *blackballed* for lying about being engaged. Every afternoon I steeled myself for the eventuality of coming back from lunch to find my office locked and some thug from Thoreau's security standing guard.

I imagined Alice shaking her head in disappointment. Bill cursing me in the three languages he speaks fluently. Throngs of campus personnel with torches chasing me off school property.

Yet, every morning was the same. Coffee on the burner. Faxes in the fax machine. Sherry the new secretary (Alice's replacement) and Brandon discussing the weekend to come or the weekend that had just passed. Brandon pretending to fix the copy machine as he held forth on the best campsites in Maine or where you could buy a good used RV and how to grill a lobster.

Meanwhile, I was left hanging and wondering what Connie was waiting for. She had her "indisputable proof." She had the goods to get my job. Not only that, but Bill was headed to Martha's Vineyard for his summer vacation. She had better act fast or she was going to blow this opportunity.

Connie wasn't my only problem. There was also Nick.

Craftily, we managed to avoid each other all week. Nick left for work every morning before dawn, while I closed down the office every night so I could be assured Nick's light would be off when I got home. I did my laundry Saturday morning, Nick did his on Saturday afternoon. We even took care to haul our trash to the curb at different hours, lest we accidentally brush shoulders over the recyclables and dissolve into a heap of steamy sex.

I couldn't wait until Patty's shower was over on Saturday night so I could tell Nick the truth. I kept holding on to his promise that he would wait. I envisioned confessing everything, Nick accepting me, forgiving me, and, finally, us beginning a wonderful life together.

But the universe has a funny way of twisting fate. Some might call it cruel.

"I met Hugh."

It is the first complete sentence Nick has spoken to me since our tryst in the bathroom and I don't know what to make of it. We are on my porch and it is Saturday afternoon, hours away from Patty's shower. Nick has his sleeves pushed up and is looking off to the thunderhead across the golf course, as if his heart is already elsewhere.

"What do you mean, you met Hugh?"

"He stopped by this afternoon, to check out the house. Took him long enough."

While I was at the dry cleaner's picking up my dress for the party, dammit. That was Murphy and his law for you.

Throwing the dress over the edge of the railing, I collapse into an Adirondack chair, my whole body now suddenly weak and achy, anticipating the worst.

Surely, Hugh told Nick the truth, that he and I were not getting married. Then again, there was that odd experience with *The New York Times*. These days, I have no idea what Hugh is capable of. He's toying with me, I think, like a mouse.

"What did he say?"

"He said he loves the house." Nick turns and folds his strong arms, laced with veins. "He loves the cabinets. The ceilings. The bookcases. The location . . . he can't wait to move in."

"But . . ." Move in? What is going on with this man? Hugh can't move in. Shoot, the last I knew he thought I was marrying Bill. "He's not . . ."

Nick cuts me off, an unfamiliar edge to his voice. "Don't bother explaining, Genie. I think I made my feelings pretty clear the other day. I thought you had, too . . . in that kiss."

In that kiss. He's right. So clear.

"Then again, like the song goes, maybe a kiss is just a kiss."

Now he's quoting *Casablanca.* He's torturing me. "It wasn't just a kiss." I can't bear to make eye contact with him so I kick a strip of peeling paint on the porch instead. "It was more. Much more."

"What you're really saying is it could have been more, if you weren't getting married. A last fling before settling down to wedded bliss."

What does *that* mean, I think, watching him pass by me and down the stairs.

"Nick, hold on . . ." Rushing to the railing, I blurt, "I made it up. I was never engaged to Hugh. What happened was, he proposed to someone else on national television and left me with the job of explaining to everyone that actually he dumped me. So I lied and said he really did propose and then things kind of got out of hand and, oh, God, I can tell you don't believe me and even if you do believe me, you probably think I'm nuts."

I'm crying, sobbing, actually, but Nick doesn't seem to care. He is standing on our front walk, hands in his pockets, with a puzzled expression. He's regarding me like I'm crazy, which makes perfect sense as right now I *feel* crazy.

"I'll rent out my apartment to Adrien. I'll be out of here by Monday."

And then he's gone.

Chapter Thirty

Patty, the big spender, has sent a limousine to pick me up and take me to Rowes Wharf, the fabulously swanky site of her fabulously swanky shower. While incredibly extravagant, the limo is also really thoughtful since I have no desire to wear my brand-new Ann Taylor übersexy Sophia silk dress with the spaghetti straps and plunging neckline while sitting on wet gum on the Green Line to Government Center.

Then again, I have no desire to go anywhere or do anything. I just want to wait for Nick. That is, if he ever returns.

Outside, the rain falls in horizontal sheets, marking a true New England nor'easter as I huddle under my umbrella and rush to the idling limo.

"Wicked *weathuh*," says my limo driver, Joe, a big beefy Southie. "People do kooky stuff in *weathuh* like this."

"I hope so," I hear myself say as the Harbor Hotel comes into view. It is a huge, redbrick building that juts into Boston bay, part of the city's refurbished waterfront. Joe informs me he'll be waiting around the corner in case I want to leave early.

"I won't want to leave early," I yell through the pounding rain.

"So says you." He gives me a thumbs-up and drives off.

"You should ask him to stay," the Harbor Hotel doorman advises. "That's what he gets paid for. If he comes back again I'll make him stick around. You never know when you'll need to go home."

There is no home, I think, not without Nick.

The party is on the fourth floor, where I find Patty wearing six-inch stiletto heels and a vintage Diane von Furstenberg wrap dress in leopard print. Her black hair is pushed back off her forehead and cascades in soft flips around her shoulders.

She's refined yet animalistic. Not many women could pull it off. "What happened to the Eileen Fisher?" I hand her my engagement gift, a set of note cards reading: *We regret to inform you that our nuptials have been canceled.*

"You know what they say. It's a jungle out there. Dress accordingly. Speaking of jungle love, where's your Greek Adonis? I invited him, you know."

"We had a falling out." I don't want to go into too much detail because this is Patty's big night and I refuse to ruin it.

"A little falling out or a big falling out?"

"A suicide plunge." Taking a deep breath, I explain about telling him the truth. "It doesn't matter because I don't think he believed me. At any rate, he said he'll be out by Monday and he's leasing the apartment to his brother."

"Genie. I'm so sorry. This is all my fault. I'm the one who made you wait."

True, I think, biting my lip to keep myself together.

"Oh, well. Now I suppose we'll find if true love will out."

"It will. You bet it will. Though, I've never understood that phrase. Just *what* is true love supposed to out?" she asks as we enter the lavish room, one wall of which is windows facing out to the stormy harbor.

The men are in tuxes, the women in glittering designer wear. There's a band and waiters in white coats serving salmon and caviar and champagne. The place smells of smoked fish and Chanel.

"It's perfect," I tell her. "All that's missing is a fiancé."

"Not anymore. There he is," she says, pointing to two men engaged in deep conversation.

I have to check once and then check again. This can't be right. There has to be some mistake. Patty would never have chosen . . .

"Hugh?"

"Hugh?" Patty takes another look. "Not Hugh. Though . . . shoot. *Is* that Hugh?"

Hearing his name, Hugh turns to us, dashing as usual in his authentic Savile Row. There is an air of triumph about him, a cockiness to his grin.

"Who let *him* in?" Patty asks.

"Todd," I say, nodding to Hugh's conversation partner. "I gotta go, Patty. Hugh's probably just told Todd the truth and I don't want to be on the receiving end of his wrath. Sorry."

Patty yanks me back. "You can't go. It's my shower. You have to stay."

It's too late, anyway. Hugh and Todd are walking toward us. Todd is smiling, slapping Hugh on the back, while Hugh is focused completely on me. I have never seen him like this. I'm almost frightened.

"Darling," he coos, taking my hand and kissing it. "I thought you'd never come." And before I can snatch my hand away, he reaches out and brings me to him, planting a soft, scotch-tainted kiss on my startled lips. He's not drunk. He's not forceful. He's intent.

"That's what I'm talking about," Todd says, clapping. "True love. Let's give it up for the other engaged couple here, okay, people?"

Several partygoers applaud. A gaggle of Hugh's groupies trip over themselves taking photos of us with their cell phones.

Hugh reluctantly ends our kiss, keeping his arm securely around my waist as if he can't be parted from my side for a minute. "I need to be alone with you, darling. There's so much I have to say."

It is all I can do to keep breathing.

"Where've you been keeping my future in-law hidden, Genie?" Todd bellows. "I was beginning to wonder whether you two were really engaged or if you just made it up to rake in the loot."

Todd and Hugh laugh heartily as the synapses in my brain short-circuit and fire off sparks.

" 'Cause that's what Patty did, you know," Todd says, bending close. "Faked it."

"I never fake it," Patty bawdily retorts. "What Patty wants, Patty gets."

I take my eyes off Hugh and shoot a look at my sweet, delicate best friend who seems perfectly fine with admitting her engagement is a ruse. She is smiling up at Todd like he's her hero. Like he's her . . . no. It can't be. Not Todd. He'd never in a million years go along with a prank like this.

"Do you mean to tell me," Hugh drawls, "that this shower is nothing but a scam?"

Patty says, "I don't know if I'd call it scamming. Payback is more like it."

Todd shrugs. "Why not scam? Look, Patty's never gonna get married. I'm never gonna get married. This is our once-in-a-lifetime chance to even the playing field with really engaged people—like you and Genie."

"Yes. Really engaged," Hugh whispers in my ear.

Wait. So Todd thinks we *are* getting married?

"I say it's a capital idea!" Hugh hoists his scotch. "A toast. To equality."

"To equality," Todd agrees, toasting him back. "Here's to screwing with society."

They clink glasses and I nearly faint. "I can't believe you, Mr. Principled, agreed to be Moe Howard."

"Let's just say that for tonight, Sister Eugenia, I'm the stooge."

Patty howls and reaches up to kiss Todd *smack* on the mouth. It's supposed to be a fun kiss, playful, but they stay like that, attached. Then Todd wraps his arms around her and they kiss some more. I have the feeling it's one of those oblivion kisses where the whole world drops away and there's just the two of them.

"This is our cue," Hugh says, taking my hand and dragging me away to the dance floor.

I'm still gaping at my brother, so tall, bending down to Patty, so tiny she is invisible, that I barely notice Hugh has me in his grasp. The band strikes up "In My Life," and, immediately, he dives in for another kiss.

"Quit it," I say, pushing him back. "What the hell do you think you're doing?"

"Doing? Why, I'm doing what I should have done years ago. I'm treating you like my lover."

This statement shocks me to where I'm tempted to make a break for it and dash to the limo. But Hugh holds me tight.

"I know what's going on," he says. "I know what you've been up to."

"What have I been up to?"

"Making me mad with desire, that's what you've been up to." He twirls me around and brings me to him again. "Bill called last week. Said Connie Robeson showed up with a copy of an e-mail I'd sent to you weeks ago, cautioning you to be careful, that we weren't really betrothed."

"That thief!" I cry. "That is so illegal for her to snoop in my personal e-mail."

"No matter. It's not important." His lips brush against my cheek and as they do, somewhere in the distance, flashes go off. Hugh's fans are lined up, watching us. "In a way it was for the best. It made me realize what a fool I've been."

"You mean, thinking Bill and I were engaged." Because, I had to admit, that was pretty foolish.

"No. I mean letting you go."

I search the room for a professional photographer beyond Patty's gaping aunts and secretaries from her firm. "Is *People* magazine here or what?"

"Oh, Genie," he says, laughing a polite Britishy kind of laugh. "I have so missed your sense of humor."

"Really? Because the other day you rolled your eyes."

"Yes, well, mustard on the collar's not actually funny, is it? Do you suppose there's somewhere we can slip off to so I can escape this infernal limelight?"

One year ago, Hugh would have died to be in "infernal limelight."

"Why do we need to be alone?"

"Because I have to explain everything." The song ends and Hugh agrees to sign a few autographs while I try to locate my exits, as if I'm on a plane and it's going down. Patty's on her cell standing by the door, so that won't work. And, cripes, there's Tony Pugliese by the other. I'd rather cross a swamp of alligators than cross him.

"Here." Hugh escorts me toward the windows and out to the balcony, begging off more signatures like he really is Mick Jagger.

Outside, a salty wind is whipping off the harbor. Moored boats are bobbing over the black waves and it's spitting nasty. Hugh takes off his tuxedo jacket and hangs it on my shoulders. "Quite romantic, isn't it?" he says, slipping my hand in his pocket to keep it warm. "I do so like inclement weather. Summons the muses, you know."

"Hugh?" I say. "Would you mind telling me what you're up to? There's no press out here. Not even adoring fans. You can be yourself. You don't have to put on a show."

"But I am being myself, love." He cocks my chin up for another kiss. "*Love.* It so fits you."

"You're freaking me out. One minute I'm the clinging girlfriend with no sexuality. Now, I'm your love. I need an explanation, Hugh."

He sighs and nods. "Yes, you do. A long overdue one, I'm afraid."

"Are you . . . mocking me?"

He shakes his head, all romantic pretense gone. "If there's anyone to be mocked here, it's me. I've been the idiot."

"That's a first." Hugh hardly ever admits he's wrong.

"Genie, I love you. I have always loved you and will always love you. I didn't realize that until I returned from England and walked into your office expecting to find the same old mousy girl, and instead discovered a strong, beautiful, and sharp woman on the verge of marrying another man."

Kissing me on the forehead, he says, "At first I felt relieved. You were off my back. We were through. I was finally free. After four long years, I was able to live my life without concern for anyone else."

Now *that* sounds more like Hugh.

"But I kept going back to you and Bill. It wasn't right that such a beautiful young woman should be stuck with such an old geezer. A philandering geezer, if the rumors are true."

Probably true.

"I was haunted by images of you and him making"—he pauses, as if shy—"babies."

"The hazards of sex," I say, pulling his coat tight.

"Right." He does his Hugh Grant bashful blinking and adds, "If there was anyone you should be doing *that* with, it's me."

I am silent, waiting for the rest.

"I decided I had to do something to stop you from marrying him. So when *The New York Times* called, looking for a quote, I just went with it. Really, it had nothing to do with the tremendous publicity potential, although that's not to say my publicist wasn't thrilled. She was beside herself."

"Oh, I bet."

"As I was telling them, *The New York Times*, about you, I had a premonition of you as my wife, standing by me, supporting me throughout my career, its ups and downs."

"Is that what you thought? That I'd be some sort of helpmate?"

"It was! I mean, what I'm trying to say, Genie, is now that you've gotten yourself so together with your new physique and independence and so on and so forth, it occurs to me what a fabulous team we'd make."

Team. Unreal. "Are you asking me to join your squash league?" I say. "Or something more?"

"I suppose what I'm asking is if you can find it in your heart to forgive me so that we can reunite."

"In other words, you want to get back together."

He closes his eyes, as if this is the most momentous decision of his life. "Yes. That's what I'm saying. I think we should start over."

Start over? Another four years? He couldn't be serious. "What about your lack of sexual attraction and all that?"

"A lie. A full-blown lie. You'd put me on the spot to come up with one good reason why I shouldn't marry you and, well, there were no good reasons."

"There were no good reasons?" I knew it. I just knew it!

"No. Not really. Unless you count my own fear of commitment, which is no excuse considering the tons of therapy I've had and the fact that I'm almost forty."

"Okay. Assuming that you are sexually attracted to me—"

"Oh, I am," he says, nuzzling my neck. "You don't know how much."

"Then what about the other woman?"

"Never."

I push him off my neck. "What do you mean, 'never'?"

Grinning like a dope, as if I will find him to be a naughty but precocious little boy, he says, "I made her up. I mean, what else could I do? Here I had a perfect opportunity to play to my audience of female readers by proposing to my girlfriend on live national television. Yet I wasn't ready to get married. I had no choice but to fake it."

This can't be. Here I'd been worried about what Hugh would do if he discovered that I'd been telling people we were getting married when all along he'd been doing the same thing. Only his fiancée was completely invented.

"You mean you haven't been sleeping around." I have to be clear on this.

"I swear."

"Not Connie or Isabel or any of the cute grad students."

"On my honor," he says, holding up his hand, "there was never anyone else. I was just pretending."

I find this absolutely incredible. "But that's what I was doing."

"See? This just proves how perfect we are for one another. This is why we need to spend our lives together." With that, he gets down on one knee.

Something cold and smooth slides over the fourth finger of my left hand and bumps against my pretend engagement ring, dwarfing it in both size and quality. Even under the dark skies, it glitters boldly. The two blue sapphires on either side standing like royal guards, securing its brilliance.

The Spencer diamond ring, given by King Edward to Hugh's great-grandmother more than a century ago. On my hand, abutting my $24.95 cubic zirconia from Bickman's Jewelers. It is quite a contrast.

"Genie. I am kneeling before you, offering all that I am and all that I have, body and soul. Tell me you'll agree to be my wife at this moment or, surely, I will die."

It was not the Sleeping Beauty Proposal. It was a real proposal. Better than I ever dreamed.

Unfortunately, it was from the wrong man.

Chapter Thirty-One

It is still raining when the limo reaches the end of Peabody Road. It's a heavy drenching rain that soaks through the skin and chills my bones and can lead to the need for all sorts of cold medicine. Despite that, I step out of my slender sandals and head to the top of the golf course for more of its punishment.

I have no idea what I'm doing or why I have this urge to bare myself to the elements. Maybe I want to re-create the happiness I felt the day I moved here. Or maybe I want to be really, truly alone on a hill in a fierce storm.

Because that's my big fear, ending up alone.

I'm beginning to learn that anything worth having in life begins by taking a risk—love, marriage, child-birth, even loving one's neighbor as thyself. Risk is the universe's way of pushing us to become more than what we are. Risk is faith at the edge. Risk is the pulsating essence of life.

Without risk, we are automatons going through our days with no purpose or meaning. We are safer, perhaps, but we are also, ironically, closer to death.

"Genie!"

The one person I want more than anyone in the world is trudging up the golf course and my heart begins to hope. Nick is in a tux, his bow tie undone, his shirt open, and he is positively soaked. Water is dripping off every inch of his body, off his head, off his nose. He must have been out in the rain all night.

"I've been looking all over for you. First I went to the party, but you were nowhere to be found. Patty didn't know where you'd gone, either."

"You came to find me?" This must be good news—unless we have a basement flooding problem again.

"The doorman at the hotel said you'd left, but you weren't home. So I looked up Hugh's address and went over there." He reaches me, almost out of breath. "I'm so glad I found you. I thought I'd lost you forever."

And then I understand. "Hugh told you my secret this afternoon, even before I had a chance to explain. You already knew my engagement was bogus."

Nick is silent. Finally, he takes off his jacket, nicely dry inside, and hangs it around my shoulders. A vicious wind whips across the course, blowing me into his arms, but he doesn't reject me. He holds me tight, his warm body like medicine for my broken heart.

"Hugh didn't have to tell me you weren't engaged. I knew from the beginning, from the first day you came to look at the house and I overheard you and Patty talking."

"Then why didn't you say something?"

"Why were you lying? That's what I couldn't figure out. There were many moments when I came close to asking you, but I decided it would be better to let you tell me the truth when you felt ready. You were never ready, Genie, until I told you I was leaving. Why didn't you trust me?"

"I am such an idiot," I murmur, burrowing my face into his damp shirt. "I've blown everything. Now you're going."

"I'm going only because Hugh proposed to you tonight for real."

Looking up, I search his eyes for clues, his mouth for his trademark knowing grin, but it's too rainy and dark to see. "He told you?"

"He showed me the ring this afternoon. I saw that and thought there was no way you'd turn him down. Todd said all you'd ever wanted in life was to marry Hugh, and it looked to me like your wish was coming true tonight."

I have to laugh at the absurdity of it all. "For someone who's completely clueless, Todd seems to think he knows a lot about me. If he knows so much, then why did he think I was engaged to Hugh all along?"

"Are you?" Nick asks, more serious than I've ever heard him.

I hold up my left hand to show him the answer and am instantly confused. Not only am I not wearing the gazillion-dollar Spencer diamond, but I'm also not wearing my $24.95 Bickman's special.

"It's gone!" I exclaim, shocked and somewhat relieved. "I lost it."

"Hugh's ring?"

"No. I never took Hugh's ring. I'm talking about the other one. The fake."

There are no coincidences. Patty was right.

"It's a sign," I say. "Proof that I've found the man I love."

Before I can make any further pronouncements, Nick bends down and kisses me. I'm not quite sure if it's really happening or if I'm hallucinating, but I feel as if we are in the midst of a swirling tempest. The rain is falling harder and harder, the wind is howling. There's a very good chance we'll be struck down by lightning and that would be fine by me because I couldn't imagine a better way to die than while being kissed by Nick.

When he tears himself away he says, "So you turned Hugh down."

"Of course." I am giddy. "Could you kiss me again? I love it when you kiss me."

"I was sure," he murmurs, his lips caressing my neck. "I was sure you would say yes. I didn't think I stood a chance. I thought I might have to fight him to the death."

Was he kidding? I never felt this way with Hugh. Never.

"You know what this means, don't you?" His strong hand slides up my waist, under his jacket, his thumb flirting where my dress is about to have a serious wardrobe malfunction. "You're free."

"I've always been free." Though that's not entirely true. What I've been is trapped, confined by cages of my own making.

"I've wanted to for . . ." He stops and concentrates. "I've longed. No, that's not right."

Then, opening those soulful dark-lashed eyes of his he says, "Genie."

"Shhh," I say, placing my finger on his lips. "I think it's time for us to get out of the rain, don't you?"

"Yes," he says, grinning at last. "It's time."

That night, Nick and I got very little sleep. We were too hungry for each other's bodies, too ecstatic over our joy of finally being able to be together that we were unable to do anything but make love and catnap and kiss and hug and whisper until the gray, rainy dawn.

"Okay, so let me get this straight," I say, running my finger down his chest. "You fell in love with me that Sunday morning Patty and I came over to look at the house."

"Love at first sight." Nick's hand traces the curve of my naked waist. "I always thought it was made up, something in movies, this phenomenon. And then I walked into the living room, saw you, and knew it was real."

"When you were nailing in molding?"

"Right."

"Before we even argued about Hugh?"

Nick lifts his mouth from where it has been lingering on my shoulder. "By then I was madly in lust. You were so passionate, the way you defended Hugh. So smart and sassy and your eyes flashed. They do that when you're angry, did you know?"

"No. You're making that up."

"I'm not. You're very sexy when you're agitated, Genie. Like that night at the Dylan contest when you got mad at Todd for spilling the secret about your virginity. You nearly drove me wild."

"Listen. I told you to forget that."

"I'll never forget it. That's why I followed you outside."

"Because I was twenty-one years old when I lost my virginity?"

He laughs. "No, though I found that endearing. That's the other reason I love you. There's a sweet side of you, Genie, and after I got past my lust for your body, I found that, in many ways, I love your sweet side more."

"But you definitely have lust for my body," I say, making sure.

"After last night you have doubts?"

"I hope never to have doubts like that ever again."

Then, pausing, I ask cautiously, "Do you think less of me for lying?"

Nick sighs and rolls on his back, hands behind his head. "I'm no fan of lies, but I've done stupid things, too. Things I could justify while I was in the moment and that later I regretted."

"So, in your opinion, it was a mistake."

"My opinion doesn't matter. I'm not judging you, Genie. You've had enough of that."

Indeed. Resting my head on his chest, I thank whatever fate or stroke of luck brought Nick into my life. "Patty says there's no such thing as coincidences."

"She's right. There is no such thing as coincidence. Everything happens for a reason." Nick kisses the top of my head, a gesture that I take as a blessing, an absolution, that my ruse has been forgiven.

We have been lingering forever in his bed. It is still raining, which is good because that means the course outside Nick's bedroom window is free of golfers who might otherwise be able to peek in and see a naked couple engaging in yet another round of inexhaustible lovemaking.

I have totally lost count. All I know is that it's way past noon and we haven't left since last night.

Running my foot up his strong leg with its dark hairs, I ask, "What I want to know is, how come you were so rude to me?"

He leans on one elbow. "Me rude to you? I think you've got that backward."

"Hardly. You dropped hints that my ring was a fake

and then you teased me about Hugh, about his six hundred acres and his pure-method house building."

"And you treated me as if I was incapable of knowing anything beyond my own T square, even asking me what I was doing in a bookstore. Now, what are you up to?"

Through no fault of my own, my hand has slipped under the sheets and is now exploring what is fast becoming familiar territory. I should be spent, exhausted, but I'm not. It's as if I've been craving this for so long that it's impossible for me to be satisfied. I fear it may take hours, days, months, even years for me to get my fill.

Fortunately, Nick appears to be up to the task.

Chapter Thirty-Two

"But Tula Abernathy's engagement party's next week! What are we going to do?"

My mother is in hysterics and for good reason. We are standing in her kitchen—the universal domestic confessional—where I have just informed her that Hugh and I have broken off our engagement, which is, technically, true.

Does it matter that we were engaged for all of two minutes? Two minutes in which I dumbly gawked at the bona fide Spencer diamond glittering on my finger, awed by its iridescent rays. No longer will I believe the advertisements. You *can* tell the difference between real and synthetic. I mean, I considered a lot of imitations and none made my heart stop like this diamond complemented by two of the most perfect dark blue sapphires.

Yes. It was hard to say no to that hunk of carbon. But it was harder to envision a life with Hugh—even after he confessed his undying love and admitted how scared he was of marriage, having been raised in, well, a rather cold family.

At first, he was incredulous when I gently refused his offer. My guess is he assumed I was still bitter because he said, "I've told you I'm sorry, Genie, I don't know how many times. Let's put it behind us and move on."

I tried to explain that I had changed. I told him how faking my engagement had liberated me from the pressure to be a bride. Maybe I'd get married someday. Maybe not. It didn't matter anymore. I had friends. Work. Family. A home. And now, thanks to my surprise bridal shower, I had a Williams-Sonoma cutting board *and* a chef's knife. What more could I want?

Well, Nick. But I didn't say that. I didn't bring up Nick at all because he had nothing to do with Hugh or my previous desire to get married. Nick was something new, something honest. Nick didn't weigh the pros and cons of commitment.

He respected true love more than that.

At least, that's what I hoped. When I said no to Hugh, I was certain I had already lost Nick.

Hugh pleaded and argued and wouldn't take no for

an answer until I said, "Sometimes if you wait too long, it's too late. Sorry." Then I gave him the ring and walked away.

Now here I am, breaking the news to my mother, who is visibly apoplectic.

"How about a drink?" my father says, his hand reflexively reaching for the vodka.

Mom stops him. This, for the record, is a Michaels family first. "No. I have to have my wits about me to think this through." She is clutching her chest, gasping, her mind racing as she mentally runs through the list of all the cancellations that need to be made.

"Don't worry, Mom," I assure her. "I have the list of guests and their phone numbers. I just wanted you and Dad to know before I started calling everyone. You won't have to do a thing."

Mom hasn't heard a word. ". . . The caterers. The band. The florists."

Dad, ever the paterfamilias, pats her gently. "Don't worry, Nance. Brides call off weddings every day. It's no big deal."

"No big deal. Ha! How would you know? You haven't done anything to prepare for this wedding. Absolutely nothing whatsoever."

"Aside from paying the bills." He shoots me a stern look.

Ouch. The bills. Better not to think about those right now.

Mom lets out a cry and starts gesturing maniacally

to the back window. Todd and Patty are coming up the walk.

And they're holding hands and swinging their arms—*swinging their arms!*—practically skipping up the garden path. Patty's in a yellow sundress and she actually has a daisy tucked behind her ear. I bet Todd picked it and slipped it there himself.

"What's *she* doing here?" Mom howls. "On today of all days."

"I asked her to come," I say calmly. "She is my best friend."

Mom is horrified. "Why? Why would you invite that horrid Patty Pugliese into our house when I am under such distress?"

"For support. Besides, I thought you liked the *horrid Patty Pugliese* now."

"I liked her when she was engaged to that Moe Howard person. But as soon as they broke up she sank her claws into my Todd. And don't tell me that wasn't her plan all along."

Probably not far wrong, knowing Patty.

Dad says, "I dunno. She's kind of fun. Very bright. Makes a hell of a living."

Mom is unaware that Todd and Patty have been inseparable since Todd played her fiancé. And I mean inseparable. I think they Krazy Glued themselves together for three days afterward.

I wouldn't know, really, since Nick and I haven't exactly been holding back on the Krazy Glue either.

"Hey, guys!" Todd bursts through the door

wearing his loud pink and yellow Hawaiian shirt and grinning like a dope. He is fitter. He even looks younger, and the same can be said for Patty. Gone are her caustic comments, her razor-sharp tongue. She is rosy and giggling and—I don't believe it—acting coy.

Dad and Mom are ashen zombies in comparison.

"Geesh. Who died?" Todd asks.

"Hugh!" Mom wails.

Todd blanches. "What?"

"Hugh didn't die," Dad says. "Your mother's being overly dramatic. What she means is that Genie and Hugh broke up. The wedding's off."

I'd assumed that Patty told him, but I think not because Todd pumps his fist and yells, "Yes! I won the bet!"

Oh, for heaven's sake. I completely forgot about that stupid bet.

Todd holds out his hand. "Cash. No check. Cash."

"What bet?" Dad asks.

Getting out my checkbook anyway, I warn Dad it's a long story and he doesn't need to be bored to death. Besides, Mom appears to have slipped into a trance and is rattling off an itemized list of wasted wedding food.

". . . seventy-four chicken almondines, fifty-two beef bourguignons, fifteen portobello steaks, gallons of shrimp, plates of salmon, crates of champagne and wine and"—she lets out a sob—"the five-tiered white chocolate and lemon wedding cake."

"Oh, Mom." I am beginning to feel really, really crappy about this. "I'll pay for it all. I promise."

Dad's incredulous. "You have no idea what those deposits are, Genie. They're huge."

"Hold on." Patty jumps in just like her old self. "There's got to be a solution to this. I'm sure the caterers won't hold you fully liable. There are three weeks until the wedding. Where are your contracts?"

Mom blinks and sniffs into her tissue. "Contracts? Donald has them."

"They're in my office at the bank. I'll send them to you Monday." Dad rubs his hands together and says, "All right. Enough of that. Let's let bygones be bygones. Anyone for a drink?"

Hold on. My old man doesn't even part with a penny if he doesn't have to. He should be plunking Patty in the car and whisking her off to the bank right now. And how come he's not throwing a fit and pounding the counter and lecturing me about being selfish and immature?

Todd says to Patty, "I need to talk to you. Alone."

"About contracts?"

"Kind of."

They step outside and Mom excuses herself to wash her face in the bathroom and redo her lipstick, thereby providing me with a perfect opportunity for a one-on-one with Father of the Year.

Dad brings out a bottle of cheap chilled chardonnay from the fridge. "So, what'll it be, Toodles? Your usual white? Or something with actual taste?"

"You knew."

"No. I don't know." He pops out the yellow plastic cork. "You might have switched to merlot since we last had drinks."

I swing around the counter so he can't flee. "Don't bluff with me, Pop. You knew all along I wasn't marrying Hugh, that I made up the whole thing."

His hand shakes slightly as he pours the chardonnay. Otherwise, he's composed. "Don't be ridiculous. Why would you do a crazy thing like that?"

The threads of evidence are weaving together to form a perfect tapestry. "That's why my condo mortgage went through so easily at the bank and why there was that special meeting with Nick. You were behind that."

"Now, Genie. Just let it be." He's trying to sound noble, but I can tell he's pleased with himself for being so smart because there's a tiny smile at the corner of his mouth.

"When did you find out?"

"Jason told me at the barbeque, right after you got so-called engaged." He looks up from his preparations and winks. "He didn't want to violate your confidence, but he was concerned you'd be too afraid to tell us and that we'd end up blowing a wad of cash. And for that I am forever in his debt. Literally."

Dad's known all this time. Since the very beginning. I'm rocked. "Does Mom . . ."

"No. Are you kidding? She'd hog-tie you if she found out the truth, so you better make sure she doesn't. I had to make sure those invitations never went out and then I had to talk her into letting me handle all the bills, which required me to contact the vendors and explain that my nutty kid was trying some sort of experiment and could they please be patient. Because, for all I knew, you were on the slippery slope to a nervous breakdown."

Oh, great. Flowers by Elsie. J&J Caterers. They think I'm . . . insane! "Why didn't you try to stop me?"

"I did. I told your mother I ran into Hugh to strike the fear of God in you. I figured that would frighten you into coming forward. No such luck."

"So you never saw Hugh on my porch."

"Of course not. Hugh was still in England, I believe. When that didn't do it, I started to worry. I couldn't for the life of me understand why you felt it necessary to tell such a lie to your own family. Your own family, Genie. How could you?"

Suddenly, my nose is hot and my chest is tightening, thinking of the hell I put him through. "I'm so sorry. I didn't mean for you to . . ." That's it. I'm about to cry.

"Now, cut that out." He reaches out and strokes my hair, his sign of forgiveness. "You know I've always had a soft spot for you, Genie. You're the middle child, the overlooked one in the family. The good girl who got the good grades and kept to herself.

"I assumed you weren't being frivolous with this fake engagement. I trusted you had a valid reason. So,

I was willing to be patient and play along until you got what you needed. I wasn't happy about it, but I did it because I love you."

Man, do I love my father. Yes, sometimes he's dreadfully boring, droning on and on about interest rates and bond returns. But mostly he's my hero.

"I just want to get this straight," I say. "There is no band. There is no caterer, right?"

"Not even a tent. They're all booked at other events for the twentieth. So you can breathe a great big sigh of relief."

I let out a great big sigh of relief. This has ended far better than I ever could have hoped.

"However," he says, giving his ice a stir. "You were wrong about one thing."

"What?"

"Nick. I may have sped up the paperwork on that mortgage, but I had nothing to do with him meeting with the bank president. That's standard procedure for our twenty-eighty clients."

This makes no sense. A 20-80 client is the banking term for the richest twenty percent of a bank's clients who generate, on average, eighty percent of a bank's profits. Investors, doctors, CEOs. Dad courts them constantly.

"But Nick's not rich. He's a carpenter."

"He's also smart. MIT grad, you know."

No. I didn't know. I know other things about Nick, very intimate things. But somehow between our bouts of passionate, sweaty sex, I never stopped to ask, "Did you happen to graduate from the Massachusetts Institute of Technology?"

"Economics major," Dad is saying. "Bored him dead. So he became a carpenter. Do you know how much sought-after carpenters like Nick can make in a year? Combine that with his investment savvy and discipline and you have a multimillionaire."

Crash!

"What broke?" Mom rushes out of the bathroom, bumping right into Todd and Patty running in from the other direction. I am frozen in place, shards of wineglass and puddles of chardonnay at my toes.

Nick. A multimillionaire? An MIT grad?

It's so . . . geeky!

"Good news!" Todd shouts. "We have solved the problem of Genie's called-off wedding."

Mom claps her hands. "I just knew you'd find a way, Todd. How?"

"You know those caterers you have to cancel? The florist and band and photographers and whatever. Don't call them. Not quite yet."

He pauses to squeeze Patty's hand. I've never seen my brother so infatuated.

"Instead of Genie and Hugh getting married, it'll be Patty and me. I've asked her and she said yes and the best part is, it's already arranged. Patty's even got her dress. We're good to go."

Crash!

This time my father's the one to drop his glass.

Epilogue

Todd and Patty were married under the willow tree in my parents' backyard on a beautiful, dry August day with puffy clouds in the blue sky and the lemony fragrance of bee balm in the air. Which was great as we couldn't rent a tent to save our soul.

Granted, we were not serenaded by a string quartet or a jazz band at the reception. Though I can't say that the neighborhood garage band, the Waverly Idiots, totally sucked. They were kind of eclectic. A sort of Red Hot Chili Peppers meets Dixie Chicks meets the Partridge Family. Danceable and yet, not.

The food, though, was fantastic. All the naan and samosas you could eat. Bombay Delight served up a feast and, frankly, I wouldn't have done it any other way. I mean, you can have chicken Kiev or beef tenderloin at any wedding. Indian takeout is definitely the way to go.

The Indian buffet was a surprising hit with many of the thousands of Puglieses who showed up and parked their cars on the sidewalk. (The Pugliese family has some sort of dispensation from the governor to do this, apparently.)

And I have to say, it was a blessing to have that many armed men around when the national and local news crews started acting belligerent. We explained and explained that Todd and Patty were getting married, not the megabestselling author Hugh Spencer.

Still, the news crews accused us of hiding him, which was ridiculous as Hugh was back in England, cursing himself for not marrying me when he had the chance.

Patty wore her Carmen Marc Valvo dress, which fit perfectly, if barely. She'd lost a lot of weight right before the wedding due to the nausea that we hope will disappear in a couple of months when she passes her first trimester.

"One whiff of a prospective husband and I get knocked up," Patty cried when the little pink plus sign appeared on her pregnancy test. "This is what I get for being a Pugliese. Now I gotta sell the Porsche and start making lasagna. It's the Pugliese way."

Despite all her railing against God and her fertility, I know she's secretly pleased. Todd, too. And it is kind of like a miracle, when you think about it. One day you're two self-centered adults going about your self-centered business. The next thing you know, you've fallen in love and now all your attention must be devoted to raising a helpless being for eighteen years.

At least, that's how my mom put it. She's still coming to terms with the fact that she's going to be grandmother to a Pugliese, a bellowing, screaming, hollering Pugliese. In anticipation of this, she has quit drinking. A hangover is one thing. A hangover with a Pugliese baby could result in criminal action.

For the record, I carefully returned every wedding gift with a note of explanation and thanks. Any money I received, I sent to All Saints' Church, with receipts to the donors. It has been a daunting task, though Reverend Whitmore now acts like he's my best friend.

Long ago, I'd given up the notion that life could change over one summer. That was only for teenagers who'd fallen in love at the beach or kids who'd suffered through some coming-of-age drama at camp, right?

But I like to think of my experience as proof that it's never too late to come of age. In one summer I had transformed from a wilted wallflower, an overlooked employee, and an inhabitant of a cramped rental into a risk-taking woman, a valued member of my workplace—a homeowner.

Most important, I was loved. Truly and passionately loved by a man I, in turn, loved back. And not just any man, Nick.

One golden fall evening, Nick and I are walking hand in hand up to the golf course. The oaks and maples that line the country club are turning red and yellow, losing their leaves, and there is a definite change of seasons in the brisk air. I button up my sweater and let Nick hold me and keep me warm as we watch the Boston skyline fade into the twilight.

I never imagined life could be so perfect.

"That's it. Summer's over," Nick says, pulling me to him.

"It was a great summer. Hot. Busy. But great."

Nick smiles. "Hot and busy. You got that right."

I give him a playful poke in the ribs and, in so doing, notice something glittering in the grass. It can't be.

"My ring!" I shout, bending down to pick it up. "My

twenty-four ninety-five cubic zirconia from Bickman's. It's still perfect."

"Ah, yes. How could I forget? I was there the day you picked it out, remember?"

This is impossible. "How did it get here? I lost it months ago. It never could have survived the golf carts and the mowing. At the very least, it should be mangled and ruined."

"Maybe you should keep it then. It might be another sign." Nick's eyes are twinkling. He's up to something.

I think about this, holding the ring up to study how the stone so perfectly catches the evening's last light, shooting off brilliant rays of pink and yellow. Not bad for a cubic zirconia. Not bad at all.

"You know what?" I say, keeping my voice bright so Nick won't know I'm about to cry. "I don't think I will keep this ring."

"What? Why not?"

"Because I don't need it. For years, I thought I did, that I wouldn't find happiness and fulfillment without a diamond ring, even a fake diamond ring, on my left hand. But I was wrong. I already had what I needed to be happy."

And with this declaration of independence, I toss the ring as hard as I can toward the city skyline.

Nick throws up his arms. "Genie! I can't believe you did that!"

"It wasn't so hard, actually. Very liberating." I slap my hips. "Aren't you proud of me?"

But he's not proud. He's in shock. I can tell because his lower jaw is open and his hands are on his head and now he's dashing across the golf course.

"That was real!" he's shouting.

"Real?" I say, laughing. "It wasn't real. That ring cost twenty-four ninety-five!"

"No, it didn't. It was . . ." He is down on the green, searching. "It was supposed to be for you. I made it myself."

"Platinum?"

"Yes," Nick says sadly.

"Diamond?"

"Two carats."

"And you made it yourself?"

Finally, out of the darkness, Nick says, "It's gone."

I try to be encouraging. "Maybe we can find it in the morning."

"And if we do," he asks slowly, "will you wear it?"

After I'm silent for a while, I say, "It's lovely. Why wouldn't I?"

"You know what I mean."

"No. What do you mean?"

"Now I'm afraid to ask. After seeing what you did with the ring, I'm worried you'll do the same to me."

"Life's all about risks, Nick. I might toss you across the golf course. I might not. You're never going to get what you want unless you ask."

He lets out a deep breath. "Would you like to get married?"

"Someday."

"I mean to me."

"To you? Hmmm. Let me think about that. Well, any man who doesn't get mad when his bride-to-be throws away his handmade platinum-and-diamond ring is bound to be the best husband ever, wouldn't you say?"

"So . . . your answer is yes?"

I take his hand and tuck my answer into his palm.

"I never threw your ring away. I never would," I murmur, as Nick gently slides his ring on my finger. "After all I've been through, I think I finally know how to spot the real thing, even if it's taken me a while."

Like they say, good things come to those who wait.

But, if you ask me, better things come to women who don't.

Acknowledgments

It was while catching up with high school friends at a Bethlehem, Pennsylvania, book signing that I came up with the idea for *The Sleeping Beauty Proposal*. A very pretty, very popular classmate of mine confessed that while she had enjoyed great success forming her small business, was blessed with many friends and close ties to her family, she felt, at age forty, something, as if she'd missed out on life by not getting married. I found this so sad.

I ran her tale of woe past my best friend since age four, Lisa, also unmarried, who told me that this was a bunch of hooey. Sure, there were disadvantages to not being married, but that didn't mean her life was incomplete. Her only regret, she said, was not being able to pay back all those brides (including me) who made her dress up in ridiculous bridesmaid's dresses. Also, not raking in the loot from showers.

Hence, the idea for the book. I've always felt that our tradition of not supplying women with the necessary kitchen gadgets, cutlery, dinnerware, etc., was outdated anyway. What's a girl supposed to do? Live on paper plates until she becomes some man's wife? No! Of course not.

To this end, we've started a "Sleeping Beauty Proposal" support group that's accessible through my Web site—sarahstrohmeyer.com. Here you can find fun tips, stories, and pictures of how to throw a "Welcome to Real Life" shower for your unmarried friend, sister, or daughter. (Or maybe yourself!) Please don't make her wait to get engaged. She needs that Cuisinart, recipe, and fabulous, glamorous party now.

Along with Lisa, I have to thank Anne Garbush, Debby Mundy, and Kathy Sweeney for their inspiring stories and words. Nor could I have survived without the moral support from my fabulous sisters and fellow authors on our blog, "The Lipstick Chronicles": Harley Jane Kozak, Michele Martinez, Elaine Viets, Rebecca the Bookseller, Margie (oh, Margie!), and Nancy Martin, who, as always, steered, advised, encouraged, and consoled me. I hope you'll check out her savvy and smart Blackbird Sisters Mysteries. They are a hoot.

My agent, Heather Schroder at ICM, pushed me to make this book as funny and real as it could be, and my editor at Dutton, Julie Doughty, was patient and thoughtful and so insightful in her editorial comments. Thanks also to Trena Keating for contributing valuable input, and to Brian Tart, the most supportive publisher ever. I'm really very lucky.

Finally, my family put up with all my late hours, grumpy moods, and cold dinners as I rewrote and rewrote. For that I owe them my undying gratitude. Thank you so much, Charlie, Anna, and Sam—especially Anna, who, as a devoted reader of women's fiction, provided superb critiques of my rough drafts.

And thank *you* for reading *The Sleeping Beauty Proposal*. Please stop by my Web site and let me know what you thought of it. I love to hear from readers.

Center Point Publishing
600 Brooks Road ● PO Box 1
Thorndike ME 04986-0001 USA

(207) 568-3717

US & Canada:
1 800 929-9108
www.centerpointlargeprint.com